John H. Vincent

Child's Story of the Bible

John H. Vincent

Child's Story of the Bible

ISBN/EAN: 9783337171698

Printed in Europe, USA, Canada, Australia, Japan

Cover: Foto ©Andreas Hilbeck / pixelio.de

More available books at **www.hansebooks.com**

CHILD'S

STORY OF THE BIBLE

REBEKAH.

CHILD'S
Story of the Bible

BY

MARY A. LATHBURY

WITH INTRODUCTION BY

BISHOP JOHN H. VINCENT

ILLUSTRATED

WITH NUMEROUS FULL-PAGE COLORED PLATES,
AND PHOTO-ENGRAVINGS

BOSTON
DEWOLFE, FISKE & CO.

'REFACE.

To Mothers.

I HAVE been asked to prepare this little aid for your use in the Home —that first and greatest of schools. The school was founded by the Maker of men, and He called mothers to be its earliest and most important teachers. He prepared a text-book for it which we call His Word, illustrating it richly and fully from life and Nature, and filling it with His Spirit. Wherever it is known, as the children become the members of the Church, the citizens of the State, the people of the World, the Book goes with them, forming the Church, the State, the World. It is not only equal to the need, but contains infinite riches that wait to be unveiled.

That no busy mother may say, "I cannot take time to gather from the Bible the simple lessons that my children need," this book of little stories—together making one—has been written. I have tried to preserve the pure outlines of the sacred record from the vivid description and the suggestive supposition that are sometimes introduced to add charm to the story, and in all quoted speech I have used the exact words of the authorized version of the Scriptures, so that the earliest impression made upon the memory of the child might be one that should remain.

The stories are not a substitute for the Word—only little approaches to it through which young feet may be guided by her who holds a place next to the great Teacher in His work with little children.

M. A. L.

INTRODUCTION.

———

WHEN the children gather at mother's knee, and the tiniest finds a place in mother's arms, and all clamor for a "story," "a story, mamma," how lovely is the picture—the living picture—that circle makes! Love, longing, wisdom, expectancy, faith, shining eyes, lips that move involuntarily, keeping time to the sweet movements of mother's lips! Blessed group! Happy mother!

When the stories mother tells are light and meaningless, full of rhyme and rollick, even their eyes are bright and faces radiant, and her own sweet face and voice give charm and weight and significance to the delicious nonsense she rehearses.

Why not give to this receptive and eager audience stories full of deepest meaning, facts, parables, myths charged with *truth?* Why not people little memories with heroes, saints, kings, prophets, apostles? Why not give stories to story-loving youngsters that will turn into immortal pictures and be transformed some day into living factors in the making of character? And why not give them as comparison the babe of Bethlehem, the boy of Nazareth, the lad of twelve years in the schools of the Temple, the man of gentle love, the preacher of righteousness, the worker of heavenly wonders, the Son of Man, the Son of God, the Prince of Peace?

The Book of books is the children's Book. It is a story book. And the stories are "true stories." And the lessons to be drawn from them are numberless, and will come up out of the treasure-house of memory when mother's eyes are closed and her voice silent.

It is a great thing to put mother and the Book together in Baby's thought ; in the big boy's memory ; in the grown-up man's heart and life.

This book is mother's book ; to aid her in doing the best and most lasting work a mother can do to sow seed and set out vines the branches of which shall reach into the world of spirits, and from which she and her children may long afterwards pluck fruit together in the eternal kingdom.

JOHN H. VINCENT.

CHAUTAUQUA, 1898.

CONTENTS.

THE OLD TESTAMENT.

(ix.)

CONTENTS.

THE NEW TESTAMENT.

CHILD'S

STORY OF THE BIBLE

THE OLD TESTAMENT

RETURN OF THE DOVE.

CHILD'S
STORY OF THE BIBLE.

CHAPTER I.

THE BEGINNING OF THINGS.

AWAY back in the beginning of things God made the sky and the earth we live upon. At first it was all dark, and the earth had no form, but God was building a home for us, and his work went on through six long days, until it was finished as we see it now.

On the first day God said, "Let there be light," and the black night turned to gray, and light came. God called the light Day, and the darkness Night, and the evening and the morning made the first day.

Then God divided the waters, so that there were clouds above and seas below, and He called the clouds heaven. It was the second day.

Then the seas were gathered together by themselves, and the dry land rose above them, and God saw that it was good. Then He called to the grass, and the plants, and the trees to come out of the ground, and they came bearing their seeds, and He called the third day good.

Then God called to the two great lights, the sun and the moon, to shine clear in the sky, which had been first dark, and then gray, and they rose and set to make day and night, and seasons and years, and the stars came also, and it was the fourth day.

Then God called for all kinds of fishes that swim in the seas, and rivers, and for all kinds of birds that fly in the air, and they came, and it was the fifth day.

And then God called for the animals to live on the green earth, and the cattle and the great beasts, and the creeping things came, and God called them all good.

After this he made the first of the great family of Man. He made them after His own likeness. He made their bodies from the earth, but their souls He breathed into them, so that Man is a spirit, living in an earthly body, and

can understand about God and love Him.   He blessed them and told them
to become many, and to rule over all the earth, with its beasts and birds, and
fishes, and it was the sixth day.

The Man's name was Adam, and the woman, who was made from a
piece of Adam's body nearest to his heart, was named Eve.

Then God's world was finished, and on the seventh day there was rest.
God was pleased with all that was made, and He made the seventh day holy,
by setting it apart from all the others.   We keep the Sabbath, or the Lord's
day still, in which his children may rest and worship.

Adam and Eve were very happy, for they had never done anything
wrong.   God gave them a beautiful wide garden, called Eden, full of flowers
and all kinds of fruit, and with a river flowing through it, and told Adam to
take care of the garden, and He sent all the animals and birds to Adam to be
named.   God told him also that he might eat the fruit of all the trees of the
garden except one—the tree of knowledge of good and evil—but if he ate of
the fruit of that tree he should surely die, and Adam and Eve loved God, and
had no wish to disobey Him, for He was their Father.

But there was a creeping serpent in the garden, and the evil spirit that
puts wrong thoughts in our hearts spoke to Eve through the serpent.

"You shall not die," he said, "but you shall be wise like God if you will
eat of this fruit," and Eve ate of the fruit, and gave it to her husband.   Then
they knew that they had sinned, and when they heard the voice of God in the
garden calling them, they hid among the trees, for they were unhappy and
afraid.   When the Lord had asked Adam if he had eaten of the fruit that
was forbidden, Adam laid the sin upon Eve, who gave it to him, and Eve
said that the serpent had tempted her to eat of the fruit.   God knew that
they must suffer for their sin, so He sent them out of the garden to make a
garden for themselves, and to work, and suffer pain, as all who came after
them have done to this day ; but He gave them a great promise, that among
their children's children One should be born who would be stronger than sin,
and a Savior from it.

After this two little children were sent to comfort Adam and Eve—first
Cain, and then Abel.   When they grew up Cain was a farmer, but Abel was
a shepherd.

They had been taught to worship God by bringing the best of all they
had to Him, and so Cain brought fruit and grain to lay upon his altar, but
Abel brought a lamb.

DRIVEN FROM EDEN.

God looked into their hearts and saw that Abel wished to do right, but Cain's heart was full of sin. Cain was angry because the Lord was pleased with the worship of Abel, and while they talked in the field Cain killed his brother. When the Lord said to Cain, "Where is thy brother?" he answered, "I know not. Am I my brother's keeper?" And the Lord sent him away from home, to wander from place to place over the earth, and find no rest, but He promised that no one should hurt Cain, or kill him as he had killed his brother, so he went away into another land to live.

Adam lived many years after this and had other children, but at last he died, when his children's children were beginning to spread over the land.

CHAPTER II.

THE GREAT FLOOD.

As the people of the earth grew to be many more and spread over the plains and hills, they also grew very wicked. They forgot God, and all the thoughts of their hearts were evil. Only Noah still worshipped God and tried to do right.

The people had destroyed themselves, and so God said to Noah:

"The end of all flesh is come ; make thee an ark of gopher wood."

He told Noah to make it of three stories, with a window in the top, and a door in the side. It was to be a great floating house, more than four hundred feet long and full of rooms, and it was to be covered with tar within and without, so that the water should not creep in.

"I bring a flood of waters upon the earth," said the Lord, "and everything that is in the earth shall die."

This was to be the house of Noah, with his wife, and his three sons and their wives, during the great flood.

Does the house seem large for eight people? God had told Noah to make room for a little family of every kind of bird and beast that lived, and to gather food of all kinds for himself and for them.

So Noah did all that the Lord had told him to do, and seven days before the great storm he heard the Lord calling:

"Come thou and all thy house into the ark," and that very day, Noah with his wife and his sons, Shem, Ham, and Japtheth, and their wives, went

THE GREAT FLOOD.

into their great black house, and through the window in the top came flying
the little families of birds and insects, from the tiny bees and humming birds,
to the great eagles, and through the door on the side came the famlies of animals, two by two, from the little mice to the tall giraffes, and the elephants,
and when all had come the Lord shut them in.

It rained forty days and forty nights, and the waters rose higher and
higher, covering the hills, and creeping up the mountains, so that every living
thing died except Noah, and all that were with him in the ark.

But after ten months the tops of the mountains were seen, and Noah
sent out a raven and a dove. The raven flew to and fro, but the dove came
back into the ark, because she found no place to rest her foot.

After seven days Noah sent her out again, and she returned with an
olive leaf in her bill, and then Noah knew that the waters were going away.

After seven days again he sent out his good little dove, and she did not
come back. So Noah was sure that the earth was getting dry, and that God
would soon tell him to go out of the ark.

And so he did. Think how glad the sheep and cows were to find fresh
grass, and the birds to fly to the green trees.

What a silent world it must have been, for there were none but Noah
and his family in all the earth. Noah did not forget how God had saved
them, and he made an altar of stone, and offered beasts and birds as a sacrifice. When he looked up to the sky there was a beautiful rainbow. It was
God's promise that there should be no more floods upon the earth. He still
sends the rainbow to show us that He is taking care of this world, and will
always do so.

Perhaps the people who lived after this—for Noah's children's children
increased very fast—did not believe God's promise, for they began to build a
great tower, or temple, on the plain of Shinar; or perhaps they had grown
proud and wicked, and wanted a temple for the worship of idols; but the
Lord changed their speech, so that they could not understand each other, and
they were scattered over other countries ; and so each country began to have
a language of its own.

CHAPTER III.

ABRAHAM—THE FATHER OF THE FAITHFUL.

The people who lived four thousand years ago were very much like children who easily forget. They told their children about the great flood, but nearly all forgot to tell them of the good God who is the Father of us all, whom we should always love and obey. Yet there is always one, if not more, who remembers God, and keeps his name alive in the world.

Abram had tried to do right, though there was no Bible in the world then, and no one better than himself to help him but God, and one day He called Abram, and told him to go away from his father's house into another country.

"A land that I will show thee," said the Lord, "and I will make of thee a great nation."

He also made Abram a wonderful promise,—

"In thee shall all the families of the earth be blessed."

He meant that sometime the Savior should be born among Abram's children's children, and that He should be the Savior of all the nations of the earth.

Abram did just what God told him to do. He took Sarai, his wife, and Lot, his nephew, and some servants, and cows, and sheep, and camels, and asses, and went into the land of Canaan. When they rested at night Abram and Lot set some sticks in the ground, and covered them with skins for a tent, and near by they made an altar, where Abram offered a sacrifice, for that was the only way they could worship God when the earth was young.

Abram went down into Egypt when there was a lack of food in Canaan, but he came back to Bethel, where he made the altar before, and worshipped God there.

He was very rich, for his cattle and sheep had grown into great herds and flocks, though he had sold many in Egypt for silver, and gold, and food. Abram and Lot moved often, for their flocks and herds soon ate up the grass. Then they rolled up the tents, and loaded the camels and asses, and went where the grass was thick and fresh.

They could easily live in tents, for the country was warm. But Abram's herdsmen and Lot's herdsmen sometimes quarreled. And so Abram spoke kindly to Lot, and told him to take his servants, and flocks, and herds, and go where the pastures were good, and he would go the other way. So they parted, and Lot went to the low plains of the Jordan, but Abram went to the high plains of Mamre, in Hebron, and there he built another altar to the Lord, who had given him all that country—to him and to his children forever.

There were warlike people in Canaan, and once when they had carried off Lot from Sodom, Abram took his servants and herdsmen and went out to fight. He had more than three hundred men, and they took Lot away from the enemy, and brought him back to Sodom. It was here that Abram met a wonderful man, who was both a king and a priest. His name was Melchisedek, and he brought Abram bread and wine, and blessed him there.

After this, God spoke to Abram one evening, and promised that he should have a son, and then while Abram stood outside his tent, with the great sky thick with stars above him, God promised him that his children's children should grow to be as countless as the stars. That was hard to believe, but Abram believed God always and everywhere.

Still no child came to Abram and Sarai, and Abram was almost a hundred years old, but God spoke to him again, and told him that he should be the father of many nations.

He told Abram that a little boy would be born to them, and his name would be Isaac, and God changed Abram's name to Abraham, which means "Father of many people," and Sarai's to Sarah, which means "Princess."

Abraham was sitting in his tent one hot day, when three men stood by him. They were strangers, and Abraham asked them to rest beneath the tree, and bathe their feet, while he brought them food. So Sarah made cakes, and a tender calf was cooked, and these with butter, and milk, were set before the men. But they were not men of this world ; they were angels, and they had come to tell Abraham and Sarah once more that their little child was sure to come. Then the angels went away, but one of them, who must have been the Lord Himself in an angel's form, stopped to tell Abraham that He was going to destroy Sodom and Gomorrah, because the people who lived there were so very wicked, and Abraham prayed Him to spare them if even ten good men could be found in them, for he remembered that Lot lived in Sodom. But the Lord never forgets. The two angels went to Sodom and stayed with Lot until morning, when they took him and all his family outside the city, and then the Lord said to him, "Escape for thy life—look not behind thee, neither stay thou in all the plain."

THE THREE STRANGERS.

And the Lord hid them in the little town of Zoar, while a great rain of fire fell upon the wicked cities of the plain, until they became a heap of ashes. Only Lot's wife looked back to see the burning cities, and she became a pillar of salt.

The next morning when Abraham looked from Hebron down toward the cities of the plain, a great smoke was rising from them like the smoke of a furnace.

At last the Lord's promise to Abraham and Sarah came true. A little son was born to them, and they called him Isaac. They were very happy, for though Abraham was a hundred years old, no child had ever been sent them.

When he was about a year old they made a great feast for him, and all brought gifts and good wishes, yet the little lad Ishmael, the son of Hagar, Sarah's servant, mocked at Isaac. Sarah was angry, and told her husband that Hagar and her boy must be sent away. So he sent them out with only a bottle of water and a loaf of bread; for God had told Abraham to do as Sarah wished him to do, and He would take care of little Ishmael, and make him the father of another nation.

When the water was gone, and the sun grew very hot, poor Hagar laid her child under a bush to die, for she was very lonely and sorrowful. While she hid her eyes and wept, saying,

"Let me not see the death of the child," she heard a voice out of heaven telling her not to be afraid.

"Arise, lift up the lad," said the voice, "for I will make him a great nation."

And God opened her eyes to see a well of water near. Then she filled the empty bottle, and gave the boy a drink, and God took good care of them ever after, though they lived in a wilderness.

Ishmael grew up to be an archer, and became the father of the Arabs, who still live in tents as Ishmael did.

But the Lord let a strange trial come to the little lad Isaac, also. His father loved and obeyed God, but there were heathen people around them, who worshipped idols, and sometimes killed their own children as a sacrifice to these idols. Abraham brought the best of his lambs and cattle to offer to the Lord; but one day the Lord told Abraham to take his only son Isaac and offer him upon a mountain called Moriah as a burnt sacrifice to God. Abraham had always obeyed God, and believed his word, and now, though he could not understand, he rose up early in the morning and took his young son, with

HAGAR IN THE DESERT.

two servants, and an ass loaded with wood, to the place of which God had told him.

They were three days on the journey, but at last they came to the high place, where the city of Jerusalem was afterward built, and to the very rock upon which the temple was built long afterward, with its great altar and Holy of Holies.

Abraham had left the young men at the foot of the mount, and went with Isaac to the great rock on the top of the mount.

"My father," said Isaac, "where is the lamb for a burnt offering?"

"My son, God will provide himself a lamb for a burnt offering," said his father, still obeying God, and believing His word, that Isaac should be the father of many nations.

Abraham made an altar of stones, and bound Isaac and laid him upon it, but when his hand was lifted to offer up the boy, the Lord called to him from heaven. "Lay not thine hand upon the lad," said the voice, "for now I know that thou fearest God, seeing thou hast not withheld thine only son from me."

Then Abraham turned and saw a ram with its twisted horns caught in the bushes, and he offered it to the Lord instead of his son. How glad and grateful Abraham must have been that morning, when he came down the mountain, with Isaac walking beside him, to think that he had still obeyed God when it was hard to do so.

Abraham was an old man when Sarah died. They had lived together a long lifetime, and he mourned for her many days. He bought a field close by the oak-shaded plain of Mamre in Hebron, and there in a rocky cave he buried her. He was called a Prince of God by the Canaanites because he lived a true, faithful life.

A few years after he also went to God, and his body was laid beside Sarah's in the cave-tomb. Ishmael came up from the south country to mourn with Isaac at the burial of their father, the Friend of God, and Father of the faithful.

ON MOUNT MORIAH.

CHAPTER IV.

ISAAC THE SHEPHERD PRINCE.

Before Abraham died, he thought much about his dear son Isaac, to whom he was going to leave all that he had. The young man had no mother, no sister, and soon he would have no father. So the old man called his old and faithful servant, and told him to go on a journey into the land of his fathers, and bring back with him a wife for his son Isaac.

The children of Nahor, Abraham's brother, lived there still, and Abraham wished for his son Isaac a wife of his own people, who should be both good and beautiful, and not like the heathen women of Canaan.

So the old servant listened to Abraham and promised to do all that he commanded.

He loaded ten camels with presents for his master's family away in Syria, and Abraham said:

"The Lord shall send His angel before thee," and from his tent door he saw the little caravan of camels and servants, as they set out across the plain, toward the land beyond the river Jordan.

There was a desert to cross and many dangers to meet, but the old servant believed in the God his master worshipped, and was not afraid.

When he came to Haran, he stopped outside the town by a well of water. It was early evening, and the women were coming each with a water-jar on her shoulder, to draw water.

The old man prayed that the Lord would show him which among these daughters of the men of the city, was the one who was to be his young master's wife.

Before his prayer was ended, Rebekah, of the family of Abraham's brother Nahor, came bearing her pitcher on her shoulder. She looked very kind and beautiful, and when she had filled her pitcher, the old man asked her for a drink of water. Then she let down the pitcher upon her hand saying:

"Drink, my lord," and asked if she should also give water to his camels. While she was giving him a drink, the man showed her some golden jewels that he had brought, and when he had asked her name, and knew that God had sent her to him for his young master, he gave them to

(14)

her, and worshipped the Lord who had led him to the house of his master's brother.

Then Rebekah ran in and told Laban, her brother, and the old servant of Abraham had a warm welcome at the door of Nahor's house.

"Come in, thou blessed of the Lord," they said.

And after they had cared for the camels and the men, there was a hurrying of servants to prepare a feast, but the old man would not taste food until he had given the message of his master. Then the father and brother of Rebekah, saw that the Lord had sent for her, and they said:

"Let her be thy master's son's wife, as the Lord hath spoken."

And the old servant bowed his face to the ground worshipping the Lord who had led him.

Then there was feasting and giving of costly gifts, and preparing to take a long journey, for the old servant was in haste to get back to his master, and Rebekah, who was willing to go, took her maid-servants and rode away into a far country to be the wife of Isaac.

When Isaac was walking in his field at sunset, thinking and praying to God, he looked up and saw that the camels were coming, and he hastened to meet them. When the old servant told Rebekah that it was his young master, she alighted from her camel, and covered herself with a long veil as was the custom of the Syrian women. When the old servant had told the story of his journey, he gave Rebekah to Isaac, and he took her to the tent that had been his mother's, and she became his wife, so that he was no longer lonely and sad.

Isaac lived to a very great age, and had two sons, Jacob and Esau. He was a gentle, quiet man, fond of his family, his flocks, and herds, and at the place where his father and mother were buried, he lived among the fields and oak groves of Hebron until he died.

CHAPTER V.

JACOB, A PRINCE OF GOD.

Jacob and Esau were the twin sons of Isaac and Rebekah.

They did not look alike as twins often do, and they were very unlike in all their ways. As they grew up, Esau loved the forests and wild places. He made bows and arrows, and was a hunter, and brought home wild birds and deer, for his father was very fond of such food. Jacob helped his father with the flocks, and learned how to cook food from his mother, who loved him more than she loved Esau.

One day Esau came home from hunting tired and hungry, and smelled the delicious soup of red lentils that Jacob was making. He begged Jacob to give him some, and Jacob, who wanted to be eldest, and have the right to the blessing that fathers gave to the first-born in those days, said:

"Sell me this day thy birthright," and Esau gave him all his rights as the first born, for a little food which he might have had as a free gift.

Jacob wanted to be counted in the great promise that God had given to Abraham, but Esau despised it.

Afterward, when Isaac was old and his eyes were dim, he called Esau, and asked him to go out into the fields and shoot a deer, and cook the venison that he loved, so that he might eat it and bless his first born before he died.

Rebekah heard it, and told Jacob to bring kids from the flock, which she cooked and served as venison. Then she dressed Jacob in the clothes of Esau, and told him to say that it was Esau who had brought the venison. Isaac said:

"The voice is the voice of Jacob," but he put his hands on him, and believed it was Esau, and blessed him.

When Esau came home and brought venison to his father, Isaac said:

"Who art thou?" and when Esau said, "I am thy son, thy first-born, Esau," the old man trembled, and told Esau the blessing had been given to another.

Poor Esau cried out with grief, "Hast thou but one blessing?" "Bless me, even me also, O my father."

(16)

JACOB'S DREAM.

And so Isaac blessed him, but he could not call back the blessing of the first-born. The Lord knew that Jacob would grow to be a good man, and love the things of God best, and that Esau would always love the things of this world best, yet it was wrong of Jacob and Rebekah to deceive, for we may not do evil that good may come.

After this Esau hated his brother, and said he would kill him.

So Isaac called Jacob, and, blessing him again, sent him away into Syria to the house of Laban, where Rebekah had lived, and where Abraham's servant went to find her for his master's son.

One night, when he was not far on his way, he lay down to sleep, with a stone for his pillow, on a hillside that looked toward his home, and he dreamed a wonderful dream. He saw a ladder reaching from earth to heaven, and a vision of angels who were going up and down upon it.

Above it stood the Lord, who spoke to Jacob, and gave to him the promise that He had first given to Abraham, and told him that He would go with him, and bring him again into his own land.

Jacob was afraid when he woke, for he had seen the heavens opened, and had heard God's voice. He made an altar of the pillow of stone, and called it Bethel—the House of God—and then he vowed that the Lord should be his God, and he added,—

"Of all that thou shalt give me, I will surely give a tenth unto thee."

When Jacob came to Haran, he saw the well from which his mother used to draw water. There were three flocks of sheep lying by it, waiting for all the flocks to gather in the cool of the day to be watered. Soon Rachel, the daughter of Laban, came leading her father's flocks, and one of the shepherds told Jacob whose daughter she was.

So Jacob rolled the stone from the well, and watered the flocks of Laban, his mother's brother. Then he kissed Rachel, and told her that he was Rebekah's son, and she ran and told her father.

There was great joy in Laban's house because Jacob had come, and after he had stayed a month with them Laban asked him to stay and take care of his flocks, and he would pay him for his work.

Since the day he had seen Rachel leading her father's flocks he had chosen her in his heart to be his wife. So he said that he would work for Laban seven years, if at the end of that time he would give him Rachel for his wife. Laban was quite willing to do so, and the seven years seemed to Jacob but a few days, for the love he had to Rachel. But, according to the custom of that country, the younger daughter could not be given in marriage

ISAAC BLESSING JACOB.

before the elder, and so Laban gave his daughter Leah also, and both Leah and Rachel became the wives of Jacob, for Jacob lived in that far away time and country of the early world when men were allowed to take more than one wife, and when each man was both king and priest over his family and tribe, and worshipped God by offering burnt sacrifices upon an altar.

After twenty years of work with Laban, in which he had earned many flocks and herds for himself, Jacob took his wives and the little sons God had sent him, and his flocks and herds, and started on a journey to his old home. Isaac was still alive, and Jacob longed to see him. He had lived long in Haran for fear of his brother Esau, and now he must travel through Edom, Esau's country, on his way to his old home.

As he was on his way some of God's angels met him, and he was strengthened. Still he feared Esau, and sent some of his men to tell his brother that he was coming.

The men came back, saying that Esau, with four hundred men, was coming to meet them.

Poor Jacob! He remembered the sin of his youth, when he had stolen the blessing from Esau, and he was afraid, and prayed God to protect him.

He sent his servants again to meet Esau with great presents of flocks, and herds, and camels, and after placing his wives and little ones in the safest place, he sent all that he had over the brook Jabbok, and he stayed on the other side to pray. It was as if he wrestled with a man all night, and when the day began to break the man wished to go, but Jacob said:

"I will not let thee go except thou bless me."

So the man blessed him there, and call his name Israel; "for as a prince," he said, "hast thou power with God and with men, and hast prevailed."

Then Jacob knew that the Lord Himself, in the form of a man, had been with him, and he had seen Him face to face.

And as the sun rose he passed over the brook. When he looked up he saw Esau and his men coming, and when he had told his family to follow him, he went straight before them, for he was no longer afraid to meet his brother.

Jacob's prayer had been answered, and Esau ran to meet his brother, and throwing his arms around him, wept on his shoulder. Then they talked in a loving and brotherly way, and Esau returned to his home with the presents Jacob had given him, and Jacob went on his way into Canaan full of joy and thankfulness. He stopped a little while in a pleasant place to rest his flocks and cattle, but he longed to see the place where he first saw the angels of

JACOB AND RACHAEL.

God, and heard the voice of the Lord blessing him, so they journeyed on to Beth-el, and there built an altar and worshipped God.

Again the Lord spoke to Jacob at Beth-el, and called him Israel, and blessed him.

After they left Beth-el, they came near to Bethlehem, where many hundred years afterward the Lord Jesus was born, and there another little son was born to Rachel, and there too God sent for her, and took her to Himself, and there her grave was made.

The little boy was named Benjamin, and was the youngest of Jacob's twelve sons, who became the fathers of the twelve tribes of Israel, and the princes of a great nation.

Jacob was almost home. His great family, with all the flocks and herds, had been long on the way, for they often spread their tents by the brooks in the green valleys, that the cattle might rest and find pasture, but at last the long caravan came slowly over the fields of Mamre to Hebron, and Isaac, whom the Lord had kept alive to see his son once more, was there in his tent waiting for him.

But soon after this he died, an hundred and eighty years old, and Esau came, and the two brothers laid their father in the cave that Abraham bought when Sarah died, and where he had buried Rebekah, and Jacob became patriarch in place of his father.

CHAPTER VI.

JOSEPH, THE CASTAWAY.

Of all the sons of Jacob, Joseph and Benjamin were the dearest to him, because they were the sons of his beloved Rachel, who had died on the journey from Syria into Canaan. They were also the youngest of all the twelve sons. When Joseph was about seventeen years old, he sometimes went with his elder brothers to keep his father's flocks in the fields. He wore a long coat striped with bright colors, which his father had given him, because he was a kind and obedient son, and could always be trusted.

Once he told his father of some wicked thing his brothers had done, and they hated him for it, and could not speak pleasantly to him.

MEETING OF JACOB AND ESAU.

Joseph had many strange and beautiful thoughts when he looked across the fields to the hills, and up into the starry sky at night. He also had some strange dreams that he told to his brothers. He said that he dreamed that they were binding sheaves in the field, and that his sheaf stood up, while the sheaves of his brothers bowed down to it.

Again he dreamed that the sun, and the moon, and eleven stars bowed down to him.

His father wondered that he should have such thoughts, and reproached him saying, "Shall I and thy brethren indeed come and bow down ourselves to thee to the earth?" and his brothers said,

"Shalt thou indeed rule over us?" and they hated him.

When they were many miles from home with the flocks their father sent Joseph to see if all was well with them. It was a long journey, and when they saw the boy coming they did not go to meet him, and speak kindly to him, but they said,

"Behold this dreamer is cometh. Let us slay him, and cast him into some pit, and we will say some evil beast hath devoured him, and we shall see what will become of his dreams."

But Reuben, the eldest, said,

"Let us not kill him ; but cast him into this pit," hoping to take him out secretly, and send him to his father.

So when Joseph came near, they robbed him of his coat of many colors, and cruelly cast him into a pit. After this they sat down to eat their bread, and looking up they saw a caravan coming. It was a company of Ishmaelites carrying costly spices down into Egypt to sell them.

Then Judah said,

"Why should we kill our brother? Let us sell him to these Ishmaelites."

Then there passed by some Midianite merchants, and who drew Joseph out of the pit and sold him to the Ishmaelites for twenty pieces of silver, and he was carried down into Egypt.

Reuben, when his brothers went back to their flocks, went to the pit to try to save Joseph, but he was not there, and Reuben cried out,

"The child is not, and I, whither shall I go?"

The brothers who had been so cruel to Joseph brought his coat to their father, all stained with blood. They had themselves dipped it in the blood of a kid to deceive him, and he mourned long, and would not be comforted, for the beloved child that he believed had been torn in pieces by evil beasts.

CHAPTER VII.

JOSEPH, A SERVANT, A PRISONER, AND A SAINT.

The king of Egypt, where Joseph was taken by the Ishmaelites, was called Pharaoh, and he had a captain of the guard named Potiphar, who bought Joseph for a house servant. Though he was the son of a Hebrew prince, Joseph did his work faithfully and wisely as a servant, and was soon made steward of the house, and was trusted with all that his master had, and the Lord made all that he did to prosper; but the wife of Potiphar was a wicked woman, who persuaded her husband that Joseph was a bad man, and he was sent to prison.

Even there Joseph won the hearts of all, until the keeper of the prison set him over the other prisoners, and trusted him as Potiphar had done. It was the Lord in Joseph who helped him to win the love and trust of those around him.

Pharaoh sent two of his servants to prison because they had displeased him.

One was his chief cook, and one was the chief butler, who always handed the wine cup to the king, and Joseph had the care of them.

They each had a dream the same night, and were troubled because they could not understand them. Joseph asked them to tell him the dreams, for God knew what they meant.

So the chief butler told Joseph that he saw a vine having three branches, and the branches budded and blossomed, and the blossoms changed into ripe grapes, and he took the grapes and pressed them into Pharaoh's cup, and handed the cup to the king.

Then Joseph said: "The three branches are three days. Within three days the king will take you out of prison, and you shall hand the king's cup to him as you used to do."

Joseph also asked the butler, to think of him when he was again in the king's palace, and speak to the king to bring him out of prison, because he had been stolen from his own land, and he had done nothing wrong that he should be put in prison.

Then the chief cook told his dream. He said that he dreamed that he carried three baskets on his head, one above another.

In the highest one was all kinds of cooked meats for Pharaoh, and the birds flew down and ate from the basket.

"The three baskets are three days," said Joseph as he said to the butler, but he told the cook that in three days he would be put to death, and hanged on a tree, where the birds would eat his flesh.

All this came true, for Pharaoh's birthday came, and he brought out the chief butler to serve at a birthday feast, but he hanged the chief cook. Yet the chief butler forgot Joseph, and did not speak to the king about him as he might have done.

At the end of two long years, Pharaoh dreamed a dream. He thought he stood by the river of Egypt, and saw seven cows looking well kept and fat, came up out of the river.

Behind them came seven other cows, looking thin and poorly fed, and the thin and poorly fed cows ate up the well-kept and fat ones.

And Pharoah had a second dream. He thought he saw seven heads of wheat growing on one stalk—and they were all full of grain. After them came seven thin heads of wheat with no grain in them; and the seven bad heads of wheat ate up the seven good ones.

In the morning Pharaoh was troubled about these dreams, and called for his wise men who worked magic for him, and they could tell him nothing.

Then the chief butler standing near the king remembered Joseph, and told Pharaoh of the young Hebrew who had told the meaning of his dream, and that of the chief cook, and they had come to pass as he had said, so Pharaoh sent for Joseph and said to him:

"I have heard that thou canst understand a dream to interpret it."

Joseph answered the king humbly and wisely:

"It is not in me," he said, "God shall give Pharaoh an answer of peace."

When the king had told his dream Joseph said:

"The dream is one," and then he showed him that the seven fat cows, and the seven full heads of wheat meant seven good years in the land of Egypt, when the harvests would be great; and the seven lean cows, and the seven empty heads of wheat, meant seven years of famine, when the east winds should spoil the wheat, so there would be nothing to reap in time of harvest and the people would want bread. He told the king that he had better set a wise man over the land, who would attend to saving the grain during the seven good years, so that the people would have bread to eat in the seven years of famine.

JOSEPH SOLD INTO EGYPT.

The king was greatly pleased with Joseph, and told him that God had taught him to interpret dreams, and had showed him things to come, and there could be no wiser man found to be set over the land.

So he made Joseph a ruler over the whole land, and next to the king in all things.

He put his own ring on his hand, and dressed him in the robes of a prince, and gave him an Egyptian name and an Egyptian wife, so that there was no one in all the land of Egypt so great as Joseph, except the king.

He built storehouses in every city, and stored the grain, until it was like the sand of the sea, and could not be measured.

In the years of plenty two sons were born to Joseph, Manasseh and Ephraim, and then the seven years of dearth began to come. When the people began to cry to the king for bread, he always said,—

" Go to Joseph ; what he says to you do."

And Joseph and his helpers began to open the storehouses, and sell wheat to the Egyptians, and to the people of all countries, for the famine was in all lands.

CHAPTER VIII.

JOSEPH—THE SAVIOR OF HIS PEOPLE.

The famine reached even to the fruitful land of Canaan, and Jacob, though rich in flocks and herds, began to need bread for his great family. So he sent his ten sons down into Egypt to buy wheat, keeping Benjamin, the youngest at home.

When they came before the governor they bowed down to him with their faces to the ground. Joseph knew them, though he acted as if he did not, and remembered his dream of his brother's sheaves bowing down to his sheaf. At first, he spoke roughly to them, and called them "spies." But they said that they were all one man's sons, and had come to buy food.

Joseph still spoke roughly to them, not because he was angry, but because he did not wish them to know him yet. His heart was full of love for them, and he was soon going to show them great kindness; but when they told him that they had left an old father and a young brother at home, and one was dead, he still acted as if they did not tell the truth.

He said that to prove themselves true men one of them should go home and bring the youngest brother, and the others should be kept in prison until they returned; and he put them all in prison.

After three days, he said one might stay while the others took the wheat home to their families, but that they must surely come back and bring the boy with them.

Then Reuben, who had tried to save Joseph from the pit long before, told his brothers that all this trouble had come upon them for their wickedness to their brother Joseph, and they said· to each other in their own language:

"We are verily guilty concerning our brother; when he besought us, we would not hear, therefore is this distress come upon us."

Joseph understood everything they said though they did not know it, for he had been talking to them through an interpreter, and they thought he was an Egyptian. Now his heart was so full that he had to go out of the room to weep. But he came back and chose Simeon to stay while the others went to Canaan to bring back Benjamin.

They took the wheat that they had bought in bags, and went away; but when they stopped at an inn to rest and feed their asses, one of the brothers opened his bag, and found the money that he had paid for the wheat in the top of his bag. Here was more trouble, and they were afraid.

When they came home to their father they told him all that had happened, and as they opened the bags, each one found his money. Jacob was deeply troubled; for Joseph was gone, and Simeon was gone, and now they wanted to take Benjamin.

Reuben who had two sons said: "Slay my two sons if I bring him not to thee."

But Jacob said Benjamin should not go down to Egypt. But the wheat was gone in a short time, and they were likely to starve so great was the famine, and at last Jacob said they must go to Egypt again for food.

Judah said they would go if Benjamin would go with them, but Jacob would not listen to this. He asked them why they told the man that they had a brother, and they replied, that the Governor had asked them if their father was yet living and if they had another brother.

"Send the lad with me," said Judah, "if I bring him not unto thee, let me bear the blame forever"

Then Jacob told them to take him and go, and also to take presents of honey, and spices, and balm, and nuts, and double the money, so as to return that which was put in their bags, and he blessed them, and sent them away.

They went down into Egypt, and stood before Joseph again. When he saw Benjamin with them he told the steward of his house to make ready a fine dinner for them, and bring them to him at noon, and he did so.

Then the brothers were afraid that they were all to be put in prison, and at the door of Joseph's house began to tell the steward how they found the money when they opened their bags, and that they had brought it back doubled; but the steward spoke kindly to them, and said that he had placed their money, and that they need not fear, for God had given it back to them.

Then he brought Simeon out, and they made ready to dine with the Governor at noon, and to give him their presents.

When he came they bowed down to him and presented their gifts, and he asked them if they were well, and if the old man of whom they spoke was still alive, and they replied that he was. When he saw Benjamin, and knew that he was truly his own brother, the son of Rachel, he said:

"God be gracious unto thee my son," and he went quickly to his own chamber, lest he should weep before them.

When he came out to them again, and they sat down to dine, he placed the sons of Jacob by themselves, and the Egyptians of his house by themselves, and the brothers were placed according to their ages—Reuben at the head and Benjamin last, and they wondered among themselves at this. Joseph also sent portions from his own table to his brothers, but the portion of Benjamin was five times greater than that of the others.

The next morning their wheat was measured to them, and the asses were loaded with it, and they went on their way, but Joseph had told the steward to put the money of each man in the top of his bag, and in Benjamin's to put his silver cup.

When they were a little away from the city, the steward overtook them, and charged them with stealing his lord's silver cup.

The men were so sure that no one of them had stolen the silver cup, that they said,

"Let him die with whom the cup is found, and the rest of us will be your slaves."

So everybody's bag was opened from the oldest to the youngest, and the cup was found in Benjamin's bag. Then they rent their clothes for grief, and loaded the asses and went back to the city, and when they came to Joseph's

JOSEPH MAKES HIMSELF KNOWN TO HIS BROTHERS.

house, they fell on their faces before him, Joseph tried to speak sternly and said :

"What deed is this you have done?"

Judah said :

"What shall we say unto my lord, or how shall we clear ourselves? We are my lord's servants."

Then said Joseph :

"The man in whose hand the cup is found he shall be my servant, and as for you, get you up in peace unto your father."

Then Judah came nearer to Joseph, and all his soul came forth into his voice as he said :

"O, my lord, let thy servant speak a word in my lord's ears!"

Then he told the story of their coming down into Egypt, and of the old father and young brother whom he had asked them about ; of the love of this father for the little one, for his mother, and his brother now dead. He reminded Joseph that he had told them to bring the boy to him, and that they had said, that if the boy should leave his father, his father would die ; but the governor had said, "Except your youngest brother come down with you, ye shall see my face no more."

Then Judah told the story of the father's grief when he found that he must let Benjamin go down into Egypt, that they might buy a little food ; how he spoke of his two sons, that were the sons of Rachel—that one had been torn in pieces, and now if mischief should befall the other, it would bring his gray hairs in sorrow to the grave. He asked Joseph what he should do when he returned to his father without the lad, seeing that his life was bound up in the lad's life, and Judah begged him, as he had made himself surety for the lad, to take him to be his slave, but to let Benjamin return to his father with his brothers,

"For how shall I go up to my father," said Judah, "and the lad be not with me?"

Then Joseph could bear it no longer. He told all the Egyptians to go out of the room, and then weeping so that the Egyptians and the people in the king's house heard, he made himself known to his brothers.

"I am Joseph, your brother," he said, "whom you sold into Egypt," and he begged them to come near to him.

"Be not grieved nor angry with yourselves," he said, for he saw that they were terrified, "for God sent me before you to save your lives by a great deliverance. It was not you that sent me hither, but God, and he hath made me a ruler throughout all the land of Egypt."

Then he told them to hasten and go to his father and tell him this, and ask him to come down at once, with all his flocks and herds, and dwell in Goshen, the best part of Egypt, for years of famine were yet to come.

Then Joseph took little Benjamin in his arms and wept over him, and kissed him, and kissed all his brothers, and after that his brothers talked with him. The king heard the story of Joseph's brothers and was pleased. He told Joseph to send wagons for the wives and little ones of his brothers, and to tell them to bring their father, and all their cattle and sheep, and come to live in Goshen where they should have the best of the land for their flocks and herds.

Joseph did as the king commanded, and also gave them food for the journey, and a suit of clothing to each brother, but to little Benjamin he gave five suits, and three hundred pieces of silver. He also loaded twenty asses with the good things of Egypt as presents to his father, so he sent them all on their journey saying:

"See that ye fall not out by the way."

When they came to Jacob in Hebron, they told him the wonderful story of the finding of Joseph, and his heart was faint, for he did not believe them; but when he had heard all Joseph's messages, and had seen the gifts, and the wagons, he said:

"It is enough: Joseph my son is yet alive: I will go and see him before I die."

So they began the long journey to Egypt, for it took a long time to travel with a great family, and with thousands of cattle and sheep. At Beersheba Jacob stopped and worshiped God, where his father had built an altar years before; and God told him in the night that he need not fear to go down into Egypt, for He would there make him a great nation, and that He would bring him back again to his own land.

So Jacob with all his children and their little ones, and all his flocks and herds came into Egypt. There were sixty-seven souls, and when they had counted Joseph and his two sons, there were seventy.

Jacob sent Judah on before to see Joseph and ask the way to Goshen, so that they might go directly there with the cattle and sheep. And when Joseph knew that his father was coming, he went to meet him in Goshen, and there he wept on his father's neck a long time, and Jacob said:

"Now let me die, since I have seen thy face, because thou art yet alive."

After this Joseph presented five of his brothers to Pharaoh, and the king spoke very kindly to them, and gave them the best of the land for their flocks, and hired some of them to oversee his own shepherds.

Joseph brought his father in also and Jacob blessed Pharaoh.

So the family of Jacob lived in peace, and were cared for by Joseph, just as the Lord had promised Jacob, when in a dream he saw the angels of God at Bethel, and heard above them the voice of the Lord blessing him, and saying :

"Thou shalt spread abroad to the West, and to the East, and to the North, and to the South, and in thee shall all the families of the earth be blessed."

Joseph carried all Egypt through the years of famine, and saved seed for the people to sow their fields in the seventh year so that they said :

"Thou hast saved our lives."

He afterwards visited his father, and Jacob made him promise that he would bury him when he died in the tomb of Abraham and Isaac, his father, in his own land.

When Jacob was near his end, Joseph brought his two little sons, Ephraim and Manasseh, to his bedside, and the old man gave them his blessing, laying his right hand upon the head of Ephraim, the youngest, and his left hand on that of Manasseh the first born, even as Isaac had given the birthright blessing to him instead of to Esau, and he said :

"The angel which redeemed me from all evil bless the lads."

Then he called all his sons together and told them what should befall them in the last days. To each one he spoke as a prophet speaks who has a vision of things to come, and he blessed them there. When he spoke to Judah, he told him that kings and lawgivers should arise from among his children until the Saviour of the world should come.

Jacob was an hundred and forty-seven years old when he died, and there was great mourning for him.

Joseph had the body of his father embalmed, as the Egyptians had the custom of doing, and after a long mourning in Egypt, Joseph and his brothers and many Egyptians who were Joseph's friends, carried the body of Jacob to Canaan, in a great procession, and buried him in the cave of Machpelah, where his fathers were buried.

After they had returned to Egypt, the brothers of Joseph said :

" Perhaps now he will hate us, and bring upon us all the evil we did to him."

So they sent to him to ask his forgiveness for all that was past. Then Joseph wept, for he had nothing but love in his heart toward his brothers, and he wished them to trust him. He comforted them and spoke kindly to them, saying :

" Fear not : ye meant evil unto me, but God meant it unto good. I will nourish you and your little ones."

And so through all Joseph's life, and he lived one hundred and ten years, he was a tender father to all his family, and a wise ruler of the people, and he died after making his family promise to carry his body back into Canaan to be buried with his fathers when they themselves should go.

" For God will surely visit you," he said, " and bring you out of this land into the land which he promised to Abraham, to Isaac and to Jacob."

CHAPTER IX.

THE CRADLE THAT WAS ROCKED BY A RIVER.

After Joseph and all the sons of Jacob had grown old and had passed away, their children's children grew in numbers until they became a great multitude.

The Pharaoh whom Joseph had served also died, and the king who followed him did not like the Hebrews. He feared them because they had grown to be strong, so he set overseers to watch them, and make them work like slaves.

He treated them cruelly, and made them lift the great stones with which they built the tombs of the kings and temples of the gods. He also tried to kill all the little boys as soon as they were born, but the Lord took care of them. Also, the king told his servants, that wherever they found a baby boy among the Hebrews, to throw him into the river Nile, but the little girls, they should save alive.

There was a man named Amrom, who, with his wife Jochebed, had a beautiful little boy whom they tenderly loved. They hid him as long as they could, and then when he was three months old and she could hide him no longer, she made up her mind to give him into the care of God. She made a little boat, or ark of stout rushes, that grew by the river. She wove it closer than a basket, and then covered it with pitch that the water might not enter, just as Noah covered the great ark before the flood.

Then she wrapped her baby carefully and laid him in the little boat, and set it among the reeds at the edge of the river Nile. God and His angels watched the cradle of the child, and the river gently rocked it. Jochebed told the baby's sister to wait near by and see what might happen to him, and this is what happened, or rather what God prepared for the baby in the boat of rushes.

The king's daughter came down to bathe in the river, and as her maidens walked up and down by the riverside, she called one of them to bring to her the little ark that she saw rocking on the river among the reeds. When she had opened it she saw a beautiful little child, and when it cried her heart was touched, and she longed to keep it for her own.

"This is one of the Hebrew's children," she said, and as the baby's sister came near she asked the princess if she should go and get a nurse from among the Hebrew women to bring it up for her, and the princess said to her, "Go," and the maid went and called the child's mother. The princess said: "Take this child away and nurse it for me, and I will give thee thy wages."

And the mother took her baby joyfully though she hid her joy in her heart, and carried him home to nurse and bring up for Pharoah's daughter.

.   And the child grew, and when he was old enough his mother took him to the king's palace, and he became the son of the princess. She called his name Moses, which means "drawn out," because she drew him out of the water.

THE FINDING OF MOSES.

CHAPTER X.

MOSES IN MIDIAN.

Moses had teachers, and was taught all the learning of the Egyptians, but his heart was with his own people. He was grieved when he saw their burdens, and heard their cries when their taskmasters struck them.

Once, when he was a grown man, he saw an Egyptian beating a Hebrew, and he struck the Egyptian and killed him, for he thought he ought to defend his people: and when he saw that the man was dead, he buried him in the sand. In a day or two Moses tried to make peace between two Hebrews who were fighting, and they answered him roughly, and one of them said:

"Who made thee a ruler over us? wilt thou kill me, as thou didst the Egyptian yesterday?"

Then Moses was afraid, and when the king heard of it, and tried to take his life, Moses fled away out of Egypt, through a desert into Midian. There he found a well and sat down by it to rest. While he sat there the seven daughters of the priest of Midian came to draw water for their father's flocks, and some rough shepherds came and drove them away, but Moses stood up and helped them, and watered their flocks. When their father knew that a noble stranger had been kind to his daughters, he asked him to come into his house, and eat bread with him, and stay as long as he would. So Moses stayed and Zipporah, one of the seven sisters, became his wife.

But Moses did not forget his people. God was preparing him to lead them out of bondage, and he learned many things, during the years that he kept the sheep of his father-in-law in the wilderness.

One day he led his flocks across the desert to Mount Horeb or Sinai. There he saw a bush all bright within as if it burned. He drew nearer to see why the bush was not consumed, and heard the voice of the Lord calling him. The Lord told him to come no nearer, and to put off his shoes, for he stood on holy ground. Then the Lord told him that He was the God of his fathers, and that He had heard the cry of his oppressed people in Egypt.

"I know their sorrows," said the voice from the midst of the fire, "And I am come down to deliver them out of the hand of the Egyptians, and to bring them up out of that land into a good land, and a large—unto a land flowing with milk and honey."

(38)

Then the Lord said that Moses must go to the new Pharaoh, for the old king was dead, and bring the children of Israel out of Egypt.   Moses was a very humble man, and he could not believe that Pharaoh would listen to him, or that the Hebrews would follow him, but the Lord said,

"Certainly I will be with thee."

And as a sign that it should be so, He said that after Moses had brought his people out of Egypt, they should serve God in this mountain.

But Moses had many fears.   He knew that he had been brought up as an Egyptian, and he feared that his people would not listen to his words.

Then the Lord showed signs to Moses to help his faith.

He turned the rod in Moses' hand into a serpent, and then when he was afraid of it, the Lord told him to take it in his hand and it became a rod again.

He also turned his hand white with leprosy, and then changed it again to natural flesh, and told Moses, that these, and other signs he should show in Egypt—to prove that he was sent of God.

But Moses felt himself to be so weak and faithless as a leader of his people, that he still cried out that he was "slow of speech, and of a slow tongue," and when the Lord said, "I will teach thee what thou shalt say," he did not believe, but begged the Lord to send by whom he would, only not by him.

Then the Lord said that Aaron, the brother of Moses could speak well, and that he should go with him to Pharoah and to his people, and should speak for him, but that the wisdom and power of God should be with Moses, and that he should do wonders with the rod in his hand.

CHAPTER XI.

THE ROD THAT TROUBLED EGYPT.

So Moses took his wife and his sons and returned to Egypt, and the rod of God was in his hand ; and Aaron, sent of God, came to meet him in the wilderness, and there Moses told him all that was in his heart, and all that God had sent him to do.

When they came into Egypt they gathered the Israelites together, and Aaron spoke to them, and they believed his words, and the signs that Moses showed them.

3

Afterward, they went to Pharoah and gave him the message of the Lord, and Pharoah said :

"I know not the Lord, neither will I let Israel go."

And he began to oppress the Israelites more than he had ever done before. They made bricks of clay mixed with straw, that hardened in the sun, and were as lasting as stone, but he forced them to find the straw wherever they could, and make as many bricks as before. This they did until no more straw could be found, and their Egyptian masters beat them cruelly because they failed to make the full number of bricks. Then they turned upon Moses and Aaron and said, that they had put a sword in the kings hand to slay them.

Where could Moses turn except to the Lord who had sent him ? The Lord heard him and made to him again the great promise, as he did at the burning bush, and Moses told the people, but they could not believe it, for they were crushed under their cruel burdens.

And now the Lord sent Moses and Aaron again to Pharoah, to show by sign and miracle, that their message was from Him. They took the rod that Moses brought from Mount Horeb, and Moses told Aaron to cast it down before the king, and it became a serpent. Pharoah called his wise men and wizards, and they did the same, only Aaron's rod swallowed up their rods, and Pharoah would not listen to their words.

But in the morning when Pharoah walked by the river the two men stood by him and said again :

The Lord God of the Hebrews hath sent me unto thee saying:

"Let my people go that they may serve me in the wilderness," and then Aaron struck the waters of the river Nile with his rod, and the waters turned to blood.

In all the land, in every stream and pond there was blood, so that the fishes died and no one could drink the water.

But because the wizards could turn water to blood also, Pharoah's heart was hardened toward Moses and Aaron.

While the people were digging wells for water, Aaron stretched forth his rod over the river again, and frogs came up from it, and spread over all the land and filled the houses of the people. This also the magicians did, but so great was the plague that the king said:

"I will let the people go."

"When shall I entreat for thee and for thy people to destroy the frogs from thee and thy houses?" said Moses; and Pharoah told him to do so the next day.

THE ROD THAT TROUBLED EGYPT.

So on the next day Moses prayed to the Lord that the frogs might go out of the land, and the Lord answered his prayer; but when Pharoah saw that the frogs had been destroyed his heart grew hard, and he would not listen to Moses and Aaron.

Then another plague was brought upon the Egyptians. The dust of the land was changed to lice that covered man and beast, and this was followed by swarms of flies that settled upon all the land except Goshen where the Israelites lived.

Then Pharoah said:

"Go, sacrifice to your God in this land," but they would not worship in Egypt, and Pharoah at last told them that they could go into the wilderness, but they must not go very far away. So Moses prayed, and the swarms of flies were swept out of Egypt, but Pharoah did not keep his word.

Then a great sickness fell upon the cattle and sheep of the country, though the flocks and herds of the Israelites were free from it; and this was followed by a breaking out of boils upon men and beasts everywhere, even upon the magicians, but Pharoah's heart was still too wicked to yield to God.

Then came a great storm of hail over Egypt, such as had never been known in that sunny land. It killed the cattle in the fields, and destroyed the grain that was grown, and broke the trees and herbs. The lightnings fell also and ran upon the ground, and when it was over the heart of Pharaoh was still hard against God.

Then Moses told Pharaoh that the face of the earth would be covered with clouds of locusts that would eat every green thing left by the storm, if he did not let God's people go. This frightened Pharaoh's servants and they begged him to send them away, and though he would not let their wives and little ones go, he said:

"Go now, ye that are men, for that ye did desire," and he drove them out of his presence.

Then at the Lord's word, Moses arose and stretched forth his rod over Egypt, and the plague of locusts came, driven by the East wind, and covered the land until there was no green thing left in Egypt.

Then Pharaoh sent for Moses and Aaron in great haste, and confessing his sin, begged to be forgiven and to be saved from, "this death only," and, at Moses' prayer, a mighty west wind drove the army of locusts into the Red Sea.

But again the heart of Pharaoh turned against God, and the Lord brought thick darkness over the land for three days, only in the homes of the Hebrews there was light. Then Pharaoh was willing to let them take their wives and their little ones, but not their flocks and herds, and because they would not leave them behind, Pharaoh drove Moses and Aaron from him in anger, saying :

"See my face no more."

But the Lord proposed to break the hard heart of Pharaoh. He told Moses to see that every Israelite should take a lamb from the flock and keep it four days. Then, at evening, he was to kill it, and dip a branch of hyssop in its blood, and strike it against the sides of his door, also over it, leaving three marks of blood there. Then he was to close his door and no one was to go out of it until morning.

They were to roast the lamb and eat of it, and be ready for the journey they were to make, and it should be to them forever the feast called the Passover. They were to eat it with unleavened bread, and the feast should be kept forever from the first to the seventh day of the month, a holy feast to the Lord.

And this is why it was called the feast of the Passover. At midnight, after the lamb was killed in each house of the Israelites, and the doors were shut, the Lord passed through the land, and wherever he saw the blood on the side posts and the top of the door, he passed over that house, and it was safe, but in every Egyptian house the first born died, from the child of Pharaoh who sat on the throne, to the child of the captive in the cell, and all the first born of cattle.

The next morning a great cry went up from the land of Egypt, for there was not a house where there was not one dead.

Then Pharaoh was quite ready to let the Israelites go.

"Take all you have and be gone," he said.

They were all ready, and rose up very gladly to join the great procession, led by Moses and Aaron, that gathered in Goshen, and started on its long journey toward the east.

They had heard of the land of their fathers, and now they were going home to be slaves no more. They were a family of seventy souls when they came into Egypt, four hundred and thirty years before, and now they went out a great nation, as the Lord had promised when he blessed their fathers.

The feast of the Passover has been the chief one held by the Israelites, from the time of their coming out of Egypt until now, and since Jesus held the Passover feast with his disciples on the night that he went forth to death, it has become to all Christians the Sacrament of the Lord's Supper.

CHAPTER XII.

FOLLOWING THE CLOUD.

"God led the people," says the Word, as they came up out of Egypt. He gave them the two leaders by whom He had broken the power of Pharaoh, and set His people free, and He also set a great cloud in the air, just above and before them, to lead them in the right way. It was to them the presence of the Lord. By day it rose white and beautiful against the blue sky, and moved slowly before them. At night it stood still while they rested, and shed light over all the camp, for there seemed to be a fire within the cloud at night. How safe and happy they must have felt away from the cruel taskmasters of Egypt, and the Lord's presence, spreading a wing of cloud over them. They were not led by a straight way to Canaan, for a warlike people lived in the land which they must pass through, but they were led at first through a country without cities or armies, where they would not trouble many people or be troubled by them. They bore with them the embalmed body of Joseph, for they had promised to bury him with his fathers in the cave of Machpelah ; and they also had much wealth in herds, and flocks, and gold, and silver. Pharaoh thought of this after they had gone, and his wicked heart grew harder than before, so he ordered his chariots and horsemen to follow them, and they found the Israelites camped by the Red Sea.

Then there was great fear and mourning in the camp when they saw the army of Pharaoh coming, but Moses cried :

"Fear ye not, stand still and see the salvation of the Lord. The Lord shall fight for you, and ye shall hold your peace."

Then the Lord told Moses to speak to the people that they go forward. He also told him to lift up his rod and stretch his hand over the sea and divide it, and the children of Israel should go on dry ground through the midst of the sea. Night was falling, and the waters lay dark before them, but the angel of God, the pillar of cloud and fire, moved from its place before them and went behind them, while Moses and Aaron led them on. Then the presence of the Lord was a cloud and darkness to the Egyptians, but it gave a light by night to the Israelites. A strong east wind drove the waters apart all night, so that there was a way through the sea, and the waters were a wall upon their right hand and on their left. Pharaoh's army saw the broad path

(44)

DESTRUCTION OF PHAROAH'S ARMY.

through the sea, and followed fast after the Israelites, but as morning dawned the Lord looked from the cloud and troubled the Egyptians. Their chariot wheels came off, and all went wrong with them.

At last the Lord told Moses to stretch his hand forth over the sea, that the waters might come back upon the Egyptians, and he did so; and as the sun rose, the sea swallowed up the Egyptian host, and their bodies were cast upon the shore. There on the other side stood the great host of Israel, and saw the salvation of God, and they believed in Him, and in Moses His servant.

Then a great shout went up from the host of Israel. Moses led them in a song of praise, and Miriam, the sister of Aaron, took a tambourine, and the women followed her in dances as they answered in a chorus of praise:—

"Sing ye to the Lord, for He hath triumphed gloriously; the horse and the rider hath he thrown into the sea."

Soon they took up their journey, the cloudy pillar going before. There was but little water by the way, and after three days of thirst, they came to the waters of Marah, but they were bitter, and the people cried to Moses,

"What shall we drink?"

Then the Lord showed him a tree which he cast into the waters, and they were made pure and sweet. Soon after they came to Elim, where there were twelve wells of water, and seventy palm trees, and there they rested.

Again they took up their journey and passed through a desert land, where they could get no food, and again they complained to Moses because he had brought them into the wilderness to die. They did not yet believe that God could supply all their need.

"I will rain bread from heaven for you," said the Lord to Moses. He was ready to provide, if they would only believe in Him and obey Him.

Moses called them to come near before the Lord while Aaron should speak his word to them. As they came near and looked toward the wilderness where the cloud stood, the glory of the Lord shone out of it. The Lord had heard them speak harshly to Moses for bringing them into a desert to die, but he said,

"At even ye shall eat flesh, and in the morning ye shall be filled with bread."

And his word came true. Great flocks of quails came up and covered the camp at sunset, so that they caught them for food; and in the morning the dew lay around them, and when it had risen, there lay on the ground a small, round, white thing, something like frost, or a little seed, and it tasted like wafers made with honey. The Lord told Moses that the people must

gather just enough to eat through the day, and no more. The morning before the Sabbath they must gather enough for two days, for none would fall
on the Sabbath. This was the bread that the heavenly Father provided for
his children through all the years of their journey from Egypt to Canaan, and
they called it " Manna."

There were hard things to bear in the wilderness. Often when they
wanted water for their little ones and their cattle, and could not find it, they
were like fretful children when they were tired and thirsty. Once, at Horeb,
Moses struck a rock with his wonderful rod, and water sprung out in a
stream.

There were enemies also in the way. The Amelikites came out to fight
with the Israelites. The strong men went to meet the enemy, but Moses
stood on a hill with the rod of God in his hand, and Aaron and Hur were
with him. While Moses held up the rod, Israel prevailed ; but when he let
down his hand Amalek prevailed.

But Moses grew tired and they placed a stone for him to sit upon, and
Aaron and Hur held up his hands on either side until the going down of the
sun, when Amalek was conquered. Moses built an altar there, and called it
" The Lord my Banner."

They were now drawing near the Mount, where Moses saw the burning
bush, and heard the Lord calling him to be the leader of his people.

They were far out of their way to Canaan, but it was in the Lord's purpose to bring them into obedience and faith before he brought them into the
promised land. They had lived long among the Egyptians, and were very
far from being like Jacob and Joseph, but there were good and true men like
Aaron, and Joshua, and Hur, who helped Moses. It was about three months
after the children of Israel left Egypt, that they came into the wilderness of
Sinai. There the "Mount of God " still lifts its great granite cliffs toward the
sky. There are high valleys midway where it is cooler than below, and there
the people encamped and waited to hear what God would say to them, for
God talked with Moses on the Mount.

He said He had chosen them, if they would obey his voice, to be a holy
nation. He told Moses to tell the people to be ready, and on the third day
He would come down in the sight of all the people on Mount Sinai.

And so it was, as the people looked there was a thick cloud upon the
Mount, from which came thunder and lightning, and the sound of a great
trumpet, while the mountain trembled as with an earthquake. Only Moses
and Aaron could approach the holy Mount, and from it God gave to Moses

the laws that the people were to live by, and Moses wrote them all down that he might read them to the people.   A company of the Elders of Israel went up and saw the glory of God afar off, but God called Moses up into the Mount, and the cloud closed him round, while the Lord gave him the laws for a great nation, and the pattern of the tabernacle which He wished him to make for a church in the wilderness.

Forty days and forty nights Moses was on the Mount with God, and then God gave him the ten great commandments written with his own hands on tablets of stone, that he might give them to the people.   They were to be kept as the rules of life for all people in all times.

Forty days and nights seemed a long time to the people camped around the Mount.   Perhaps they thought Moses would never come back to lead them, for they began to think of the gods of Egypt, and asked Aaron to make one for them.   So to please them he told them to bring him their gold ornaments, and he melted them and made a golden calf such as the Egyptians worshiped, and before it they made an altar, and they worshiped the calf.

The Lord who sees all things told Moses to go down to the people for they were worshiping an idol.   So Moses went down a little way and met Joshua, and they both went down and saw the people feasting, and singing, and dancing, and Moses cast the tablets of stone upon the ground and they were broken.   The heart of Moses, too, was almost broken, but he destroyed the golden calf, and punished the people for their great sin, and then went up to the Mount to plead for the life of his people.

"O this people have sinned a great sin," he cried, "and have made them gods of gold, yet now if thou wilt forgive their sin, and if not, blot me, I pray thee, out of the book which thou has written," so great was the love of Moses for his people.

There was a time of repentance among the people after this, and Moses and his servant Joshua reared a tent outside the camp and called it the Tabernacle of the congregation.   It was for worship until the true Tabernacle should be built according to the pattern given in the Mount.   All who sought the Lord went to worship there, and the pillar of cloud came and stood at the Tabernacle door while Moses talked with God, and all the people saw it and worshiped.

Moses prayed again for the people, and the Lord said :

"My presences shall go with thee, and I will give thee rest."

The Lord called Moses again into the mount, and told him to bring with

MOSES DESCENDING FROM THE MOUNT.

him two tablets of stone and He would again write the ten commandments upon them.

So Moses hewed them from the rock and took them up into Mount Sinai. Then the Lord came down again in a thick cloud and talked with Moses, and wrote upon the tablets of stone.

After forty days Moses came down to the people bringing the commandments with him, but his face shone with a strange light that the people never saw before, and they were afraid of him. It was something above the light of the sun, for Moses had seen the Glory of the Lord.

While they still camped around the mount they began to build the Tabernacle. Moses told the people to bring gold, and silver, and brass, and wood. They also brought precious stones, and oil for the lamp, and fine linen, and they gave so willingly that at last Moses told them that there was more than enough.

These were put in the hands of two wise men whom the Lord had chosen and taught to do the work, and they had willing helpers among the people, for wise hearted women did spin with their own hands, and bring what they had spun, of blue, and purple, and scarlet, and fine linen to make the hangings of the Tabernacle.

If you would know all the beautiful and costly and curious things that were made for this church in the wilderness, you will find them described in the last chapters of Exodus.

The Israelites camped a long time in the high valleys around the Mount of God, and at last set up the Tabernacle. It was so made that it could be taken down and carried with them when they journeyed, for it was a beautiful tent. Over it the pillar of cloud stood. Whenever it moved the people followed, and when it stood still, they rested. Within the Tabernacle they placed a beautiful chest of wood overlaid with gold, which ever after held their most precious things, the tablets of stone written upon by the Lord himself.

This "Ark of Testimony," as it was called, had rings at the sides through which men laid strong rods by which to carry it, and so had the golden table for bread, and the golden altar of incense. There was a beautiful seven-branched candlestick of pure gold in which olive oil was burned for a sacred sign, and there was a brazen altar for burnt offerings, and a great brazen bowl for washing, and other things to be used in the worship of the Sanctuary.

There were beautiful garments, also, for the priests, Aaron and his sons, and for Aaron there was a wonderful breast-plate of gold set with twelve precious stones, bearing the names of the twelve tribes of Israel.

When all was finished, and the Tabernacle was set up, the cloud that veiled the presence of the Lord came and covered it, and the glory of the Lord filled it, so that Moses could not enter; but the Lord spoke to him from the cloud, and told him how the priests should order the worship of the Lord there.

Afterward, Aaron and his sons offered burnt offerings for their sins, and the sins of the people, in the way the Lord had commanded, and fire from the Lord came down and consumed the offering.

When the people saw the answer of the Lord they fell on their faces before him.

In the second month of the second year the cloud rose from over the Tabernacle, and then the people knew it was time to go on their journey. So they took down the tent of the Tabernacle and put all things in order for the journey. Each of the twelve tribes descended from the twelve sons of Jacob marched by themselves, carrying banners, and having captains. In the midst of them all marched the Levites carrying the Ark and the different parts of the Tabernacle, and when the cloud stood still, they stopped and set up the Tabernacle, while the people formed their camp all around it in the order of their tribes.

Still the manna fell with the dew at night, and the people gathered it in the morning, and when they tired of it, the Lord sent them quails again.

Over and over the people complained and rebelled, but the Angel of the Lord's Presence still hovered over them, and led them toward the promised land. Forty years they were on the journey that was so easily made by the sons of Jacob when they went back and forth to buy wheat in the time of famine ; and forty-two times did they encamp on the way, yet the mercy of the Lord never failed them, and they were brought into their own land at last. Then the cloud was no longer needed to go before them, but long after, when they built a beautiful temple at Jerusalem in which to put the sacred Ark of Testimony, the cloud came again and filled the temple with the glory of the Lord.

CHAPTER XIII.

IN THE BORDERS OF CANAAN.

While the host of Israel was in camp at Paran, the Lord told Moses to send men before them into Canaan to spy out the land.

So he sent twelve men who walked through the land and saw the people, and the cities and the fields and the fruits. They were forty days searching the land and they brought from the brook Eschol a cluster of grapes so large that two of them bore it on a staff between them. They also brought some pomegranates and figs.

When they came into the camp they said that the country where they had been was good, and flowing with milk and honey, but the people were strong, and the cities had very high walls. They said they saw giants there.

Caleb, who was one of the twelve, and a good and true man, said:

" Let us go up at once and possess it, for we are well able to overcome it," but the men who were with him were afraid of the giants, and said they felt like grasshoppers before them. Then there was great weeping among the people all that night, and they said,

"Let us make a captain, and let us return into Egypt." Moses and Aaron were greatly troubled, but the two good men, Caleb and Joshua, stood up and encouraged the people, saying that they need not fear, for the Lord had given them the land, yet they were ready to stone Caleb and Joshua.

Then the Lord spake to Moses from the Tabernacle, and the people saw his glory. He said the people were unbelieving and disobedient, and for this reason they could not enter the promised land. He said, that all who were twenty years old and upward would die in the wilderness, except Caleb and Joshua, who had followed the Lord wholly. He also said that the people would be forty years in the wilderness, and only the youth and the children would live to enter Canaan.

There was mourning and repentance then because of the word of the Lord, and the people promised again to believe and obey, but over and over they lost faith and rebelled, and great storms of trouble fell upon them.

Once the earth opened and many were swallowed up ; a sudden sickness destroyed thousands. Near Mount Hor, where Aaron died, fiery serpents ran among the people, and all who were bitten by them died ; but there was

THE RETURN OF THE SPIES.

full forgiveness and cure for those who turned to the Lord. When the fiery serpents entered the camp Moses lifted a brazen image of a serpent up on a pole so high that it could be seen all over the camp, and whoever looked upon it lived. It was a sign of the coming Saviour.

Between the marches and the battles with heathen tribes, some of whom were giants, Moses wrote in a book the laws that God gave him for the government of the people. They were wise laws, the keeping of which would bring health, peace and blessedness to the people. He gave the book to the Levites who carried the Ark, and they were to keep it always beside the Ark, and often read it aloud to the people.

Moses said many things to the people, and as Jacob blessed his twelve sons, so Moses blessed each of the twelve tribes that descended from them, for he was near the end of his long life. The Lord had told him that He should take him to Himself before the people entered Canaan, and that Joshua must lead the people into the promised land. So when they had reached the borders of Canaan, and were encamped near the Jordan, the Lord called his tried servant up into Mount Nebo, that he might see the land beyond the Jordan, where the twelve tribes were to find their promised home. Then the Lord gave him a view of the land, and there he died, as Aaron died on Mount Hor.

No one saw Moses die, and no one knows where he was buried, for the Lord buried him. He was one hundred and twenty years old, and yet as strong as a young man   After his death Joshua became the leader of Israel.

CHAPTER XIV.

A NATION THAT WAS BORN IN A DAY.

The time had come for the people to cross the river Jordan, and enter their own land, and the Lord told Joshua to prepare the people for their last journey before going over Jordan. Joshua first sent two men over the river to see the land.

They went to the walled city of Jericho, and to the house of a woman named Rahab. The king heard that they were there and sent for them, but the woman hid them under the flax that she was drying on the roof of her

CROSSING THE JORDAN.

4

house.   Afterward she let them down by a rope through a window (for her house was built on the town wall), and they escaped.   They promised Rahab before they went, that if she would hang a long line of scarlet thread from the window on the wall, that when they came to take the city she should be saved and all her family because of her kindness to them.

After they had returned to the camp they told Joshua that the Lord would surely give them the land, for the people were afraid of them.   Then they rose up and marched to the banks of the Jordan and waited for Joshua to lead them over.   Some of them remembered how they had passed through the Red Sea, and others had heard it from their parents, and they now waited to see the salvation of God.   Joshua told them to follow the priests, and the Levites who would bear the Ark of the Covenant, so when Joshua said :

"Behold the Ark of the Covenant of the Lord of all the earth passeth over before you into Jordan," the people followed.

The Jordan lay spread before them like a lake, for it was the time of year when it overflowed all its banks, but when the feet of the priests who bore the Ark were dipped in the edge of the water, the waters from above stopped and rose like a wall, while the waters below flowed away into the Dead Sea, and left a wide path for the people to walk in, and the Ark stood still in Jordan until every one had passed over.   Then twelve men, one out of every tribe, took a stone from the bed of the river and carried it over for a memorial altar, so that when any should ask in years to come, "What do these stones mean?" someone might tell them how the Lord led Israel through Jordan into their own land.

After the Ark had come up from the bed of Jordan, and there was not one of all the thousands of Israel left behind, the waters came down from the place where they had stayed, and flowed down into the Dead Sea, and over-flowed the banks of Jordan as before.

The stones were heaped in Gilgal where they camped, and directly be-fore them rose the walls of Jericho, and here they kept the passover.   For forty years they had been fed with manna from heaven as they camped or journeyed in the wilderness, but now they began to eat the grain and the fruits of the land, and the manna fell no more.

Nearly five hundred years before the family of Jacob left this land to go down into Egypt where Joseph was.   They grew to be a great people, but they were slaves.   Then the Lord sent Moses to make them free, and they began the long journey, which at last brought them to their own land.

Forty years they were on the journey, and all this time they were pilgrims, but on the day that the Jordan ceased to flow, and parted while they passed over into the land promised to their fathers, they became a nation.

The land was before them, and they had only to obey the Lord and his servant Joshua to conquer and possess it.

As they filled the valley of the Jordan before Jericho, the hearts of the heathen fainted for fear, for they knew that only the Lord could divide a river to let his people pass.

Joshua went out of the camp to look at Jericho, the walled city. It was shut up for fear of the Israelites, and there was no one to be seen.

Suddenly Joshua saw a warrior standing with a drawn sword in his hand.

"Art thou for us," said Joshua, "or for our adversaries?" and the warrior angel answered,

"Nay! but as Captain of the host of the Lord, am I now come," and Joshua fell on his face before him.

He knew then that it was the Lord who would conquer Jericho, and he was told how the people were to help him.

So Joshua called the priests, and told them to take up the Ark, and he told seven priests to go before it bearing trumpets of rams' horns. Then the army of Israel, ready for war, followed, half of them marching before the Ark, and half of them coming after, and as the trumpets gave a great sound, they marched once around the city, and then went to camp. This they did once every day for seven days, but on the seventh day they marched around the city seven times, and as the priests blew the trumpets for the last time, Joshua cried with a mighty voice,

"Shout! for the Lord hath given you the city."

Then as a great shout went up from the people, the walls of the city fell down flat, so that the soldiers of Israel went up, every man straight before him, and took Jericho.

And Rahab was not forgotten. The Lord cared for her little house on the wall, and she, with all her family, were brought into the Camp of Israel.

And so by the conquest of Jericho the new nation of Israel began to possess its land.

CHAPTER XV.

SAMSON THE STRONG.

All the days of Joshua—and he lived to be an hundred and ten years old—the Israelites were conquering the people who lived in Canaan, and dividing it among the tribes. Joshua was a father to them, as Moses had been, and when at last they were at rest, each tribe within its own borders, and they had begun to build their houses, and plant their fields, Joshua spoke words of loving counsel to the people, and they set up a stone under an oak tree, as a sign that they would always serve the Lord and keep the law, and then he went to be with God. After his death Israel was ruled by wise men called judges, who helped them to conquer the land little by little. Some of them were good men and brave warriors as Othniel and Gideon and Jephthah, and one was a prophetess named Deborah, a noble mother in Israel, and one was a mighty man of strength, Samson, the son of Manoah.

The people of Israel had turned away from the Lord, and could no longer conquer their enemies, but the Philistines had conquered them, and had been their masters for forty years, when the Lord sent Samson to deliver them. He was not a wise man like Moses or Joshua, but he had great strength, and the Lord used him against the Philistines.

Once a young lion came roaring against him, and he caught it and rent it in two, as if it had been a kid. When he passed the same way afterward he saw that the bees had built a nest in the body of the lion, and it was full of honey. At his marriage feast—for he married a Philistine woman—he made a riddle for the young men to guess:

"Out of the eater came forth meat, and out of the strong, come forth sweetness."

They tried for seven days to guess the riddle, but they could not, and then they told Samson's wife to find it out for them, or they would burn her house. She begged him with tears to tell her, and at last he told her of the honey comb in the body of the lion, and she told the young men, so that at the end of the seventh day they said to Samson,

"What is sweeter than honey?" and "what is stronger than a lion?"

He saw that he had been betrayed, so he paid his debt, a suit of clothes to each guest, and went home to his father's house. Afterwards when he

THE YOUNG SAMSON.

found that his wife had been given to another he tied firebrands to the tails of three hundred foxes, and sent them among the wheat fields of the Philistines so that the fields were set on fire.

Once the men of Gaza tried to kill him when he was within their city, but he rose at midnight and took the city gates, with its posts and bar, and carried them away on his shoulders to the top of the hill. Again the Philistine lords had promised a great deal of money to a woman, if she would get Samson to tell her what made him so strong, so she begged him to tell her. Three times she thought she knew the secret, and told the Philistines, but they could not bind him. At last he was tired of her questions, and said to her plainly—that from a child no razor had ever touched his hair. If it should be cut he would be as weak as other men. Then she watched and cut his hair while he slept, and the Philistines bound him and carried him to Gaza, where they made him blind, and forced him to grind in the mills of a prison house. The Philistines were glad because Samson was their prisoner at last, and so they came together in a great feast to sacrifice to their god Dagon, for they said,

"Our god has delivered Samson into our hands." While they were merry they said:

"Let us send for Samson to make sport for us," and he was brought out of the prison. It was very sad to see the strong judge of Israel, weak and blind, led by a little lad, and making sport for the people in front of their temple. All the lords of the Philistines were there, and upon the broad roof of the temple were about three thousand people watching Samson while he showed his strength, for his hair had grown and his strength was returning. At last as he was standing between two great pillars that held up the roof, he prayed, lifting his sightless eyes to God:

"O Lord God, remember me, I pray thee, and strengthen me only this once."

Then he clasped his arms around the pillars on either side of him, and bowing himself with all his might, saying,

"Let me die with the Philistines," he drew the great pillars with him, and the house fell with all that were upon it, on all that were within it. So died Samson who judged Israel twenty years, yet a woman, Deborah, who was also one of the judges in Israel, was stronger than he, for the Lord looketh on the heart.

THE DEATH OF SAMSON.

CHAPTER XVI.

RUTH.

In the days when the judges ruled in Israel, there was a famine in the land, and an Israelite, who lived in Bethlehem, took his wife and his two sons into Moab where there was food. After a while the Israelite died, and the two sons married women of Moab.

After two years the sons died also, and their mother, Naomi, longed for her home in Bethlehem, for there was no longer a famine there. So she took Ruth and Orpah, her sons' wives, and started on the journey into the land of Israel.

But before they had gone far Naomi said:

"Go! return each to her mother's house; the Lord deal kindly with you, as ye have dealt with the dead, and with me."

She kissed them, and they wept and would not leave her.

"Turn again, my daughters," she said, "why will ye go with me?"

And Orpah kissed Naomi, and went back to her own mothers' house, but Ruth, whose heart was with Naomi, would not go back.

"Entreat me not to leave thee," she said, "or to return from following after thee, for where thou goest I will go; and where thou lodgest I will lodge; thy people shall be my people, and thy God my God; where thou diest I will die, and there will I be buried; the Lord do so to me, and more also, if aught but death part thee and me."

And so they came to Bethlehem, and the old friends of Naomi greeted her tenderly, and welcomed her back. It was about the beginning of the barley harvest.

There was a good and great man in Bethlehem named Boaz, and he was of the family of Naomi's husband. He had a field of barley where the reapers were at work, and Ruth asked Naomi if she should not go and glean after the reapers, to get grain, for they were poor.

Naomi said, "Go, my daughter," and she went.

When Boaz came out of the town into his field and greeted his reapers, he said to his servant having charge of the reapers,

"What maiden is this?" and he told him that she was the Moabitish girl who had come back with her mother-in-law Naomi.

(62)

RUTH GLEANING.

Then Boaz spoke very kindly to Ruth, and told her to stay with his maidens, and freely drink of the water drawn for them, and Ruth bowed before him and asked why he should be so kind to a stranger. He told her that he knew all her kindness to her mother-in-law since the death of her husband, and how she had left her own family and country to come among strangers, and he blessed her, saying,

"A full reward be given thee of the Lord God of Israel, under whose wings thou art come to trust."

Then he told her to sit down and eat bread with them, and he helped her to the parched corn with his own hands, and when they returned to work he told his young men to let her glean among the sheaves and reprove her not, and to let some handfuls fall purposely for her to glean. When Ruth went home Naomi said,

"Where hast thou gleaned to-day?" and Ruth told her. Then Naomi blessed Boaz, and told Ruth that he was one of their near relatives.

And so Ruth gleaned in the fields of Boaz through all the barley and the wheat harvest. When all the reaping was done, the grain was threshed on a piece of ground made very smooth and level. The sheaves were beaten, and then the straw was taken away, and the grain and chaff below it was winnowed. By this the chaff was blown away and only the grain was left.

When Boaz winnowed his barley Naomi told Ruth to go down to his threshing floor and see him for he had a feast for his friends.

So after the feast Ruth came near to him and said,

"Thou art our near kinsman," and Boaz said,

"May the Lord bless thee my daughter," and with many kind words he gave her six measures of barley to take to Naomi.

Boaz remembered that it was the custom in Israel for the nearest relative of a man who had died, to take care of the wife who was left, and so he went to the gate of Bethlehem where the rulers met to hold their court, and spoke to the elders and chief men about Ruth. He also wished them to be witnesses that he was going to take Ruth to be his wife. Then the rulers all said,

"We are witnesses," and they prayed that God would bless Ruth and make Boaz still richer and greater.

So Ruth became the honored and beloved wife of Boaz, and they had a son named Obed.

Obed grew up and had a son named Jesse; and Jesse was the father of David, King of Israel, who was first a shepherd lad of Bethlehem.

RUTH AND NAOMI.

More than a thousand years after Ruth lived there was born in Bethle-hem, of the family of Boaz and Ruth, a little Child, who came, to be the Saviour of the world, and the shepherds in the fields, where, perhaps, Ruth gleaned, and David kept his sheep, heard the angels tell the good news and sing

" Peace on earth, good will to men."

CHAPTER XVII.

SAMUEL—THE CHILD OF THE TEMPLE.

The Tabernacle that was built in the wilderness, and was brought into Canaan by the priests was set up at Shiloh in the very centre of the land of Canaan, and once every year the tribes came to it to worship and offer sacrifices. After it had come to Shiloh to stay it was called the temple. .

When Eli was high priest a man named Elkanah came up from Ramah to worship, and Hannah his wife went with him. She was a good woman, and very sorrowful, because she saw other wives with sons and daughters around them, and she had none. Her husband was loving and kind and said: "Am I not better to thee than ten sons?" but she prayed to God for a son. While she was at Shiloh she prayed in the temple, and Eli saw her lips move, though he heard no voice. At first he spoke harshly to her, thinking she had been drinking wine, but she told him that she had not taken wine, but was praying.

"I am a woman of sorrowful spirit," she said, "and have poured out my soul before the Lord." Then Eli blessed her and said :

"Go in peace, and the God of Israel grant thee the prayer that thou hast asked of him." Then Hannah was no longer sad.

Her prayer was answered, and the Lord sent her a little son, and when he was old enough, she took him to the temple, for she had promised the Lord that the child should be His. So Elkanah came bringing sacrifices, and the young child was with them. Hannah told Eli that she was the woman whom he saw praying in the temple.

„ For the child I prayed," she said, "and the Lord has answered my prayer. Therefore I have lent him to the Lord; as long as he lives he shall

THE CHILD OF THE TEMPLE.

be lent to the Lord." Eli was very glad and gave thanks to the Lord, and took the little boy to help him in the service of the temple. Every year his father and mother came to bring offerings to the Lord, and his mother always brought him a little coat which she had made.

Over it was a linen garment called an ephod, such as the priests wore. Eli was an old man, and his sons, though they were priests, were not good men, and he believed the Lord had sent him one who would be good, so he loved little Samuel as if he were his own.

One night when Eli was laid down to sleep, and Samuel also, while the light was still burning in the golden candlestick before the Ark, Samuel heard a voice calling him, and he answered, "Here am I," and ran to see what Eli wanted. But Eli said that he had not called, and Samuel lay down again. When the voice called again, Samuel went again to Eli's bed, but Eli told him to lie down again, for he had not called him. When the voice called the third time, Samuel said: "Here am I, for thou *didst* call me."

Then Eli told the boy to lie down once more, but if he heard the voice again to say,

"Speak Lord, for thy servant heareth."

And when the voice called again, "Samuel, Samuel," the boy answered, "Speak Lord, for thy servant heareth."

Then the Lord told Samuel that the sons of Eli had become very wicked, and their father had not kept them from the evil, and therefore He could not accept their offerings.

When Eli asked Samuel what the Lord had said to him, the boy told him all and hid nothing from him, and Eli bowed his spirit before the Lord, and said:

"It is the Lord, let Him do what seemeth Him good."

After this all the people of Israel knew that the Lord had called Samuel to be a prophet. And as he grew up the Lord was with him, and he was a judge over his people all his life.

As for Eli and his sons, the word of the Lord soon came true. When the Philistines came against the Israelites in battle, the Elders of Israel said : "Let us bring the Ark of the Lord out of Shiloh to us, that it may save us out of the hand of our enemies." And so they took it from the holy place to the camp of Israel. Then the Philistines fell upon the camp and scattered the men of Israel. They also took the Ark of God, and the two sons of Eli were among the thousands slain.

Eli, who trembled for the Ark of God, sat outside the city gate, by the wayside watching. He was nearly a hundred years old, and his eyes were dim, but when a messenger came with the bad news, he fell backward in his seat and died. His heart was broken.

Where was Samuel? Perhaps he was praying in the temple for the return of the Ark of the Covenant.

Wherever the Ark went among the Philistines, there went also trouble and death. When they put it in the temple of their fish-god Dagon, the great idol fell down before it and was broken. And when it was taken to another city, the people were smitten with sickness, until at last the Philistines said:

"Send away the Ark of the God of Israel, and let it go to its own place."

After seven months they sent it with gifts of gold to the Israelites. They placed it on a new cart drawn by two cows, and the cows, guided by the Lord alone, took a straight way into the land of Israel. How glad the people were when they looked up from their reaping in the fields, and saw the Ark coming safely back to them. The Philistines watched it from afar to see if it would be guided of God to its own place or not and then they returned to their city.

Samuel gathered the people to the Lord after this, and though they had sinned greatly, and had gone after the gods of the heathen around them, they repented and returned to the faith of their fathers, and were faithful all the days of Samuel. He went from year to year on a journey to three cities of Israel, and judged the people in those places, but his home was in Ramah, the city where he was born, and where Hannah had brought him up for the Lord.

CHAPTER XVIII.

THE MAKING OF A KING.

When Samuel was old he made his sons judges in his place, but they were not holy men like their father.

They loved money, and would judge unjustly, if money were given to them as a bribe. So the people came to Samuel at Ramah and said,

"Give us a king to judge us."

And Samuel prayed to the Lord, and the Lord told him to do as the people had asked him to do, for they had not rejected him as judge, but the Lord as their King, and now they must learn what kind of a king would reign

over them.   So Samuel told them what they must be ready to do for their
King, for a king was often a hard master, and ruled his people cruelly,
taking the best of their fields, and their harvests, and their flocks for themselves, and the finest of their sons and daughters to be his servants ; but they
said,

"We will have a king over us, that we may be like other nations, and
that our king may judge us, and go out before us and fight our battles."

When Samuel told these things to the Lord he said, "Make them a
king," and Samuel sent the people to their own cities.

Samuel did not choose a king for the people himself, but he waited for
the Lord to send him the man He had chosen, and the Lord said to him as
he went to a city called Zeph, to hold a sacrifice,

"To-morrow about this time I will send thee a man from the land of
Benjamin, and thou shalt anoint him to be captain over my people Israel."

On the next day as Samuel came out to go up to the hill of sacrifice he
met a tall, noble looking young man, who, with his servant, was looking for
the lost asses of his father, Kish, the Benjaminite.   He had come far, and
had heard that Samuel, the seer was in that place, and he hoped he would
tell him where to go for the asses that were lost.

Samuel knew from the Lord that this was the man God had chosen, so
he told him to go up with him to the sacrifice, and the next day he would let
him go.

He told him that he need not be troubled about the asses, for they were
found, but the desire of Israel was set upon him.   Saul, for that was his
name, did not understand him until he was invited to feast with thirty of the
chief men, and Samuel had talked with him upon the house-top.   Early the
next morning they both rose and went out of the city, and while Saul sent his
servant on before, Samuel anointed Saul with oil, and kissed him saying, that
the Lord had anointed him to be Captain over his inheritance.

As a sign that the Lord had done it, he told Saul three things that would
happen to him on the way home, and charged him to go to Gilgal, where he
would meet him and sacrifice to the Lord for seven days.   As Saul turned
to leave the prophet, God gave him another heart, and all the signs came to
pass that day.

At Mizpah Samuel called all the tribes together, that the man who was
to be their king, might be chosen in their sight, and when Saul, the son of
Kish, the Benjaminite was chosen he could not be found; he had hidden from
the people ; but when they brought him out before them, he was taller than

THE SHEPHERD BOY OF BETHLEHEM.

any of the people from his shoulders up, and looked a king indeed. For the first time in all their history they cried,

"God save the King!"

Then Saul went home, and there went with him a body of men whose hearts God had touched, while Samuel wrote in a book the order of the kingdom and laid it up before the Lord.

CHAPTER XIX.

THE SHEPHERD BOY OF BETHLEHEM.

After Saul had been king of Israel for a few years, Samuel was deeply troubled about him, for he had hoped that he would be as truly a king as he looked, but he had a strange and wilful spirit that led him to turn away from the counsel of the Lord and follow his own way.

Samuel had been grieved again and again by Saul's rashness, until at last he said to him when he had taken the spoil of the enemy to sacrifice to the Lord,

"To obey is better than sacrifice ; because thou hast rejected the word of the Lord, He hath also rejected thee from being king," and he went to his house and mourned over Saul, for he had loved him.

At last the Lord told Samuel to cease from mourning for Saul, for He had rejected him, but to fill his horn with oil, and go to Bethlehem where Jesse lived, for He had chosen one of the sons of Jesse to be king in place of Saul.

Samuel went to Bethlehem leading a heifer, as the Lord had told him to do, that he might hold a sacrifice. He told the elders of the city to make ready for the sacrifice, and when he had found the house of Jesse, he called him and his sons. Jesse was the grandson of Ruth and Boaz, and owned the fields, no doubt, where Ruth gleaned. When Samuel saw Eliab, the son of Jesse, he said :

"Surely the Lord's anointed is before Him," but the Lord said :

"Look not on his countenance or on the height of his stature, because I have refused him, for the Lord seeth not as man seeth, for man looketh on the outward appearance, but the Lord looketh on the heart."

Then Jesse called Abinidab, but Samuel said :

"The Lord hath not chosen this." Then he made Shammah to pass before him, but Samuel said:

"Neither hath the Lord chosen this."

Jesse made seven of his sons to pass before Samuel, but Samuel said: "The Lord hath not chosen these."

"Are here all thy children?" said Samuel.

"There remaineth yet the youngest, and he keepeth the sheep," Jesse replied. Then Samuel said:

"Send and fetch him, for we will not sit down till he come hither."

So Jesse sent out into the sheepfolds on the hillsides outside the city to bring the lad David in. What did the boy think when he found his father and his brothers waiting, with the old prophet in the midst? What did it mean that the eye of the seer was set upon him, as were the eyes of all in the house?

Samuel saw a noble youth, "ruddy, and of a beautiful countenance, and goodly to look to." He had been told that he must not look on the outward appearance "for the Lord seeth not as man seeth," and so he waited a little until the Lord said:

"Arise, anoint him, for this is he." Then he took the horn of oil, and anointed him in the midst of his brethren, and the spirit of the Lord came upon David from that day forward, and Samuel went back to his house in Ramah.

It may be that his father and his brothers did not understand that the boy had been called to be king over Israel, but a new spirit of wisdom, and love, and strength came upon David, and though he went back to his father's flocks with no thought of being greater than his brothers, he went with a new song in his heart which he sang to the little harp he had made while watching the sheep. Long after when he was King of Israel, he made, in memory of these days the beautiful Psalm to be sung in the temple beginning,

"The Lord is my Shepherd, I shall not want."

CHAPTER XX.

THE POWER OF A PEBBLE.

Saul the sullen was still king over Israel, although he had departed from the Lord, and in His sight he was no longer a king. He was very gloomy and dark in his mind, for he had driven the Lord's spirit away, and his light was gone.

His servants tried to amuse him, and told him of David, the son of Jesse, who was a skillful player on the harp, and a brave and handsome youth. So Saul sent for David, and David, bringing presents from his father, came to the king's house.

Saul was greatly pleased with David, and asked Jesse to let his son stay with him, for when the evil spirit was upon him, if David played upon his harp the darkness left him. But this did not last, and after a while David went back to his flocks, and Saul forgot him.

Then the Philistines rose against Israel again. Their camp was on a mountain side, and Saul gathered his warriors on the side of another mountain and there was a valley between them.

Out of the Philistine camp a giant came one day, Goliath of Gath. He talked loud and often in order to terrify the Israelites, asking them to send out a man to fight with him, but he was not truly brave, for he had carefully covered his great body with armor of brass, so that no spear or sword could touch him He defied Israel every morning and evening for forty days, and no one was found who would dare to go out alone to fight him. David's elder brothers were in camp, and Jesse, their father, called David from the flocks to take food to them. He found the army of Israel ready to go into battle, but Goliath came out as he had done each day and defied the Israelites, who ran in terror at the sight of him. The spirit of David was moved at this, and he said:

"Who is this Philistine that he should defy the armies of the living God?" "The man who killeth him," said one, "the King will enrich him, and, will give him his daughter and make his father's house free in Israel."

Then Eliab, David's eldest brother, spoke sternly to David asking him why he had left his sheep to come down and see the battle, and called him naughty and proud, but David still talked with the men, for the spirit of the

(74)

Lord was strong within him. When Saul heard of him and sent for him, David said :

"Let no man's heart fail because of him ; thy servant will go and fight with the Philistine."

Saul frowned at David and said :

"Thou art not able to go against this Philistine ; thou art but a youth, and he is a man of war."

Then David told the king how he had killed both a lion and a bear that had come down upon his father's flocks, and that he could also conquer the Philistine.

"The Lord that delivered me out of the paw of the lion, and the paw of the bear," said David, "He will deliver me out of the hand of this Philistine." And Saul said : "Go ! and the Lord be with thee." Then Saul armed David with his own armor, but David said :

"I can not go with these, for I have not proved them," and he put them off.

And this was the way David armed himself to meet the giant.

He took his staff in hand, and chose five smooth stones from the brook and put them in his shepherd's bag, and with his sling in his hand, he drew near to the giant. Goliath came on also, his armor-bearer carrying the shield before him, but when he saw the youth David, he despised him, for he was without armor, or sword or spear, only his staff.

"Am I a dog, that thou comest to me with a staff," said Goliath, and then he told him that he would soon give his flesh to the birds and the beasts.

"Thou comest to me with a sword, and a spear, and a shield," said David, "but I come to thee in the name of the Lord of Hosts, the God of the armies of Israel whom thou hast despised."

Then the Philistine came down upon little David to destroy him, and David ran, not away from him, as the men of Israel had done, but straight toward him, taking a pebble from his shepherd's bag as he ran. Quickly putting it in the sling, he whirled it in the air once, twice, and then it went swift and straight to the mark. It sunk into the forehead of the giant, and he fell dead upon his face. Then David ran and stood upon the dead Philistine and cut off his head with the giant's great sword, and when the Philistines saw that their champion was really dead, they fled, pursued by the shouting hosts of Israel.

Saul had forgotten the youth who played upon the harp before him, for when he sent for him after the battle he said,

"Whose son art thou, thou young man?" and David answered,

"I am the son of thy servant Jesse, the Bethlehemite."

And Saul took him to live with him from that day.

CHAPTER XXI.

FAITHFUL UNTO DEATH.

Saul had a son named Jonathan, and he loved David as his own soul. He took off his princely robes, even to his sword, and his bow, and his girdle, and made David wear them; and David acted wisely in all that the king gave him to do. There was great joy and much feasting over the Death of Goliath and the flight of the Philistines, and wherever Saul went, the women came out of the cities to meet him, singing and dancing, and the song with which they answered one another was,

> "Saul hath slain his thousands,
> And David his tens of thousands."

Saul did not like this, and an evil spirit of jealousy came upon him, and he thought "What can he have more but the kingdom."

The next day the evil spirit came upon Saul in the house, and David played on his harp to quiet him, but Saul hurled a spear at David, hoping to fasten him to the wall with it. This he did twice, but the Lord guided the spear away from David, just as he guided the pebble to Goliath, and he was unhurt. Saul was afraid of David. He was afraid that God was preparing him to be king over Israel, so he sent him into battle, hoping he would be killed, but the life of David was in the Lord's hand, and no enemy could destroy it.

After a great battle, in which David had been victorious, the evil spirit came again upon Saul, as he sat in his house with his spear in his hand, while David played on the harp. Again he tried to kill David, but the spear struck the wall and David slipped away.

THE POWER OF A PEBBLE.

It was clear that David could not live near the king, and so he talked with Jonathan, his friend, who said,

"God forbid, thou shalt not die," but David said,

"Truly there is but a step between me and death."

Then they made a promise to each other before the Lord that should last while they lived. They promised to show "the kindness of the Lord" to each other while life should last.

Jonathan told David that he might go away for three days, and they went out into a field together. They feared the anger of Saul when he found that David was absent from the feast of the new moon. So Jonathan told David to return after three days and hide behind a great rock in the field. Then Jonathan said he would come out and shoot three arrows from his bow, as if he were shooting at a mark, and he would send his arrow-bearer to pick them up. If he should call to the lad, "The arrows are on this side of thee," David would know that Saul was not angry, and would not hurt him, but if he cried, "The arrows are beyond thee," David would know he was in danger and must go away.

On the second day of the feast, Saul asked why David was not there, and Jonathan told him he had asked permission to go away for three days. Then Saul was very angry. He blamed his son for loving David, for, as Saul's son, Jonathan should be king after his death, but he never would be if David lived, and he commanded Jonathan to bring him that he might put him to death. When Jonathan asked what evil David had done that he should be put to death, Saul cast his spear at his own son. Then Jonathan knew there was no hope for David, and left the table in sorrow.

The next day he went out to the rock in the field with his armor-bearer and sent him on before. When he shot an arrow, he cried:

" The arrow is beyond thee; make haste! stay not!"

And David, in his hiding place heard it, and knew that he must flee for his life.

Then Jonathan gave his bow and arrows to the lad to take to the town, and David came out from his hiding place, and they kissed each other and wept together. But at last Jonathan said:

" Go in peace: as we have sworn both of us in the name of the Lord, saying, The Lord be between me and thee, and between my children and thy children forever."

And David went away to hide from Saul, and Jonathan went back to the king's house.

For seven years Saul hunted for David to take his life, and David, often hiding in caves in the wilderness, could not see his friend Jonathan, but they were faithful in their friendship, and when at last Saul was slain in battle, and Jonathan also, David came to mourn over his friend, saying :

"I am distressed for thee, my brother Jonathan : very pleasant hast thou been unto me ; thy love for me was wonderful, passing the love of women."

CHAPTER XXII.

DAVID THE OUTCAST.

For seven years King Saul hunted David from one end of the land of Israel to the other.   The evil spirit of jealousy and hate had full possession of him, and David, with a few faithful men, was driven from one stronghold to another, until he cried, "They gather themselves together ; they hide themselves ; they mark my steps when they wait for my soul.   What time I am afraid I will trust in thee."

He had escaped again and again from the hand of Saul, and now he was down in the desert country by the Dead Sea, hiding among the cliffs and caves of Engedi. Saul heard of it and took three thousand men to hunt for him among the rocks of the wild goats.   He was very tired after climbing the rocks, and seeing a cave, he went in to lie down for a little sleep.   He did not know that David and his men were in the cave hiding in the dark sides of it.   Then his men whispered to David :

"Behold the day of which the Lord said unto thee : 'I will deliver thine enemy into thine hand that thou mayest do to him as it shall seem good to thee.'"   Then David arose and crept near to Saul, and—did he kill the man who had so often tried to kill him ?

No, he bent down and cut off a part of Saul's robe.   Even this seemed wrong to David.

"The Lord forbid that I should do this thing unto my master," he said "to stretch forth my hand against him, seeing he is the annointed of the Lord," and in this way he kept his servants from harming Saul, and after Saul awoke he went out of the cave.

David also went out of the cave and cried,

"My Lord the King!"

5

THE GARMENT OF SAUL.

And when Saul turned David bowed down to him and asked him why he listened to men who said that he wished to harm the king, and then he told him how the Lord had given him into his hand in the cave, but he would not touch the Lord's annointed to harm him.

"See, my father," he cried "see the skirt of thy robe in my hand. I have not sinned against thee, yet thou huntest my soul to take it."

Much more he said, and asked the Lord to Judge between them, and Saul's hard heart was moved so that he wept aloud.

"Is this thy voice, my son David," he said, "Thou art more righteous than I, for thou hast rewarded me good, whereas I have rewarded thee evil," and he made a covenant with David. For though he made no promise to spare David's life, he made David promise to spare the life of his children when he should be made king.

But a year was hardly past before the evil spirit was again upon Saul, and he went out with three thousand men to hunt for David. Saul's camp was on a hill, and David saw where it was. At night he took Abishai, one of his warriors, and went down from the cliffs to Saul's camp, where Saul lay sleeping in a trench, and the spear stuck in the ground by his pillow, while all his men lay around him. Abishai wished to strike him through with the spear, but David said,

"Destroy him not, for who can stretch forth his hand against the Lord's anointed and be guiltless? The Lord shall smite him, or his day shall come to die, or he shall fall in battle and perish; but take thou now the spear that is at his pillow, and the cruse of water, and let us go."

And they took them and went away. A deep sleep had fallen upon the camp of Saul from the Lord, so that no one saw them.

Then David went up to his stronghold, and from the top of the cliff he cried to Abner, the captain of Saul's men, and asked why he had not defended his Master, and where was the king's spear, and his cruse of water?

Then Saul cried as before,

"Is this thy voice, my son David?"

"It is my voice, my lord, O King," said David, and again he plead his cause with his old enemy, but who could trust to the repentance of Saul? He cried,

"I have sinned; return, my son David, for I will no more do thee harm, because my soul was precious in thine eyes this day. I have played the fool, and erred exceedingly."

But David trusted him no more, and went and made friends with a Philistine prince that he might live within their borders.

Samuel the prophet was dead, and there was no one to give counsel to the darkened soul of the King when trouble fell upon him. The Philistines had come with a great army, but Saul was afraid, for the Lord's spirit was not with him. He tried to seek the Lord through the priests, and through dreams, but the Lord answered him not. Then he went to a witch by night, and asked her to bring up the spirit of Samuel. The witch could not bring up Samuel, but the Lord sent him to speak to Saul, and the woman cried out with terror when she saw the prophet of the Lord, and knew also that it was the King who had called for him.

"I am sore distressed," said Saul, "and God is departed from me. What shall I do?"

Then Samuel told him plainly that the kingdom was taken from him and given to David, and that on the next day he and his sons should fall in battle, and the Israelites into the hands of the Philistines.

Saul, forsaken and despairing, fell to the earth fainting, but was revived by the woman, who gave him food so that he went away through the dark to the camp of Israel.

In the battle of the next day the Philistines conquered. The three sons of Saul were slain, and Saul himself, when chased by the Philistines, fell upon his own sword and died.

When a messenger brought news of the battle to David he rent his clothes for grief, and in the chant of lamentation that he made, he mourned for his faithful friend Jonathan, and had no word of blame for his enemy Saul, neither did he triumph over him.

CHAPTER XXIII.

EVERY INCH A KING.

After Saul's death David came back to live with his own people, for he was of the tribe of Judah. He went to Hebron, the old home of Abraham, Isaac, and Jacob, for the Lord had told him to go there, and the men of his tribe came to Hebron and anointed him king. The other tribes did not come, for Saul's son and the captain of his host, Abner, were still holding the king-dom. But when both were killed by an enemy, then all the other tribes came to Hebron and made a league with him, so seven years after Saul's death David became king over all Israel. He was then thirty years old and his reign lasted forty years.

Then David began to establish the kingdom. There was a rocky height not far from Hebron with a valley all around it that was still held by the Jebusites, one of the tribes of Canaan that the Lord said must not be left in the land. The city was Jerusalem, and the stronghold was Zion, and close by Zion was the mount to which Abraham had once gone to offer up Isaac. David wanted this stronghold for the chief city of the kingdom, and so he took it, and it became the city of David. He built a beautiful house for him-self there, and King Hiram of Tyre sent skilled workmen, and cedar trees, and they built a house of cedar for him. But stronger than the wish to have a house for himself was the longing to see the Ark of God set within the curtains of the Tabernacle in the city of David. It had been in the house of Abinadab in Kirjath-Jearim for seventy years, ever since it was sent home by the Philistines who captured it. Because the people had grown cold toward God, they did not wish to hear the reading of the law, or be led by his counsel. Now David called together the flower of all Israel, thirty thousand men, and they went to bring the Ark to the city of David. While on the way a man who had laid his hand upon the Ark when it was unsteady was smitten and died, for no one but the priests and Levites could touch the Ark of God. David feared to bring it further, and so he placed it in the house of Obed-edom which was near by. It was there three months, and great blessing came to the house because of it. When David heard this he went joyfully down to bring the Ark to his city, and it was with sacrifices, and shouting, and the sound of trumpet that it was brought and set in the Tabernacle that had been made ready for it. And so the worship of the Lord was established in Jerusalem, which was to be the great altar for the sacrificial worship until the sacrifice should be taken away, and the kingdom of Christ established on the earth.

But David was not satisfied.

"See," he said to Nathan the prophet, "I dwell in a house of cedar, but the Ark of God dwelleth within curtains."

That night the Lord spoke to Nathan and told him what to say to the king. He promised to establish the royal house of David, and give final peace to the people, and also to build a house for the worship of the Lord, but he said that David's son, who should be king after him, should build a house to his name, and of him the Lord said, "I will be his Father, and he shall be my son."

Then King David went in to the Tabernacle and thanked the Lord for His promise to him and to his son, and asked His blessing upon them. Though he reigned forty years, he never forgot that his work was not to build the temple of the Lord, but to prepare for it. So he subdued enemies, built cities, made leagues with friendly nations, gathered much wealth of wood, and stone, and gold, and silver and precious stones for the house of the Lord, and trained choirs of singers for the service. He also kept his heart open toward the Lord, so that he was able to write some wonderful poems that were set to music and sung by the temple choirs. We call them the Psalms of David.

Though David had grown rich and great, he did not forget his promise to Jonathan. He called Ziba, who had been Saul's servant and said to him,

"Is there not yet any of the house of Saul that I may show the kindness of God to him?"

Then Ziba told him of a man who was lame in both his feet, who was the son of Jonathan. David sent for him, and gave him all the land of Saul, and a place was made for him at the king's table among his own sons, and it was his while he lived.

CHAPTER XXIV.

DAVID'S SIN.

The army of Israel was at war with the Ammonites, and Joab was the chief captain. David did not go out with the army, but stayed in his house in Jerusalem. One evening he was walking on the flat roof of his house, as the people of that country always do, and he saw a little way off a very beautiful woman. He sent a servant to ask who she was, and found she was the wife of Uriah who was in the army with Joab, fighting the Ammonites. Then a great temptation was set before David, and instead of going to the Lord to be saved from it, he sent to Joab, asking him to send him Uriah, the Hittite. So Uriah came, and David talked kindly with him, and found him a good and faithful man. When he went back to Joab he took a letter from David, who asked that he be set in the front of the battle. So Joab placed him there, and when the two armies met Uriah was killed, and Joab sent a messenger to tell David. After her mourning was ended, Bathsheba, the wife of Uriah, became the wife of David, but the Lord was displeased with David. He also knew David's heart and how to deal with him, so he sent Nathan the prophet to him.

"There were two men in one city," said Nathan, "one of them rich and the other poor. The rich man had many flocks and herds, but the poor man had nothing, save one little ewe lamb, which he had bought and nourished up; and it grew together with him and with his children : it did eat of his own meat and drink of his own cup, and lay in his bosom and was unto him as a daughter. And there came a traveller unto the rich man, and he spared to take of his own flock to dress for the wayfaring man that was come to him, but took the poor man's lamb and dressed it for the man that was come to him."

David was very angry at the man who could do such a cruel thing, and he said to Nathan,

"The man that hath done this thing shall surely die ; and he shall restore the lamb fourfold, because he did this thing, and because he had no pity."

Then Nathan said to David, "Thou art the man," and he told him how greatly the Lord had blessed him in making him King over Israel, and in delivering him from the hand of Saul, and how he had slain a faithful servant and taken his wife for himself; therefore evil would befall him.

David said, "I have sinned against the Lord," and the Lord saw that his repentance was real, and forgave the sin, but that David might never forget and sin again, the Lord took the little child that was born to him and to Bathsheba. While it was sick David fasted and lay all night upon the earth, and would not rise to taste food. This he did for seven days while the little child was sick, but when they told him that his child was dead he arose and bathed and dressed himself and went to the house of the Lord to worship, and returned to take his food. Then his servants wondered at it, and replied,

"While the child was yet alive I fasted and wept, for I said, who can tell whether God will be gracious unto me that the child may live. But now he is dead, wherefore should I fast? Can I bring him back again? I shall go to him, but he shall not return to me."

After this another child was born to Bathsheba, and they named him Solomon, which means "Peaceable."

And David wrote a prayer of repentance for his sin. It is the fifty-first Psalm, and has been the prayer of penitent souls for nearly three thousand years.

CHAPTER XXV.

DAVID'S SORROW.

David had a very beautiful son named Absalom. From the crown of his head to the soles of his feet there was no fault to be seen in him. His hair was thick and long, and his beauty was much talked of through all Israel. But the Lord who looks upon the heart saw that the heart of Absalom was wicked and false. He killed his brother Amnon, and then fled to another country and stayed three years. When he returned he tried to see his father, but David would not see him for two years. Then Absalom forced Joab to bring him to the king's house by setting Joab's barley field on fire. He was false as well as handsome, and won his father's heart by pretending to be humble.

After this Absalom began to live more like a king than a prince. He had fifty men to run before his chariot when he rode, and he stood in the city gates and talked with the men who came to see the king about their rights. He told them that if he were ruler over the land every man should have all that he wanted, and deceived many by a false show of friendship.

Then he asked the king if he could go to Hebron to pay a vow to the Lord by offering sacrifice there, and David told him to go in peace, and he went. But he had cruelly deceived his father. He had sent spies through all the land to persuade them to join him at Hebron and make him king. He also took two hundred men out of Jerusalem to help him, and one of them was David's counsellor. They had arranged to have all the people, as soon as they heard anywhere the sound of the trumpet, to cry,

"Absalom is king in Hebron."

Then it came to the ears of David that his people had been led away by deceit to follow Absalom, and David, who had been fearless before Goliath and before great armies of other nations, was afraid. His heart was broken at the treachery of his son, and he said to his servants,

" Arise, and let us flee ; make haste and go, for fear Absalom may come and fight against the city with the sword."

His servants were ready to fight for him, but he fled in haste over the brook Kedron and went toward the wilderness, with all of the people of the city with him, until there was a great multitude, and in the midst the priests and the Levites bearing the Ark of God, but when David saw this he said,

(86)

SAUL ATTEMPTS THE LIFE OF DAVID.

"Carry back the Ark of God into the city. If I shall find favor in the eyes of the Lord He will bring me again. Let Him do to me as seemeth good to Him."

So the priests and the Levites returned to the city with the Ark of God.

It was a sad procession that went over the Mount of Olives led by David, weeping as he went, with his head covered and his feet bare. Some enemies of the house of Saul came out and troubled him by the way, but there was no anger in the heart of David toward any. He believed the hand of the Lord was upon him, and he said,

"It may be the Lord will look on mine affliction."

Absalom came to Jerusalem, and while he was asking his chief counsellor what to do, he was persuaded by a friend of David, who had stayed behind, to wait until he had gathered a larger army before he followed after David. This gave him time to send word to David to cross over Jordan before Absalom should overtake him. The chief counsellor, when he saw that his advice was not followed, went to his own house and hanged himself, for he knew that the Lord was bringing his counsel to naught.

After David had passed over into Gilead the people of that land brought food, and dishes, and beds to the sorrowful king and his tired people, and they were cared for in the city of Mahanaim. Then Joab, the captain, gathered the men together to go and meet Absalom and his army, and as they passed out of the city David stood in the gate and charged all the captains as they passed, saying

"Deal gently, for my sake, with the young man, even with Absalom."

So they went out to battle, and it was in a wood. God had given David's army the victory, and twenty thousand men of Absalom's army were slain. Absalom, who rode on a mule, was caught by his long thick hair in the branches of an oak tree, and the mule went away and left him hanging there.

A man ran and told Joab that he had seen Absalom hanging in an oak.

"Why didst thou not smite him there?" said Joab.

The man said he would not have done it for a thousand shekels of silver, because David had charged them all not to touch the young man Absalom.

But Joab turned away, and when he had found Absalom in the oak, he, with the ten young men who were with him, killed Absalom, and they buried him in the wood.

Then Joab sent two messengers to carry news of the victory to the king, who sat between the city gates, while a watchman stood over the gates on the

THE DEATH OF ABSALOM.

city wall. When the watchmen saw the two men running, one after the other, he cried out and told the king. The first man cried as he came, "All is well," but when the king said, "Is the young man Absalom safe?" he could not answer, and when the second messenger cried, "Tidings, my lord, the king," again David asked,

"Is the young man Absalom safe?"

The enemies of my lord the king and all that rise against thee to do thee hurt be as that young man," said the messenger.

Then the king went up to the room over the city gate and wept, and as he went he cried,

"O my son Absalom! my son, my son Absalom! would God I had died for thee, O Absalom, my son, my son!"

The people who had come back joyful because the enemy had been conquered were distressed by the grief of the king, so that Joab persuaded David to come down to the gate and meet the people.

After this those who were left of the followers of Absalom begged the king to come back to Jerusalem, and so he came, and thousands came to meet him. He had only forgiving words for those who had injured him, and for Barzillai and the men of Gilead who had fed them and shown them great kindness in the darkest hour of the king's life, and who came a little way on the journey with them, he had grateful words and blessings.

And so the king came to his own again. He was now getting to be an old man, and the love of his people made his last days blessed.

His warriors said, "Thou shalt go no more out with us to battle, that thou quench not the light of Israel."

Once he sinned against the Lord by numbering his people. He wanted to know how many men in his kingdom could bear arms in battle, and he forgot that victory over the enemy was not with the many or the few, but with the Lord, who is the strength of his people. When he saw that he had done wrong he confessed it and begged for forgiveness, but a pestilence spread over all the land, and came near to Jerusalem, and the angel was stayed by the Lord's hand just over the threshing floor of Araunah. This was the broad flat top of Mount Moriah where long before Abraham had built an altar on which to offer Isaac.

When David saw the angel he said,

"I have done wickedly, but these sheep, what have they done? Let Thine hand, I pray thee, be against me, and against my father's house."

Then the prophet Gad said, "Go up, rear an altar to the Lord in the

DAVID MOURNING FOR ABSALOM.

threshing-floor of Araunah," and David went as the Lord commanded.

When they reached the mount Araunah offered David the piece of ground with the oxen for a sacrifice, but he would not take them as a gift.

"But I will surely buy it of thee at a price," said David, "neither will I offer burnt offerings to the Lord my God of that which doth cost me nothing."

So he bought the piece of ground and paid for it six hundred shekels of gold. Twice had the Lord blessed this spot with a miracle of salvation, and twice an altar had been built there, and looking upon it, David said,

"This is the house of the Lord God, and this is the altar of burnt offering for Israel," and he prepared to build there the temple of Solomon,—the altar of the world.

CHAPTER XXVI.

THE BUILDING OF THE GOLDEN HOUSE.

The time was near when David must leave his people and go to his God, and his chief thought was about the house of the Lord that he had longed to build, that the Ark of God might be at rest, and that the people might have a place of worship for all time to come. He knew that his son Solomon was to build the temple, but he was still young, and David made ready as far as he could for the building of the house. There were men at work in the quarries, cutting great stones, and there were men in the forests of Lebanon cutting and hewing cedars, and others gathering iron and brass, and gold, and silver for the treasury of David. He also spent much time dividing the sons of Levi into companies, so that they could in turn serve with the priests in the temple, and ordering the times and manner of service, for he believed that this temple would be a house of prayer for all nations. David had been a man of war, for he had been called to destroy idol worship in the land of Canaan, and to make it the land of Israel, in which the one true God should be worshipped forever, but Solomon's reign was to be one of peace, and the Lord chose a man of peace to build his house.

David had another son, Adonijah, who tried to make himself king as Absalom did, but David heard of it, and had Solomon proclaimed king before his own death, lest trouble should arise after. When Adonijah heard the shouts of the people, and the sound of the trumpets he was afraid, and expected Solomon would kill him, but Solomon said if he would only show himself a good man no harm should come to him.

The last things that David did were to call his princes and chief men together and tell them that the Lord had promised many years before, that Solomon should build the house of the Lord during his reign ; and also that his children's children should rule over Israel, and he begged them to keep the Lord's commandments, that they might keep the good land that had been given them.

He also charged Solomon before them all to serve God with all his heart, but if he failed to do so he would be cast off forever.

David gave Solomon all the plans and patterns for the house of the Lord, as the Lord had given them to him ; also the gold and silver stored up for time of building. He also told the people, when he had called them together, what he had stored for the work of the temple, and asked them who were willing to give also. Then the people brought gifts, as they did when the Tabernacle was built, and gave them to the Lord. David led them in a great thanksgiving service, and they offered three thousand sacrifices.

Solomon was again anointed king in the presence of all Israel, and took the throne of David; and David died, honored and loved by his people, and he was buried in his own city.

When Solomon went to Gibeon to sacrifice the Lord came to him in a dream and said,

"Ask what I shall give thee."

Solomon was wiser than all the sons of David, and yet he did not feel himself to be so. He said,

"I am but a little child ; I know not how to go out or come in, and thy servant is in the midst of a great people that cannot be numbered. Give therefore thy servant an understanding heart to judge thy people, that I may discern between good and bad, for who is able to judge this thy so great a people."

And the Lord said,

"Because thou hast asked this thing, and hast not asked for thyself long life, neither riches, nor the life of thine enemies, lo, I have given thee a wise and understanding heart, and I have also given thee that which thou hast not asked—both riches and honor; and if thou wilt walk in my ways as thy father David did, then I will lengthen thy days."

The Lord was true to his word. Solomon had wisdom beyond all the old and the learned men of his kingdom, and many came to him for counsel who were not of Israel, for he was famous among the nations. Some of these nations wished to be ruled by him, and brought him many precious things as gifts; they had been conquered by David, and now they wished to be ruled by Solomon. He had thousands of servants and he knew how to direct their work. Away up in the mountains of Lebanon they worked with the servants of Hiram, King of Tyre, getting the cedar timbers ready for the temple, while Hiram's artisans in gold, and silver, and brass, and fine linen came to Jerusalem to work on the temple, and Solomon sent Hiram wheat, and olive oil, and wine. So wise were the workers in stone and wood that when the temple was built there was no sound of a hammer or any tool heard on Mount Moriah. Each stone was ready to fit into its place, and each piece of wood to fit another.

The house was not like any that we have ever seen. It was not large, but it was very precious. The cedar boards that lined the walls were carved in flower patterns, and covered with gold. The floor also was covered with gold. He divided the temple in two parts, as the Tabernacle had been, with a rich curtain of blue and purple and crimson. The innermost room was called the most holy place, and was for the Ark, and its walls were beautiful with cherubim, and palm trees, and flowers, overlaid with gold, as was the floor also. Within this most holy place stood two cherubim fifteen feet high. They were of olive wood covered with gold, and they stood with wings spread forth so that they touched each other, and also touched the wall on either side, and their wings overshadowed the mercy seat where the Ark of the Lord was to rest. All the carvings upon wood were covered with gold, and precious stones were set among them for light and beauty.

Solomon's workmen made two great pillars of brass to stand before the house, and a great brass altar for the burnt offerings. They also made ten basins of brass that were set upon wheels, and one very great one called the "sea" which stood on twelve brass oxen.

They also made many things for the use of the temple—candlesticks, and spoons, and censers all of pure gold, and there was also a golden altar and a golden table.

Solomon was seven years building the house of the Lord, and when it was finished, and its outer courts made ready, he called all the elders and chief men of Israel together to carry the Ark of God to its place. So the Ark, borne by the priests, and holding the tables of the law, was carried into the most holy place, and set under the wings of the cherubim. After the priests came out a cloud filled the house of the Lord so that the priests could not go in. It was the glory of the presence of the Lord.

Then Solomon stood before all the people and gave thanks to God and asked him to take the temple for his own house to dwell in, and kneeling down, he prayed that wherever the children of Israel might be, at home, or captives in a strange land, that the Lord would hear them when they prayed toward his house, and that all prayer offered in it might be heard and answered.

Then fire from heaven fell upon the great altar, and the sacrifice was consumed, and all over the great pavement of the court the people bowed and worshipped the Lord, saying, "For He is good, and His mercy endureth forever."

There were offerings and feasting for fourteen days, and then the people went to their homes to think of the wonderful things they had seen. And there were sacrifices offered morning and evening each day, on the Sabbath, and at the three great feasts of the year—the feast of the passover, the feast of the harvest, and the feast of tabernacles.

Solomon also built a wonderful house for himself, and another called the "house of the forest of Lebanon," where he kept his armor. The roof was upheld by cedars of Lebanon, standing like mighty pillars beneath it. So famous did his work and his wisdom become that a queen from a distant land called Sheba came to visit him. She came with a caravan of servants and camels bringing costly presents of spices, and gold, and precious stones. She asked him many things that she had longed to know, and he answered all her questions, and told her strange and wonderful things, so that after she had seen all his palace, and his servants, and the service of his table, and the beautiful ascent by which he went up to the temple, she said that the half had never been told her in her own country. They exchanged costly presents, and she went back to her own land.

Solomon had many ships upon the sea that brought riches from every land. He learned much of the world in this way, and as he grew older and from his throne of gold and ivory judged his people, he dropped many wise sayings that were written in a book by the scribes and are now called the "Proverbs of Solomon."

But in Solomon's latter days his wives, who were daughters of heathen kings, turned his heart from the Lord. When his father sinned he repented at once, and his heart never turned to idols, but with all his wisdom, Solomon was weak of will, and built temples for his wives to worship idols in.

THE QUEEN OF SHEBA BEFORE SOLOMON.

The Lord had made a promise to David that his sons should inherit the throne, and He kept the promise, but he allowed the kingdom to be divided. The two tribes who lived near to Jerusalem—Judah and Benjamin—were left to Solomon's son Rehoboam, but the ten tribes chose a man named Jeroboam to be their king. The men of Rehoboam, led by their king, went out to fight with the ten tribes, but the Lord would not let them. He spoke to them through a prophet and they went home.

So now there were two kings in Israel, and Rehoboam's kingdom was called the kingdom of Judah, and that of Jeroboam was called the kingdom of Israel; but after the kingdom was divided no kings ever reigned who could be compared with David and Solomon.

CHAPTER XXVII.

ELIJAH THE GREAT HEART OF ISRAEL.

During the reign of Jehoshaphat, fourth king of Judah, and Ahab, sixth king of Israel, after the division of the kingdom, there came out of Gilead Elijah, a prophet of the Lord. Two of the kings of Judah, and all of the kings of Israel had been wicked men, and the Lord sent Elijah to Ahab, king of Israel, to tell him that there should be no rain for years in the land of Israel, and then only as Elijah should ask for it. Ahab was more wicked than the kings that reigned before him, and had built a temple for the god Baal in Samaria.

Because he would seek to destroy Elijah, the Lord told His prophet to go to the brook Cherith that ran into the Jordan, and there He would take care of him. "Thou shalt drink of the brook, and I have commanded the ravens to feed thee there," said the Lord.

And so it was. Morning and evening the ravens came bringing bread and meat, and the brook brought him water out of the rock, but as there was no rain, the brook at last dried up, and there was a great famine.

Then Elijah was told to go to Zarephath, for a woman there had been told to feed him, and he went at once. As he came near the city gate he saw a woman gathering sticks, and he asked her to bring him a cup of water and a little bread. She told him that she had but a handful of meal in a

6

barrel, and a little oil in a cruse, and she was going to bake it for herself and son, that they might eat it and die.

Then Elijah said, " Fear not ; go and do as thou hast said, but make me thereof a little cake first, and after that make for thee and thy son, for thus saith the Lord God of Israel, 'The barrel of meal shall not waste, neither shall the cruse of oil fail until the day that the Lord sendeth rain upon the earth.'"

She believed Elijah, and did as he commanded, and they ate for a whole year, and the meal and the oil lasted all that time.

After this the woman's son grew very sick, so very sick that he appeared to be dead, and the woman cried to the prophet in her distress,

" O thou man of God, art thou come unto me to call my sin to remembrance and to slay my son ?"

Then he said, " Give me thy son," and he took him up to his own room and laid him upon his bed and prayed over him. Then he stretched himself upon the child three times and cried,

" O Lord my God, I pray Thee let this child's soul come unto him again ! "

And God heard Elijah, and the soul of the child came to him again, and he revived.

Then he gave the boy to his happy and grateful mother, saying, " See, thy son liveth."

In the third year of the famine the Lord said to Elijah,

"Go, show thyself to Ahab, and I will send rain on the earth."

As Elijah went he met a good man named Obadiah, who was governor of the king's house. This man worshipped the Lord, and when Ahab's wicked wife, Jezebel, tried to kill all the Lord's prophets he hid a hundred of them in two caves and kept them alive with bread and water. He was seeking grass and water for the king's horses, and when he saw Elijah he fell on his face and said,

" Art thou my Lord Elijah ? "

" I am," said Elijah, "go, tell thy lord, 'Behold, Elijah is here.' "

Obadiah was in distress at this command, for he knew that the king would kill Elijah if he found him, and he could not think that Elijah would be brave enough to meet the king, or he thought perhaps the spirit of the Lord would carry him away, and he alone would have to meet the anger of the king.

"As the Lord of hosts liveth," said Elijah, " I will surely show myself unto him to-day."

So Obadiah told Ahab, and Ahab went to meet Elijah, and said to him, "Art thou he that troubleth Israel?"

"I have not troubled Israel," he said, "but thou and thy father's house, in that ye have forsaken the commandments of the Lord, and thou hast followed Baalim."

Then he told Ahab to call all Israel to Mount Carmel which overlooks the sea, and to bring there also the four hundred and fifty prophets of Baal, and the four hundred prophets of the groves.

So the king called them together, and Elijah cried to the people, "How long halt ye between two opinions? If the Lord be God, follow Him; but if Baal, follow him.

And the people, afraid of the king and his wicked wife, answered not a word.

"I, even I only, remain a prophet of the Lord," said Elijah, "but Baal's prophets are four hundred and fifty men." And then he told the people how it could be proven which was true—the God of Israel, or Baal.

He told the prophets of Baal to make an altar and place wood and a sacrifice upon it, and he also would do the same, and they should call upon Baal, and he would call on the name of the Lord, and "the God that answereth by fire, let him be God."

This the priests of Baal were willing to do, and they cried around their altar from morning until night, "O Baal, hear us," but there was no voice, and no answer by fire.

Elijah watched and waited, sometimes telling them that perhaps their god was asleep, and could be waked; or that he had gone on a journey, or was talking with somebody, and then they became wild and leaped upon the altar and cut themselves with knives.

After many hours Elijah called the people to him, and he repaired a broken altar of the Lord that stood there with twelve stones for the twelve tribes of Israel, and made a trench all around it. Then he placed wood on the altar and told the people to pour four barrels of water over the sacrifice. This they did three times, and the water ran down and filled the trench around the altar, and the people saw that Elijah could not by any means make a fire there.

Then, as it was the hour of the evening sacrifice in the temple, Elijah knelt by his altar with his face toward Jerusalem, and prayed to his God that He would hear him, and show the people that they were called from the worship of idols to the service of the living God.

What a wonderful sight was that, when fire fell from heaven and burnt up the sacrifice, and the wood, and the altar, and even the water in the trench around the altar !

And the people all fell on their faces at the sight, and cried,

"The Lord He is the God! The Lord He is the God!" Then Elijah told them to take the prophets of Baal and destroy them, and they did so.

"There is a sound of abundance of rain !" said Elijah to the king, and then he went to the very top of Carmel, and threw himself upon the earth, hiding his face between his knees, while he sent his servant to look toward the sea, and watch for the coming of the rain.

This the servant did seven times, each time coming to his master and saying, "There is nothing," but the prophet told him to look seven times more, and when he came back the seventh time he said,

"Behold, there ariseth a little cloud out of the sea like a man's hand."

Then he sent his servant to Ahab, saying,

"Prepare thy chariot and get thee down, that the rain stop thee not."

The little cloud grew to be a great one, and filled all the sky until it was black with clouds and wind, and there was a great rain. And as Ahab rode in his chariot, Elijah, who was strong with the spirit of the Lord and glad for His great victory over sin, ran before the chariot to the gates of the city.

Jezebel the queen was furious when she heard that the priests had been destroyed. She sent word to Elijah that he would be treated the same way on the morrow, and so Elijah fled for his life, and leaving his servant in Beer-Sheba on the southern border of Israel, he went a day's journey into the wilderness. There he sat down under a juniper tree, and for the first time his heart grew weak within him.

"It is enough," he said, "Now, O Lord, take away my life, for am I not better than my fathers."

Perhaps he was discouraged because he was tired and hungry, for he fell asleep, and when he awoke it was because an angel touched him, saying, "Arise and eat," and he looked, and there was a cake just baked on the hot coals, and a bottle of water close beside him. So he ate and drank, but he was not yet rested, and he fell asleep again. The angel waked him the second time telling him to eat and drink, for the journey was too great for him. Then he ate and drank again, and went on the strength of that food forty days and forty nights, till he came to Horeb, the mount of God, where the Ten Commandments were given to Moses, and there he lodged in a cave.

ELIJAH AND THE ANGEL.

He was still gloomy and discouraged, and when the Lord said, " What doest thou here, Elijah ?" he said,

" I have been very jealous for the Lord God of hosts, for the children of Israel have forsaken thy covenant, thrown down thine altars, and slain thy prophets with the sword, and I, even I only am left, and they seek my life to take it."

Then the Lord told him to go out and stand on the mount before the Lord, and he passed by. There was a great wind that split the mountains, and broke the great rocks, but the Lord was not in the wind, and after the wind an earthquake, but the Lord was not in the earthquake ; and after the earthquake a fire, but the Lord was not in the fire ; and after the fire a still, small voice.

When Elijah heard that, he wrapped his face in his mantle and stood at the door of the cave, and the Lord asked again, " What doest thou here, Elijah ?" and Elijah answered him just as he did before,

Then the Lord told him to go back and anoint a new king over Syria, also a new king over Israel, and Elisha to be prophet in his place.

Elijah went, and he found Elisha ploughing with twelve yoke of oxen. He cast his mantle over Elisha, and Elisha followed him and became his servant.

When Elijah came back to his own country he found there had been war between Israel and Syria, and Ahab had grown hard of heart again. He and his wicked wife Jezebel had taken the vineyard of Naboth away from him because Ahab wanted it for a garden, and they had caused the death of Naboth, so when Elijah came he found Ahab in the vineyard, and said,

" Hast thou killed and also taken possession ?" and he told him that he should die where Naboth died.

" Hast thou found me, O mine enemy !" cried the king.

" I have found thee," answered Elijah, and he spoke to him the word of the Lord, that he should be destroyed out of Israel with his whole family.

Then Ahab repented, and the Lord spared his life two years, but later his wife Jezebel came to a dreadful end, with the seventy sons of Ahab.

When the time came for the Lord to take his servant to himself, Elijah wished to be alone, but Elisha his servant would not leave him. He followed his master from one town to another until they came to the river Jordan. Then Elijah took off his mantle, and folding it, struck the waters and they were divided, so that they went over on dry ground. Then Elijah said,

ELIJAH AND THE CHARIOT OF FIRE.

"Ask what I shall do for thee," and Elisha prayed that a double portion of his Master's spirit might rest upon him.

"If thou see me when I am taken from thee it shall be so unto thee," he said, "but if not, it shall not be so."

And as they went there appeared a chariot of fire, and horses of fire, parting them from each other, and Elijah went up in a whirlwind to heaven. Now Elisha wished his master to know that he saw him, so he cried,

"My father, my father! the chariot of Israel and the horsemen thereof!" and he saw him no more.

Then he took Elijah's mantle that fell from him, and struck the waters of Jordan again, and they parted, and he went over, and he knew that the power of the old prophet's spirit had been given to him.

Fifty young men, sons of the prophets, saw him return, and they said,

"The spirit of Elijah doth rest on Elisha," and they bowed themselves to the ground before him.

CHAPTER XXVIII.

THE LITTLE CHAMBER ON THE WALL.

Elisha did many wonderful things in the strength of the spirit that Elijah's God gave him. He changed the waters of Jericho, so that they were no longer poisonous, by casting salt in the spring.

He brought water for the thirsty armies of three kings who had gathered to battle, by telling them to dig ditches in a valley of Edom, and watch for the water to come, without wind or rain. When the morning dawned the valley was full of running water.

He helped a poor widow to pay a debt and take care of her two sons by telling her to borrow empty pots and pans of all her neighbors, and pour into them her one little pot of oil. The oil increased until all the pots and pans were full, and she had plenty to sell.

He saved the sons of the prophets from death by casting meal into the pot when a poisonous nut had been mingled with the food, and he fed a hundred people with the bread that was brought as a portion for himself.

But the most beautiful story in the life of Elisha is that of the Shun-amite mother and her son. The mother was a noble lady of Shun-em, who

THE FEEDING OF ELIJAH.

believed in God, and in the good man who passed her house so often, and she said to her husband,

"Let us make for him a little chamber on the wall." And so they did, and when Elisha came again he lodged there. He was grateful to these kind people, and asked the woman what he should do for her—if she would ask anything of the king, but she only said,

"I dwell among mine own people."

Then the prophet, knowing that she had no child, promised that she should have a son, and though it was hard to believe, the little son was sent to her, and she was very happy. But one day when he went out in the field where his father and his men were reaping, he cried out, "My head, my head!" and they carried him in to his mother. She held him in her arms until noon, and then he died and she laid him in the prophet's chamber. Perhaps the heat of the harvest time had been too great for one so young. Did the mother cry out and call her husband? No, she called for a servant and a donkey, and rode as fast as she could to Mount Carmel where Elisha was. His servant saw her coming, and Elisha sent him to meet her and ask if it was well with her and her husband and her child, and she said,

"It is well," though her heart was breaking.

"Did I ask a son of my lord?" she said as she came to Elisha and fell at his feet. Then he knew that the child was ill or dead, and he would have sent his servant to lay his staff on the child, but the mother cried,

"As the Lord liveth, and as thy soul liveth, I will not leave thee," and he arose and followed her.

When he came to the Shun-amite's house he went into his little room where the dead child lay upon his bed, and, shutting the door, prayed to the Lord. Then he stretched himself upon the child, and breathed upon him until life began to creep back into the little cold body, and when he had done this twice the child opened his eyes Then Elisha called the mother, and when she had fallen at his feet in grateful joy, she took up her child and went out.

ELIJAH RAISES THE WIDOW'S SON.

CHAPTER XXIX.

A LITTLE MAID OF ISRAEL.

There was war almost all the time between Israel and Syria. A band of Syrians from Damascus would often come into a village of Israel and take the people away for slaves. One little girl who was carried off by the Syrians became a slave in the house of a Syrian general called Naaman, and was a maid to Naaman's wife.

Naaman was a great man, and beloved by all, but he had a disease that could never be cured. It was leprosy. He could go about, but he could not touch others without giving them the disease which turns the skin white and dead, and finally eats the flesh away.

The little maid said to her mistress one day,

"Would God my lord were with the prophet that is in Samaria! for he would recover him of his leprosy."

When this was told to Naaman he talked with the king, who sent him to the king of Israel with a letter, but the king of Israel was angry.

"Am I God to kill and make alive, that this man doth send unto me to recover a man of his leprosy?" he cried, but when Elisha heard of it he said,

"Let him come now to me, and he shall know that there is a prophet in Israel."

So Naaman came with his horses and chariot to Elisha's house, but the prophet did not even come to the door, but sent his servant with this message,

"Go wash in Jordan seven times, and thy flesh shall come again to thee, and thou shalt be clean."

But Naaman went away in a rage. He expected Elisha to come out, and that there would be a fine scene while he called on the name of God, waved his hand over the leprous spots, and made a cure.

"Are not Abana and Pharpar, rivers of Damascus, better than all the waters of Israel? May I not wash in them and be clean?" he said.

Then some of his servants came near to him and said,

"My father, if the prophet had bid thee do some great thing, wouldst thou not have done it? How much rather, then, when he saith to thee, 'Wash and be clean.'"

(108)

Then he went down and dipped himself seven times in Jordan, and his flesh became like the flesh of a little child, and he was clean.

After this he, with all that were with him, went humbly back to Elisha and said,

"Now I know that there is no God in all the earth but in Israel." And he urged the prophet to take gifts from him, but he would not.

But Naaman begged of Elisha two mule-loads of earth to take to his own country. He wanted to build an altar upon it to worship the God of Israel, and he thought it must stand on the soil of Israel.

Did Naaman ever send the little maid of Israel to her home? We do not know, but surely he was kind to her in some way.

CHAPTER XXX.

THE TWO BOY KINGS.

There were many kings over Israel from the days of Solomon until the time when they were carried away captives to Babylon. The kingdom was divided soon after Solomon's death, and a king reigned in Jerusalem over the kingdom of Judah, and another in Samaria over the kingdom of Israel. There were a few kings who tried to follow that which was right, but the most of them were men who were given to idolatry, and who did not help the people to remember the true God. The Lord sent them prophets to remind them of Him, but they were often driven away or ill treated. There were a few good kings of Judah, such as Asa and Jehoshaphat, and Hezekiah, and among them were two who became kings when they were very young.

When Ahaziah, King of Judah, was killed, his mother, who was a wicked woman, killed all his sons, that she herself might be queen. All but a baby boy who was hidden with his nurse in the temple, and tenderly cared for by the good high priest and his wife for six years. Then when he was seven years old the priests and the Levites brought out little Joash and anointed him king. They formed a guard all about him, and when the high priest had crowned him there was a great cry around the temple of "God save the King."

The old queen heard this and came to see what it meant. When she saw the little Joash standing by a pillar with a crown on his head she cried out that the people were plotting against her.

The people did by her as she had done by her grandsons—they took her life.

Then there was great rejoicing. The house of Baal was torn down, and the Lord's gold and silver brought back to the temple, and the good high priest began the worship of God in the temple after the manner of former days.

When Joash was old enough to understand he longed to make the temple beautiful again, for it was falling into decay, so he called for money throughout his kingdom. Everyone was asked to drop a silver piece in the chest that was set at the temple door, and more than enough was brought to re-build the temple, and while the high priest lived the king worshipped there with all the princes of Judah, but as soon as he died they went back to idol worship, and killed the new high priest in the court of the temple because he told them that the Lord would bring great trouble upon them. And so it came to pass in less than a year the Syrians came and killed the princes, and took away the gold and silver treasures of the temple. Joash himself became very sick, and his own servants took his life as he lay helpless.

It was quite different with little Josiah. He was only eight years old when he was crowned King of Judah, and he had no one so good as the high priest Jehoida, who was the teacher of Joash, to help him to do right. Even the holy writings that were given to Moses were lost, and the people did not ask to hear them read. But the Lord had not allowed His word to be destroyed, and when Josiah was having the temple repaired the high priest found the rolls of parchment on which the law was written, and sent it to the king by a servant of the king who was a writer. Josiah was full of interest in the ancient book, and wished to know what was in it, and his servant read it to him.

When he found that he and his people were not living as God had commanded in the law, he sent to inquire of the Lord what He would have them to do, and they went to Huldah, the prophetess. She told the king's messengers that a great calamity would fall upon the kingdom because they had turned away from the true God, but because the king's heart was tender and full of desire to follow the Lord, it should not come during his lifetime.

Then the king called all the chief men of Judah, and the people of the city, both great and small, with the priests and the Levites, to the Lord's house, and there he read in their hearing the word of the Lord. It was like a new book to the most of them, but they were ready to follow the king in making a solemn promise to the Lord to do His commandments, and bring back the true worship.

So they had a great feast of the passover, to which all the people came with offerings, and there was no passover in all the history of the kings of Judah and Israel that was like this one that was held in the eighteenth year of the reign of Josiah.

After he had prepared the temple for worship, and had destroyed the altars of the idols, he went out to meet the King of Egypt in battle and was killed, and there was a great mourning for him in all the land, for he had been a good king—kind to his people and faithful to his God. Jeremiah the prophet made a great lamentation for him, for he knew that one of Josiah's sons would be the last king of Judah, and that for their sins the people would be driven out of their own land to be captives in Babylon for seventy years.

CHAPTER XXXI.

THE FOUR CAPTIVE CHILDREN.

Nebuchadnezzar, King of Babylon, came with his armies and besieged Jerusalem, just as Jeremiah the prophet had foretold. He took the king and the princes of Judah captive, and carried away their precious things from the temple and the palaces into his own land, and put them in the temples of his gods. Before twenty years had passed the whole nation had been driven into captivity, and their holy house had been burned, and the ark of the covenant lost or destroyed. As the kingdom of Israel had also been scattered, the whole land lay desolate, and the walls of the cities were broken down.

When the King of Babylon first beseiged Jerusalem he carried away the finest of the princely families to serve him. They were the flower of Jerusalem—young men of noble face and form; well taught in the learning of the Jews, and skilfull in the sciences of that time. They were also chosen for their natural ability to learn the language and the wisdom of the Chaldeans.

Among these were four boys named Daniel, Hananiah, Mishael and Azariah. The king gave these boys into the care of his chief officer, who set teachers over them and treated them very kindly, while the king sent them each day meat and wine from his own table. The Chaldeans offered these things to idols, and then ate of them themselves ; they also used some meats for food that were unclean to an Israelite, so that the four children of Judah determined that they would not touch the king's meat and drink.

Daniel spoke to the chief officer about it, and though he had learned to love Daniel very much, he was afraid to have the boys refuse the king's food.

"I fear my lord the king," he said, "who hath appointed your meat and your drink, for why should he see your faces sadder than the children which are of your sort? Then shall ye make me endanger my head to the king."

But Daniel turned to Melzar, the steward, and begged him to prove them by giving them only vegetables to eat and water to drink for ten days, and "Then," said he "let our countenances be looked upon before thee, and the countenance of the children that eat of the portion of the king's meat: and as thou seest, deal with thy servants." And he proved them for ten days.

At the end of that time their faces were fatter and fairer than the faces of all the others who ate portions from the King's table, and they were allowed to eat the food they had chosen.

They also grew in wisdom and judgment. Daniel had the gift of understanding visions and dreams, and the gift came from God, and not from the study of magic. Among all the young men these four were most pleasing to the king, and they were called to the palace to stand before him.

Not long after this the king had a dream that seemed very wonderful to him, but he could not remember it. He called all his magicians, and astrologers, and wise men together, and told them that they must tell him what his dream was, and the meaning of it, or he would destroy them. There was no man wise enough to tell him, and he ordered that all the wise men of Babylon should be killed, Daniel and his friends among them.

Daniel asked the captain of the king's guard why the king was so hasty with his decree, and the captain told him.

Then Daniel went to the king and told him that if he would give him a little time he would tell him his dream and its meaning, and he went to his three friends and together they prayed the God of Heaven to show them the dream and its interpretation.

That night Daniel saw in a vision from God the same thing that the king had seen and had forgotten. It was a great image standing before the king, and shining like the sun. The head was of pure gold, the breast and arms of silver, and the rest of the body of brass ; while the legs were of iron, and

IN THE FIERY FURNACE.

the feet were part of iron and part of clay. As he looked a great stone cut from a mountain by unseen hands was hurled at the image, striking its feet and breaking them. Then the image fell and broke into pieces so fine that the winds blew them away, but the stone grew to be a great mountain that filled the earth.

Then Daniel gave thanks to God for showing him the dream, and went to the king.

He told the king that the God of Heaven alone had revealed the dream, for no man could know it, and he told him what the dream had been. He also told him that God had shown him the meaning ; that the head of gold was the king himself, who reigned over the greatest kingdom on earth, but after him new kingdoms would rise, and the silver, the brass, the iron and the clay stood for these ; but in the days of the kingdom of iron and clay the God of heaven would set up a kingdom which should never be destroyed, but it would destroy all the kingdoms that had gone before it. This kingdom—the great stone cut without hands from the mountain—meant the Kingdom of Christ.

The king was so astonished at Daniel's wisdom—for it was the dream he had forgotten brought back and interpreted—that he fell on his face before Daniel and reverenced the God of heaven. He made Daniel chief ruler in his realm and gave also great honors to his friends.

Nebuchadnezzar soon forgot God, for he set up a great golden image on the plain of Dura, and called a feast of dedication. He had all his princes and governors there, and his captains, and judges, and rulers. The musicians were there also, with many kinds of instruments, and a herald was there who cried in a loud voice the command of the king. It was a call to worship the golden image. At the first sound of the bands of music all were to fall down before the golden image, or failing to do so, be thrown into a fiery furnace.

Among the rulers were the three friends of Daniel, whose names had been changed by the king to Shadrach, Meshach, and Abednego. They did not fall before the golden image, and some jealous Chaldeans who saw them went and told the king. Then the king, who had a fiery temper, was angry, and sent for the three young men. He told them the bands should play again, and if they failed to worship the golden image they should be cast into the furnace, "and who is that God that shall deliver you out of my hands?" he asked.

DANIEL IN THE LIONS' DEN.

"We are not careful to answer thee in this matter," they said, "If it be so, our God whom we serve is able to deliver us from the burning fiery furnace, and he will deliver us out of thy hand, O king."

Then the king in a great rage called his mighty men to bind the young men, and after the furnace was heated seven times hotter than before, they were thrown in. So great was the heat that the men who threw them in were killed by it in the sight of the king. As he watched the great door of the furnace the king rose up and said,

"Did not we cast three men bound into the midst of the fire?"

"True, O king," said his lords and captains.

Then the king with his eyes fixed upon the glowing door of the furnace said,

"Lo I see four men loose, walking in the midst of the fire, and they have no hurt, and the form of the fourth is like the Son of God."

Then he went near the door of the furnace and cried,

"Shadrach, Meshach, and Abed-nego, ye servants of the most high God, come forth and come hither!"

Then they came out before the king and all the people, who saw that the fire had no power over their bodies, for no hair of their head was burned, and no smell of fire was upon their garments.

Then the king was very humble, and acknowledged the God of heaven, "because there is no other God" he said "that can deliver after this sort." And he promoted the young men to still higher places in his kingdom.

CHAPTER XXXII.

THE MASTER OF THE MAGICIANS.

The Lord saw that the heart of Nebuchadnezzar was lifted up with pride because he was king of a great people, and had conquered many weaker nations. He was proud of his royal city, Babylon. The walls of Babylon were sixty miles in length, and in them stood one hundred brazen gates. There were wonderful palaces, and statues, and bridges, and gardens. The river Euphrates ran through the city, and near the king's palace was a hill covered with trees and flowering plants from many lands, called the Hanging Gardens.

Babylon was built on a plain, but the king had these gardens made for his wife, who had come from a country of hills.

The king was praised so much by the princes and rulers that he thought only of his own power and riches, and became proud and cruel. So the Lord sent him a dream. He saw a tree great and high, standing in the midst of a wide plain. It grew until it reached the heavens, and its branches spread to the ends of the earth. It was thick with green leaves, and heavy with fruit; the birds lived in it, and the beasts lay in its shadow, and all things living came to it for food. Then he saw an angel coming down from heaven crying,

"Hew down the tree, and cut off his branches; shake off his leaves, and scatter his fruit; let the beasts get away from under it, and the fowls from his branches; nevertheless, leave the stump of his roots in the earth, even with a band of iron and brass, in the tender grass of the field; and let it be wet with the dew of heaven, and let his portion be with the beasts of the grass of the earth; let his heart be changed from a man's, and let a beast's heart be given unto him, and let seven times pass over him."

This dream was given that the king might be taught that the Lord alone is King.

Daniel, named by the king Belteshazzar, was called to interpret the dream, and the Lord gave him power to do it.

"The tree that thou sawest," said Daniel, "it is thou, O king, that art grown and become strong; for thy greatness is grown and reacheth unto heaven, and thy dominion to the end of the earth."

Then Daniel told the king that he must be driven from men to dwell with the beasts of the field; to eat grass with the oxen, and be wet with the dews of heaven, until he had learned that the Most High rules in the kingdom of men, and gives to whosoever He will. But as the roots of the tree were left in the ground, so his kingdom should be preserved for him until he had learned that the heavens do rule.

At the end of a year the king's heart had not been made humble, for as he walked in his palace he said to himself:

"Is not this great Babylon that I have built for the house of the kingdom by the might of my power, and for the honor of my majesty?"

And while he yet spoke there fell a voice from heaven, saying:

"O, King Nebuchadnezzar, to thee it is spoken; the kingdom is departed from thee."

And within an hour the word of the Lord came true. For seven years he was without reason, and was an outcast from his kingdom. But at the end of

7

that time his eyes were lifted to heaven and his reason returned, and his kingdom was restored to him, for he had learned that God alone is great, and "Those that walk in pride He is able to abase."

Belshazzar was the next king of Babylon. He made a great feast, and a thousand of his lords were bidden to sit around his tables in the great hall of the palace. While he drank the wine he thought of the holy vessels of gold and silver that his father had brought out of the Temple at Jerusalem, and he sent for them, and into these golden bowls that had been consecrated to the worship of God he poured wine and gave it to his princes and to his wives, while they praised the gods of gold, and silver, and wood, and stone.

While they were feasting, and laughing, and singing, there came a man's hand and wrote some strange words on the wall of the great hall where they sat. The king saw the hand as it wrote, and he was so much afraid that he trembled and grew very weak. He called for his wise men and they could not read the writing, but the queen remembered that in the time of Nebuchadnezzar there was a man whom he made master of the magicians because he had power to interpret dreams and make all doubtful things clear.

So Daniel was brought before the king, and the king told him that if he would read the writing on the wall he should be clothed royally and be made the third ruler in the kingdom.

"Let thy gifts be to thyself," said Daniel, "and give thy rewards to another, yet I will read the writing unto the king, and make known to him the interpretation."

Then Daniel reminded the king of that which fell upon his father Nebuchadnezzar, when he had grown proud and hard-hearted toward God and men, and, though he knew all this, he also had lifted himself up against the Lord of heaven, and had defiled the holy vessels of the Temple by drinking from them to gods which could neither see or hear, and because of this the message had been written on the wall. And this was the interpretation of the strange words,—

"God hath numbered thy kingdom and finished it. Thou art weighed in the balances, and art found wanting. Thy kingdom is divided, and given to the Medes and the Persians."

The king clothed Daniel in scarlet, and gave him a chain of gold, and proclaimed him third ruler in the kingdom, but the same night Belshazzar was slain, and Darius the Median took the kingdom.

The new king set one hundred and twenty princes over the kingdom, and over these he set three presidents, the first of which was Daniel. The king

THE HANDWRITING ON THE WALL.

loved Daniel for the wise and good spirit that was in him, and this stirred up jealousy in the hearts of the Babylonian princes, and they watched Daniel to see if they could find something against him to tell the king, but they could not, for he was faithful in all his work.

Then they agreed to plot against him, and they went to the king and persuaded him to make a decree that whoever should ask any petition of any god or man for thirty days, except of the king, he should be thrown into the den of lions, and they asked the king to sign the decree, so that it could not be changed, and he signed it.

When Daniel heard of the decree, and knew that the king had signed it, he went into his own house, and to his chamber. There the windows were always open toward Jerusalem, and he kneeled down as he had done every day since he was taken from his own land, and prayed to God with his face toward the Temple in Jerusalem. And the men who were plotting against him watched him.

Then they hurried to the king, saying,

"That Daniel, which is of the captivity of Judah, regardeth not thee, O, King, nor the decree that thou hast signed, but maketh his petition three times a day."

The king was greatly disturbed at this, and set his heart on the deliverance of Daniel, and labored till sunset to do it. But his princes said it could not be done, because, according to the law of the Medes and the Persians, no decree made by the king could be changed.

So Daniel was condemned to be cast into the den of lions, but the king said,

"Thy God, whom thou servest continually, he will deliver thee."

Then a stone was laid over the mouth of the den, and the king sealed it with his own signet, and with that of his lords, that the purpose might not be changed.

That was a long night for Darius the king. He could neither eat nor sleep, and he would hear no music, but very early in the morning he went to the den of the lions and with a very sorrowful voice cried :

"O Daniel, servant of the living God ! is thy God whom thou servest continually able to deliver thee from the lions ? "

Then up from the pit came a strong, cheery voice saying :

"O king, live forever ! My God hath sent his angel, and hath shut the lions mouths, that they have not hurt me."

Then there was joy in the king's heart and he had Daniel brought up out of the den, and no hurt was found upon him, because he had believed in God, but the men who had accused Daniel were cast into the lions' den and destroyed.

Darius acknowledged the God of Daniel before all his kingdom, and commanded the people to honor Him, so that Daniel and his people suffered no more from their enemies during the reign of Darius. After the death o Darius, Cyrus was made king of Persia, and he also was kind to Daniel. The Lord gave him a tender heart toward the captives of Judah who had been in his land for seventy years, so that he sent them back into their own land and helped them to rebuild their city and their Temple

---

CHAPTER XXXIII.

THE STORY OF JONAH.

More than eight hundred years before the birth of Christ a prophet named Jonah lived in the land of Israel. He had given the Lord's messages to his own people, and they had listened to them, and a part of their country had been saved by obeying the Word of the Lord as it was brought to them by Jonah.

But when the Lord wished to send Jonah to warn a great city in Assyria to repent of their sins, he did not wish to go. Nineveh was a very old and a very great city. It was built soon after the flood, but was still at a high point of glory and wealth in the time of Jonah.

It was a heathen city, but God is the Father of all who live, and cares for all His children, though they may not know or care for Him.

Perhaps Jonah was afraid, for the people were strong and warlike, and they would not wish to hear about their wickedness. So Jonah ran away to the sea shore and took a ship from Joppa to go to Tarshish. He had not gone far from shore when a storm of wind rose, and the wind tossed the ship on the great angry waves until it was very nearly wrecked

The men were afraid, and each prayed to his God, and threw out the goods they were carrying in order to make the ship lighter.

Where was Jonah? He was below the decks asleep. When the captain found him he cried out,

"What meanest thou, O sleeper? Arise, call upon thy God, if so be that God will think upon us, that we perish not."

Then they began to wonder if the storm had not been sent upon them for the wickedness of some one in the ship, and they cast lots to see who it could be. The lot fell upon Jonah. Then they asked Jonah his name and country, and of his journey. He told them all about it. Then the men were more afraid, for they knew that he had tried to run away from the Lord, and they said,

"What shall we do unto thee, that the sea may be calm unto us?"

"Take me up and cast me forth into the sea," he said, "so shall the sea be calm unto you, for I know that for my sake this great tempest is upon you."

It was not easy for the men, who were kind-hearted, to throw into the sea a man so honest and so willing to die, so they rowed very hard, and tried their best to reach the shore, but they could not. So they prayed to Jonah's God to forgive them, and then threw Jonah into the sea.

But the Lord meant not only to teach Jonah a lesson, but to teach, through Jonah, a lesson to His children who should live in the ages to come. He was to make him also a sign of the coming Christ.

When Jonah believed he was sinking down into the green depths of the sea to die, a great fish, prepared by the Lord, opened his mouth and took him in. We cannot understand all the ways of God, but we know that "nothing is impossible with God," and that he was able to keep his servant alive even in such a strange place as this.

For three days and three nights he was kept in his living prison, and was able to pray to God, and to know where he was.

"The waters compassed me about," he said, "even to the soul; the depth closed me round about, the weeds were wrapped about my head. I went down to the bottoms of the mountains; the earth with her bars was about me forever."

Then he praised and thanked God, for he knew that he meant to save him. And when the Lord spoke to the fish, it threw Jonah out upon the dry land.

The second time Jonah heard the voice of the Lord telling him to go to Nineveh and preach the words that should be given him to say, and this time he obeyed.

It was a long journey to Nineveh, and when Jonah reached it he found that the city was so great that it would take three days to walk around the walls.

JONAH THROWN ON THE DRY LAND.

The walls were a hundred feet high. And so broad that three chariots could be driven on them side by side. The walls had fifteen hundred towers, each two hundred feet high. Inside the walls lived hundreds of thousands of people, many of them rich merchants or princes and nobles who lived in palaces, and thought only of their own pleasure and glory. They had grown very selfish and wicked.

When Jonah had walked a day's journey into the city, he began to cry in the streets the message God had given him,

"Yet forty days, and Nineveh shall be overthrown!"

The people began to tremble and be afraid of the strange voice that went up and down the long streets crying out these terrible words. They began to believe in Jonah's God, and to repent.

They repented in the eastern way, by putting on a garment of coarse sackcloth, and sitting in ashes. All did this, even to the king, who took off his beautiful robes and sat down in ashes before the Lord. He also proclaimed a fast to all the people, and urged them to "turn every one from their evil way."

When the Lord saw that they turned away from their sins, for He could look into their hearts, and read all their thoughts, He was satisfied, and said he would not destroy Nineveh.

But Jonah, who could not read the hearts of men, was not satisfied. He was very angry. He wanted to have the Ninevites see that he was a true prophet, for if no destruction came upon them he feared that they might call him a false prophet. So he complained to God, and said,

"Now, O Lord, take, I beseech Thee, my life from me, for it is better to die than to live!"

The Lord's gentle word to Jonah was,

"Doest thou well to be angry?"

Jonah went outside the city walls, and made for himself a little house of the branches of trees and waited to see if the city would be destroyed. It was very hot and Jonah was deeply troubled, and the Lord, who is full of love and pity for His children, caused a gourd vine with large leaves to spring up and grow over the dried branches of the little house that sheltered Jonah, and he was very glad and grateful. But the Lord, who always looks upon the heart, saw that the heart of Jonah was not yet wholly right, and the next morning he allowed a worm to eat the gourd until it withered. Then the sun beat down upon Jonah's head until he fainted and wished to die, saying, as he had said before,

"It is better for me to die than live !"

But the Lord was patient with him, and said,

" Doest thou well to be angry for the gourd?"

And Jonah replied ungraciously,

" I do well to be angry, even unto death."

Then the Lord in his love and pity answered,

" Thou hast had pity on the gourd, for the which thou hast not labored, neither madest it grow ; which came up in a night and perished in a night; and should not I spare Nineveh, that great city, wherein are more than six-score thousand persons that cannot discern between their right hand and their left hand, and also much cattle ?"

Jonah did not know all that was in the mind of the Lord, though he was a prophet.   He did not know that he was one of the signs of the Lord's first coming, for Jesus spoke of Jonah as a "sign," that as he was three days and three nights within the great fish "so shall the Son of man be three days and three nights in the heart of the earth."

CHAPTER XXXIV.

ESTHER, THE QUEEN.

About five hundred years before Christ King Ahasuerus (Xerxes) reigned over Persia.   In the third year of his reign he gave a royal feast to all the princes and nobles of Persia and Media, in Shushan, the royal city. It lasted one hundred and eighty days, and was very costly, for the king wished to show the great men from all his provinces the riches and glory of his kingdom and of his palace.

At the end of these days he made another feast to all who were in Shushan, a feast of seven days, and which included great and small.   The palace garden was hung with awnings of white and green and violet, fastened with cords and silver rings to pillars of marble.

Wine was given to the guests in golden cups as they sat on couches of gold and silver, and the pavement of the court was of many colored marbles.

In another part of the palace Vashti, the queen, also made a feast for the women.

On the seventh day the king sent his seven chamberlains to bring Queen Vashti before him, wearing her royal crown. He wished to show to his people and princes the beauty of the queen, for she was very fair to look upon.

But the queen refused to obey the king's command, and he was angry. He asked the seven princes who stood next to him in the kingdom what he should do, and what the laws of the Medes and Persians (which could not be broken) would say in such a case.

The princes did not speak of any law, but one of them told the king that the conduct of Vashti would do them great harm through all the kingdom, for women hearing of the act of the queen, would despise and disobey their husbands. They advised, therefore, that a commandment should go forth from the king and be written among the laws of the Medes and Persians, that Vashti should no more come before the king, and that her royal estate should be given to another better than she.

This pleased the king, and he did as Memucan, the prince, had advised, and he sent letters into all parts of his empire to people of various languages, that every man should rule in his own house.

Then the king's servants, the nobles, advised the king to send officers to every part of his kingdom to find some one worthy to take the place of Queen Vashti, and the plan pleased the king, and he did so.

There was in Shushan a Jew named Mordecai, who had been brought away from Jerusalum with the captives when Nebuchadnezzar conquered the city. He had an adopted daughter named Hadassah. This was her true name, although the Persians called her Esther. She was the daughter of Mordecai's uncle, and when her father and mother died, Mordecai took her for his own. She was very beautiful, and as good as she was beautiful, for Mordecai had taught her to be faithful to the true God, though living among a strange people.

When Mordecai heard that the king was seeking for a maiden worthy to be a queen through all his provinces, he brought Esther and placed her in care of Hegai, who had the care of that part of the king's house where the women lived. Hegai was very kind to her, and gave her seven maids to serve her, and the best place in the house for her own.

Mordecai had told Esther not to speak of her Jewish family, but every day he walked before the court of the women's house to ask how she did and what had become of her.

Out of all the maidens brought from the city and the kingdom Esther was chosen by the king to be queen in the place of Vashti, and he placed the royal crown upon her head, and proclaimed a great feast that he called Esther's feast, when he gave gifts and made a holiday for all the people to rest and be happy in all his provinces.

Mordecai sat daily at the king's gate, and once while there he heard of a plot to kill the king by two of his chamberlains, and he sent word secretly to Esther, and she told the king in Mordecai's name, so that these two men were hanged, and the account of it was written in the king's book of records.

About this time the king gave great honors to a man named Haman. He set him above all his princes, and when the king's servants who were at his gate knew it they all bowed down and gave great honor to Haman, whenever he passed, for the king had so commanded them; but Mordecai would not bow to Haman. When Haman saw this he was full of anger toward Mordecai the Jew, and he made a wicked plan to destroy not only Mordecai, but all his people.

So he came with wily ways and cunning speech to the king, saying,

"There is a certain people scattered abroad and dispersed among the people in all the provinces of thy kingdom, and their laws are diverse from from all people, neither keep they the king's laws, therefore it is not for the king's profit to suffer them. If it please the king let it be written that they be destroyed, and I will pay ten thousand talents of silver to the hands of those that have the charge of the business, to bring it into the king's treasuries."

Then the king gave his ring to Haman as a sign that he would pledge his word to do what he asked, and said,

"The silver is given to thee, the people also, to do with them as it seemeth good to thee."

Then Haman had letters written and sealed with the king's seal ring, saying to the rulers of every province in the kingdom that all Jews, both young and old, throughout the kingdom, must be destroyed in one day, and their goods, and money, and lands be taken for a prey, and the thirteenth day of the twelfth month was set in which to destroy them.

After the messengers were sent out the king and Haman sat down to drink wine, but the city was troubled.

Then Mordecai rent his clothes in sign of mourning, and went out into the streets of the city clothed in sack-cloth uttering a loud and bitter cry. He cried even before the king's gate.

All through the kingdom there was great mourning among the Jews, and they fasted and wept in sack-cloth and ashes.

When Esther heard that Mordecai was clothed in sack-cloth she was deeply grieved, and sent some garments to clothe him, but he would not receive them. Then she sent for the king's chamberlain Hatach, and gave him a command to Mordecai to tell what caused his grief.

Hatach found him at the king's gate, and Mordecai told him all that had happened to him, and of the great sum of money that Haman had promised to pay into the king's treasuries for the Jews to destroy them. He also gave him a copy of the decree to show Esther, and told Hatach to charge her that she go before the king and make request for her people.

Hatach took these words to Esther, and Esther sent a reply by Hatach, saying that it was known in all the king's palace that no man or woman could come into the king's presence in the inner court who had not been called, and for any who so entered there was but one law, and that was that they be put to death, unless the king hold out to them the golden sceptre. She had not been called to see the king, she said, in thirty days.

Hatach gave this message to Mordecai, and he again sent word to Esther that she could not hope to escape the decree, as she too was of the Jews. He told her that deliverance must come to the Jews in some other way, but she and her family would be destroyed, and then he added,

"Who knoweth whether thou art come to the kingdom for such a time as this?"

Then Esther made her resolve, and sent word to Mordecai to gather all the Jews in Shushan together to fast night and day, while she and her maidens fasted also.

"And so I will go in unto the king," she said, "which is not according to the law, and if I perish, I perish."

And Mordecai went his way and did as Esther had commanded.

It was the third day when Esther arose from her fast before the Lord and put on her beautiful royal robes and stood in the inner court of the king's house in sight of the royal throne.

When the king saw Esther standing in the inner court he was not displeased, but his heart was turned toward her, and he held out to her the golden sceptre that was in his hand.

"What wilt thou, Queen Esther?" he said, "and what is thy request? it shall be even given thee to the half of the kingdom."

HAMAN DENOUNCED BY THE QUEEN.

"If it seem good unto the king," said Esther, "let the king and Haman come this day unto the banquet that I have prepared for him."

So the king commanded Haman, and they came to the queen's banquet. The king knew that Esther had a favor to ask of him, so he said again :

"What is thy petition? and it shall be granted thee; and what is thy request? even to the half of the kingdom it shall be performed."

But Esther was wise. She begged as her petition and request that the king and Haman would come to the banquet she should prepare the next day also, and she would then do as the king had said.

Haman went home very happy and proud that he had been so honored by the queen, and told his wife and his friends of all the glory and honor that had come to him.

"Yet all this availeth me nothing," he said, "so long as I see Mordecai the Jew sitting at the king's gate."

Then his wife and his friends urged him to build a high gallows and ask the king on the next day to hang Mordecai upon it. "Then go thou merrily with the king unto the banquet," they added.

This pleased Haman, and he ordered the gallows to be made.

That night the king was restless, and he could not sleep, and he commanded that the book of records be brought and read aloud to him. Then he found that it was written that Mordecai had saved the king's life when it was threatened by his two chamberlains.

"What honor and dignity hath been done to Moreecai for this?" he asked, and his servants replied:

"There is nothing done for him."

"Who is in the court?" cried the king. Now Haman had come in to speak to the king to have Mordecai hanged.

"Haman standeth in the court," said the king's servants, and the king said,

"Let him come in."

As Haman came in the king said,

"What shall be done to the man that the king delighteth to honor?"

Haman thought in his heart, "To whom would the king delight to do honor more than to myself," and then he replied, thinking all the time of himself.

"For the man whom the king delighteth to honor let the royal apparel be brought which the king useth to wear, and the horse that the king rideth upon, and the crown royal which is set upon his head, and let this apparel and horse be delivered to the hand of one of the king's most noble princes, that they may array the men withal whom the king delighteth to honor, and bring him on horseback through the street of the city, and proclaim before him, ' Thus shall it be done to the man whom the king delighteth to honor.' "

Then the king said, " Make haste, and take the apparel and the horse as thou hast said, and do even so to Mordecai, the Jew, that sitteth at the king's gate ; let nothing fail of all that thou hast spoken."

Haman did as he was commanded, for he could do nothing else, and after it was all over Mordecai took his place again at the king's gate, but Haman hastened home mourning, and with his head covered.

The next day he came to the queen's banquet with the king, and again the king said,

" What is thy petition, Queen Esther ? and it shall be granted thee ; and what is thy request ? and it shall be performed, even to the half of my kingdom."

Then the queen made her request, saying,

" If I have found favor in thy sight, O king, and if it please the king, let my life be given me at my petition, and my people at my request : for we are sold, I and my people, to be destroyed, to be slain, and to perish. But if we had been sold for bondmen and bondwomen I had held my tongue, although the enemy could not countervail the king's damage."

" Who is he, and where is he," cried the king, " That durst presume in his heart to do so ?"

Then Esther said, " The adversary and enemy is this wicked Haman."

Haman was overcome with fear at this, and the king was so angry that he rose up and went out into the palace garden. Haman stood up to make a plea for his life, and when the king came in he found Haman fallen at the queen's feet.

One of the king's chamberlains who knew what the king wished told him of the gallows at Haman's house that had been made for Mordecai, and the king said, " Hang him thereon," and they did so, and the king's anger was pacified.

That day the king gave Haman's house to the queen. Mordecai came before the king that day also, for Esther had told him how he was related to her, and the King gave to Mordecai the ring that he had once given to Haman. Esther's petition was not yet finished, so she fell down at the king's feet and asked for the life of her people, and that the decree might be changed.

Then the king held out his golden sceptre to Esther, and she arose. She spoke noble words of petition for her people, and the king told Mordecai to write in the king's name and seal with the king's seal letters that should make the decree void.

So the scribes were called in and the letters were written and sealed with the king's ring, and sent out to every province in the kingdom.

Mordecai went out of the palace that day clothed in royal garments of violet and white, fine linen and purple, and a great crown of gold upon his head, and there was joy in Shushan, and there was joy among the jews all over the land. They hanged the ten sons of Haman, and destroyed their enemies by the king's permission, so that they had rest from persecution. They also set apart two days for a feast of thanksgiving through all time, and the feast of Purim is kept by all Jews to this day, as it was first confirmed by the decree of Esther.

And Mordecai was next to the king and honored by his brethren the Jews as long as he lived, for he always sought their peace, and was as a father to them.

CHILD'S

STORY OF THE BIBLE

———

THE NEW TESTAMENT

THE HOLY CHILD AND THE WISE MEN.

CHILD'S STORY OF THE BIBLE.

THE NEW TESTAMENT.

CHAPTER I.

THE ANGELS OF THE ADVENT.

THERE was an old priest named Zacharias, who lived in the hill country of Hebron, where Abraham the father of the Jewish people used to live. He went to Jerusalem when it was his turn to serve in the temple, and once while he was offering the incense of sweet spices on the golden altar, he saw through the rising smoke an angel standing on the right side of the altar. The good priest was frightened, but the angel said,

"Fear not, Zacharias, for thy prayer is heard," and he promised that to him and his wife Elizabeth should be born a little son, whose name should be John. He was coming to prepare the way for the Messiah, and must not drink wine or strong drink, for he was to be filled with the Holy Spirit.

It was too wonderful for Zacharias to believe, and when he went out of the temple he was dumb, and all the people who waited for him knew that he had seen a vision. He did not speak while he stayed to minister in the temple, and when his time of service was ended he went to his home in Hebron.

A few months later the angel Gabriel went to the little town of Nazareth, high up among the hills of Galilee, and spoke to a young girl named Mary. She had never seen an angel, and she also was afraid when he said to her,

" Hail, thou that art highly favored, the Lord is with thee ; blessed art thou among women. Fear not, Mary, for thou hast found favor with God." And then he told her that she should become the mother of a Holy Child, who should also be the Son of the Highest, and a King whose kingdom should have no end, and His name should be Jesus. He also told her of her cousin Elizabeth away in Hebron, to whom a little son was promised.

Then Mary said these beautiful words to the angel:

8   (135)

"Behold the hand-maid of the Lord; be it unto me according to Thy word," and the angel went away into heaven.

Mary was so full of wonder at the angel's words that she set out on a journey to see Elizabeth. It was eighty miles to Hebron, but it was early summer, and as Mary went through the green valleys and fruitful plains, and along by the flowing Jordan, she thought about the angel's words, and prayed to God to make her good and wise. She was not afraid, though the journey was four days long, for she knew God was with her.

On the fourth day she passed Jerusalem, the Holy City, and went on and up into the Hebron Hills to the house of Elizabeth. When they told to each other the wonderful words of the angel Gabriel they were full of joy, for they knew that the coming of the Christ was near, and that the Lord had trusted them with the heavenly secret. They were filled with the Holy Spirit, and Mary broke out into a beautiful song of praise.

Mary stayed three months with her cousin Elizabeth, and learned many things, for the old priest and his wife were wise and good. When she went back to Nazareth she told no one of her vision, not even her mother or Joseph, the good carpenter, whose promised wife she was. But the angel came one night to Joseph and spoke to him through a dream of the Holy Child that was to be born.

Now Joseph and Mary were of the family of King David, and they knew that the prophets had long ago talked of a King who was to come and restore the kingdom, and reign on the throne of David. They even told where he was to be born, in Bethlehem, the "City of David." And though the Jews had become the servants of the Romans, yet it was time, according to the promise, that the new King should come and set them free, and many were looking for His coming.

Perhaps Joseph and Mary thought of these things when the time came for them to go to Bethlehem, for the Emperor of Rome had made a decree that all Jews should be enrolled, that he might know how many were in his empire. So all Jews, who had gone to live in other parts, returned to their own tribe and city to be enrolled among their own people.

When Joseph and Mary came to Bethlehem they found it full of people who had also come home to write their names for the Emperor, and there was no room for them in the inn. It was winter, and while Joseph wondered what he should do the keeper of the inn showed them the stable where the gentle oxen and asses were kept, and where it was much quieter than in the noisy yard and crowded rooms of the inn.

It was here in a humble stable that the Lord of Heaven was born upon earth, and cradled in a manger. He chose the stable instead of a palace, and a bed of straw instead of a bed of down, for He had come to be the Brother of the poor and the Saviour of the world.

Out in the fields near by were some shepherds watching their flocks. It has been said that the flocks kept in the Bethlehem fields were for the sacrifices in the temple, and were watched night and day the year long, while other flocks were kept in their folds in winter.

While they sat on the rocks, wrapped in their cloaks and sheepskin jackets, with a fire of brushwood to keep the beasts away, perhaps they thought of young David, who once kept his sheep there, and killed a lion and a bear to defend his flock; or they watched the stars and wondered at their beauty.

But suddenly an angel stood by them, and a great light shone round about them, and they were terrified. But the angel spoke kindly to them saying :—

"Fear not, for behold I bring you good tidings of great joy, which shall be to all people. For unto you is born this day, in the city of David, a Saviour which is Christ the Lord." And the angel told them how they would know it to be the Holy Child—because it lay in a manger. Then, in a moment the air was full of angel faces, and heavenly voices sang this song of praise to God and promise to all people :—

"Glory to God in the highest, and on earth peace, good will toward men!" And they went away into heaven.

The shepherds looked at one another and then one said; "Let us go to Bethlehem." And they went in great haste. There they found Mary and Joseph with the Holy Child lying in a manger, just as the angel had said. They told the people of Bethlehem about the angels they had seen and the words they had heard, and they were very much astonished. But Mary was silent, and kept all these things in her heart to think about and to pray about.

As for the shepherds they went back to their flocks praising God.

When the Holy Child was eight days old his parents called His name Jesus, as the angel had commanded, and they dedicated him to the Lord. Later they took him up to the Temple at Jerusalem to make the offering that all Jewish mothers made, some money, if it was the first boy-child, and a lamb, or a pair of doves. Joseph bought for Mary a pair of doves, and they went up the white steps of the beautiful porch of the Temple, and passed the long rows of marble pillars into the court of the Gentiles where they could look up and see the Temple itself with its white marble pillars and golden roof shining in the sun.

Mary gave her doves to the Priest at the gate of the Court of the Women, and he took them away to be offered on the altar, while Joseph took the Holy Child into the Men's Court for the Priest to bless as he dedicated Him to the Lord. When all was done and they were going away, an old man named Simeon saw them, and begged to hold the child. He was a good man who had longed to see the Christ who was to come, and now the Spirit of God told him that this was He. He thanked God, and said :

"Lord, now lettest Thou thy servant depart in peace, according to Thy word, for mine eyes have seen Thy salvation."

He also spoke as a prophet of the days to come, and just then a very old woman who lived in the Temple, Anna, the prophetess, came and gave thanks to God, and told the people that the Redeemer had come to Israel. All these things Mary kept in her heart, as she had kept the words of the angel, and wondered why she had been chosen to be the mother of the Holy Child.

Seven months before this time a little son had been born to Zacharias and Elizabeth. The neighbors wished to name him for his father, but Elizabeth said, "Not so ; but he shall be called John." When they asked his father what it should be, he wrote an answer (for he had been dumb ever since he talked with the angel in the Temple) and they read, "His name shall be called John." Then his mouth was opened, and he began to speak and to praise God, and his friends wondered what the child would be when he grew to manhood. His father became a prophet for a time, and said some strange things about him that were written down. He said that John should be called a prophet of the Highest, and go before the Lord to prepare His ways.

John grew, and he also grew strong in spirit, and while he was yet young he went to live in the deserts where he was taught of God to be a prophet and a preacher.

CHAPTER II.

FOLLOWING THE STAR.

While Joseph and Mary and the Holy Child were still staying in Bethlehem, some Wise Men came from and Eastern country to Jerusalem, asking,

"Where is he that is born King of the Jews? for we have seen His Star in the East, and are come to worship Him."

No one knows who these men were, but it may be that they were Jews who lived in Persia, as David had done long before, and were learned in all the wisdom of the Chaldeans, who studied the stars, and believed that they had much to do with the lives of people on the earth. These wise men were called Magi. They had heard that a great One would be born about this time, and that He would be the King of the Jews.

When they saw a strange and beautiful Star near the earth away toward Jerusalem they prepared to go and see if it would lead them to the King. Their servants loaded the camels with food and water and some costly gifts, for they were rich men, and mounted on beautiful saddles covered with blue and crimson cloth they rode away toward Jerusalem. They had deserts of yellow sand to cross, and they were tired at the end of the hot day, but at night they saw the beautiful Star shining before them low in the sky, and watched it from their tents on the sand where they rested for the night, and rose to follow it before it faded in the morning. They were glad when they came to the fresh green mountain country of the Jews, and rode through the flowery valleys till they came to the gates of Jerusalem. Perhaps they expected to hear all about the new King, and to find the people feasting and rejoicing, but they did not.

When they asked, "Where is He that is born King of the Jews?" the people were surprised, and only wondered who these men were who looked liked princes from a foreign court, for they had armed servants, and from their camels hung tinkling silver bells, and swinging tassels of silk and gold.

They searched Jerusalem for the king, and Herod heard of it and was troubled. He wished always to be king himself. He set the scribes to searching for the prophecies of the Messiah's birth. They knew very well where to find them, and they read to the king these words from the prophet Micah :—

FOLLOWING THE STAR.

" But thou, Bethlehem Ephratah, which art little among the families of Judah, out of thee shall One come forth unto me that is to be the ruler of Israel ; whose goings forth are from of old, from ancient days."

Then the king sent for the wise men, for he had a secret plan. They came in their best robes, hoping perhaps, to find the newly born King in the beautiful palace of Herod on Mount Zion, but they found only the gloomy old King Herod waiting for them. He asked them when they first saw the Star, and when they had told him, he sent them to Bethlehem and said,

" Go and search diligently for the young child, and when ye have found him, bring me word again, that I may come and worship him also."

They were very glad to hear about Bethlehem, and as they came down the marble steps of Herod's palace it was evening, and there, low down before them in the sky was the Star ! They went out through the Bethlehem gate toward the south, and followed the Star again over the hills until the white walls of Bethlehem shown in the moonlight before them, and they saw the Star standing still and shining down upon a little house within the walls. Then they rejoiced with exceeding great joy, for they had come to the end of their long journey, and they had found the King ! When they came to the house where Mary and Joseph were staying they told their servants to unpack the presents of gold, and frankincense, and myrrh, and they went in. Then they found the lovely young mother and the Holy Child, and they fell down before Him and offered their gifts.

They did not go away at once. They slept in Bethlehem that night, and the Lord showed them in a dream that they must not go back to tell King Herod that they had found the Christ. They told Joseph of their dream, and went away by another road that led past Hebron to their own country.

CHAPTER III.

THE FLIGHT INTO EGYPT.

It seems very strange that in a few hours after the wise men had gone over the hills to their own country, that Mary and Joseph and the Holy Child should be swiftly following the same road. The night after the wise men had been warned in a dream to go to their own country, Joseph was warned also

THE FLIGHT INTO EGYPT.

in a dream to take the young Child and His mother and go into Egypt. He was told to stay until he had orders to return, for Herod would seek to take the Child's life. Their flight was in the night, and Mary's heart beat fast as she held her baby close and rode down the steep path from Bethlehem with Joseph walking beside her. They did not rest until they were far on their way. It was nearly a week before they reached the river that was the border of Egypt, but when they crossed it King Herod's soldiers could not harm them.

They had gold that the wise men had given them, and Joseph knew how to make many things of wood, so they lived quietly in Egypt waiting until the Lord should call them back.

Herod was very angry when he heard that the Magi had gone away without telling him anything about the young King ; so angry that he ordered his soldiers to destroy every baby boy in Bethlehem. So all the little boys of Bethlehem under two years of age were killed by the order of this wicked king, and the Holy Child whom Herod believed would be destroyed with them was safely borne in His mother's arms along the road to Egypt, while Joseph walked beside them and led the patient ass, and angels went with them unseen to be their guard by night and by day.

They lived in Egypt about a year, and then the sick and unhappy old king died, and an angel came to Joseph one night in a dream, and said,

"Arise and take the young Child and His mother and go into the land of Israel, for they are dead which sought the young Child's life."

They were glad to know that they could come home again, and they came, perhaps with a company of merchants, into their own land. Joseph would have settled in Judea, the part of the land of Israel in which stands Jerusalem, and Bethlehem, the city of his ancestors, but Herod's son had been made king over Judea, and Joseph was told in a dream to go into Galilee.

In Galilee was Nazareth, where both Joseph and Mary lived when they were married, and there they went and were at home again, and there Jesus grew to manhood.

IN HIS FATHER'S HOUSE.

CHAPTER IV.

THE BOY OF NAZARETH.

Nazareth was a little town high among the hills of Galilee. It still stands there, but it is not so large a town as it was when Mary and Joseph and the Child Jesus lived there. Then Galilee was full of cities and villages, and men and women were busy among its fields, and vineyards, and gardens, and the shores of the beautiful Lake of Galilee were lined with the boats of fishermen.

Nazareth was more quiet than the crowded cities by the Lake. A great green plain lay below it, and a narrow road winding among the limestone rocks led up to it. Its streets were narrow and steep, and steps of stone led from house to house. A fountain of pure water breaking out of a rock was the meeting place of the women of Nazareth, who came with their tall pitchers for water and bore them away upon their heads. Here Mary often came tenderly leading the Holy Child. Perhaps He gathered the bright wild flowers that grew thick around the fountain and along the stream flowing from it. When he grew a little older He could climb the rocks around His home, or go with His mother and Joseph to the top of the hill from which they could see the snowy peak of Hermon, or the long line of shining blue sea beyond the hills on the west, or they would point out a slowly moving caravan of heavy laden camels from Tyre and Sidon by the sea on their way to Damascus.

Sometimes He would go with Joseph to the woods when a certain piece of wood was needed, for Joseph was a carpenter, and in a lower room of his humble house of rough white stone there was a long bench and the tools of a wood-worker. Here, perhaps, the Holy Child played with the curled shavings that fell from the bench, and watched the making of the plows, the yokes, the doors, and the lattices until He was old enough to help in the making of them.

He learned to read and write while a young child at home, as Jewish children did, and His reading book was the Old Testament, which was the Jews' Bible. Then He went to school at the Synagogue, which was the Jews' Church, and there, we may be sure, He was a gentle, obedient pupil, and a loving, unselfish playmate. While he read He may have had many strange thoughts about the prophecies in the Book that were promises of the Messiah, the King that was to reign in righteousness.

When He was twelve years old His parents took Him with them to the Feast of the Passover at Jerusalem.   Great companies of people went from all parts of the Jews' country, and from every country in which they had settled, to keep the feast that the Lord had commanded when they were led out of Egypt.   The very journey to Jerusalem was a festival, for their friends joined the company from almost every house in Nazareth, and on horses, and camels, and asses, the men walking beside them, a happy group set forth from home to keep the Passover week in the city of the great King.   It was the first visit of the boy Jesus to Jerusalem, and as He walked strong and beautiful beside Joseph, what tender and holy thoughts, what questions about the future must have filled the mind of Mary.   He was going to see His Father's House, the beautiful Temple where the thousands of Israel gathered every year for worship and of which He had read in the Book of the Law, for He was now old enough to be called a "Son of the Law," and verses from the Bible folded in little boxes, had been tied upon his arm and his forehead by the village Rabbi, as a sign that He was old enough to think for Himself and go to the religious Feasts at Jerusalem.

When they reached the great public roads they found other companies of pilgrims going up to the Holy City, and by their banners they knew the tribe and city from which they came.   There was music, also, of timbrel and pipe and drum as the songs of Zion were sung along the way, or at evening when they camped in the fields.

When they had climbed the steep Jericho road and the Mount of Olives, a glorious sight opened before them.   There lay the City of David shining in the sun, its thick walls set with towers ; its marble palaces, and castles, and gardens, and, most wonderful of all, the Temple with its hundreds of white marble pillars, its beautiful porches and arches, and, rising within its richly-paved courts, the Holy Place with the sun like fire upon its roof of gold. The people shouted and sang a song of joy.   Perhaps they sang that song of David beginning :

"I was glad when they said unto me
' Let us go into the house of the Lord, '
Our feet shall stand within thy gates,
O Jerusalem ! "

Like thousands of others they pitched their tents outside of the walls, perhaps on the slopes of Olivet, and after eating the Passover supper together went daily into the Temple.   To the Boy of Nazareth this must have been the one charmed spot in all Jerusalem.   Other boys loved to watch the strange people from far countries, and wander among the bazars, but Jesus stayed in the Temple. He saw the white-robed priests, the altars, and the sacrifices ; He saw the great curtains of purple and gold that hid the Holy place, and He heard the Temple choirs answer each other in song ; He also saw the old Rabbis who taught and answered questions daily in the outer courts, and stood long among the listeners.

When the company from Nazareth began the journey home, and had gone as far as the plains of Jericho, Mary looked for her boy. She had not been troubled about him, for she thought He was walking with the other children, or with relatives, but when Joseph found that he was not with them they went back over the long, steep road full of fear and anxiety. They searched Jerusalem through, asking everybody they knew if they had seen the Boy Jesus.

When they had been searching for three days, and Mary's heart was almost broken, they went again to the Temple, and looking through a crowd gathered around the Rabbis, Mary saw her Boy. She pressed through to speak to Him, but He was speaking. She listened, and her heart must have stood still to hear His simple, yet wonderful words. Sometimes he asked questions which the old teachers could not answer, and when he replied to the questions of the learned teachers His wisdom astonished all who heard Him, for it was not like the wisdom of the Rabbis, who used many words to explain the Word of God.

When Jesus saw His mother and came to her, she said,

" Son, why hast Thou so dealt with us ? Behold thy father and I have sought Thee sorrowing."

" How is it that ye sought me ?" He said, "wist ye not that I must be about my Father's business ?"

They did not quite understand how He could so easily forget them, and yet Mary, perhaps, remembered that the angel had told her that He should "be called the Son of God," and that He was at home in His Father's house.

But He was content to go home and be subject to His parents, so that through all the world children may learn how He lived, and try to live like Him.

He found that His Father's house was greater than the Temple, and under its starry roof, and wandering over its wide courts paved with grass and flowers, He learned more than the Rabbis could teach Him. And every day He grew in wisdom as He grew in stature, and "in favor with God and man."

CHAPTER V.

THE YOUNG CARPENTER.

There are many years of the life of Jesus of which the Gospel story tells us nothing. He lived with Mary and Joseph in Nazareth, and was preparing for the great work for which He came. He learned easily all that other boys were taught in the synagogue school, and no doubt caused His teacher to wonder at such wisdom coming from a boy. He was so humble and teachable that no one could accuse Him of setting Himself above His companions, and so winning and unselfish that He was loved by all. The school days ended, perhaps, when He was fourteen, and He was asked, as every Jewish boy was asked, to choose what trade He would learn, for every boy had to learn a trade. He chose to learn the trade of His father, and began to work with him making the many things that were then used by the people. Few houses, if any, were made of wood, for the white limestone was then, as now, used in making the houses of Nazareth, but they were finished with wood, and wood was used not only for boats, tables, benches, yokes and carts, but also for plows, saddles, and many things we now make of other material Can you make a picture in your mind of this tall, beautiful youth standing near His father ready to serve in any humble way in the work they were doing?

There was no service so small that He did not willingly do it, and no labor so rough and common that He did not make it noble and beautiful by the doing. But He was always thinking—thinking. The world around Him was full of pictures and stories through which heavenly truths shone, and they formed themselves in His mind, and when He began to teach He used them to help others with. We call them parables. Wherever He saw the flowers, the grape vines, the olive and the fig trees, the wheat fields, the shepherds and their flocks, the fishermen and their nets, He read high and holy lessons that were much more simple, and true, and beautiful than those taught by the Rabbis.

The more He thought about the teaching of the Rabbis, the more He saw how false and hard it was. The Law given by Moses was full of the good thoughts of God, but the Jewish teachers had only taught the outward form, and had not given the people the inward spirit. It was like bringing to

(148)

the hungry a beautiful dish with no food in it, or to the thirsty a costly cup with no water in it.

As He grew older He would sit sometimes long into the night on some hillside watching the stars, and with his great heart going out beyond the hills to the people of the world in longing love and in desire for their salvation. He wanted to show them how God loved the world. He wanted to take the empty forms of the Law and fill them full of the Spirit—the real thought and love of God. He wanted to take away the burdens on the minds of the people, which were heavier than those that Pharoah laid upon their bodies long before, and give them the rest and peace of God. He wanted to take away their endless rules and give them one rule—to do by others as they would have others do to them. And He wanted to add a new Commandment to the Law—that they love one another.

In this way, by living with His mind in heaven and His body on earth He came to know that He was the Christ of God, and that He must go out from Nazareth to be a Teacher of Truth, and begin to build The Kingdom of Heaven among men. But His friends thought that He was fitted to be a Rabbi and teach in the Temple with the Doctors of the Law. He waited many years, caring for His mother and His younger brothers and sisters after the death of Joseph, and then He left Nazareth.

CHAPTER VI.

THE VOICE IN THE WILDERNESS.

Jesus was thirty years of age when He left Nazareth to begin His work as a Teacher of the Truth. It was the age set by the older teachers for a young man to begin his work.

His cousin John, the son of Elizabeth and Zachariah, was six months older than Jesus, and he had begun his ministry on the lower Jordan. While Jesus had been living quietly at Nazareth preparing for his work, John had been away in the wilderness beyond the Dead Sea alone with the Spirit of God. He was a prophet who could be taught by God only. When his time to speak came he came out of the wilderness to a place on the banks of the Jordan, just above Jericho, called The Fords. Many people crossed at this place, and he stood on a bank above the river crying, "Repent, for the Kingdom of Heaven is at hand."

Like those who had made a vow to the Lord, John had never cut his hair, he wore a coarse garment woven of camel's hair, and lived on the simple food of the wilderness—locusts and wild honey. He seemed never to think of himself, but always of One who was coming. He said that he was only a "Voice," preparing the way for the Messiah, as Isaiah had prophesied centuries before, and the "Messenger" that had been promised through Malachi.

"Behold I will send My messenger, and he shall prepare the way before me."

He did something which seemed new and strange to the people. He called them to a change of mind—a turning away from sin, and, as a sign that they had done so, he baptized them in the river Jordan. He was getting the people ready for the coming of Christ, who was to begin the Kingdom of Heaven on earth.

Thousands were flocking down to the river to hear the new prophet. They went from all parts of Palestine, and Jesus, knowing that his hour had come, went also. He wore a white tunic gathered at the neck and reaching to his feet, and on it the large blue mantle of thick stuff that was worn in cold weather, for it was in the winter of the year 31.

We cannot know all about His parting with His mother, and the three days' journey to the Fords of Jordan, but we know that He came and stood with others on the banks while John preached.

On this day John's words were different. He had said that the Christ was coming, but to-day he said,

"There standeth One among you whom ye know not, whose shoe's latchet I am not worthy to unloose."

After this Jesus came down to the water's edge to be baptized, and John, though he had not seen Jesus since he was a young boy, knew Him. Ready to fall at His feet, John cried,

"I have need to be baptized of Thee, and comest thou to me?"

Jesus replied in a low voice,

"Suffer it to be so now, for thus it becometh us to fulfill all righteousness," and so reverently John baptized his Master.

As Jesus stepped from the water's edge to the river bank a strange and beautiful thing happened. Out of the warm, blue sky a white dove came circling down around the head of Jesus, who stood silent in prayer. With eyes lifted to heaven He saw the dove, which was the form in which the

JOHN THE BAPTIST AT JORDAN.

Spirit of God descended upon Him, and John saw it also, and both heard a voice from heaven saying,

" Thou art my beloved Son, in whom I am well pleased."

This was the answer to Jesus' prayer. Only Jesus and John understood the meaning of these words, for they heard with the spirit. To others it seemed like thunder out of a clear sky, and they were full of wonder about the strange young man who had been baptized with such a beautiful and singular sign following. They also remembered what John had said, that the Christ was now standing among them, and perhaps this was he! And they wondered what John meant when he said that though he baptized with water, the coming Christ would baptize them with the Holy Spirit and with fire.

It was of little use to wonder about the Messiah, however, unless they could remember and do all that John had said to them about being honest and true in their hearts, for that was the only way to prepare for the kingdom that was near at hand. He told the rich to share with the poor ; the people who handled money to be honest, and the soldiers to harm no one with word or hand, and to be contented with their wages.

When they were willing to give up the sins that John showed them they took the sign of baptism from John, which meant that they wished to be washed from their sins, and begin life in a new way.

CHAPTER VII.

JESUS IN THE DESERT.

The people were looking for the promised Messiah, and would have welcomed John as the Christ if John had not always said "One mightier than I cometh." "I am not the Christ." The sign of the Dove filled them with new thoughts.

While they were thinking Jesus went up the river bank alone. The power of the spirit was upon Him, and His great work before Him, and He wished to go for a time as far as possible from every human being. He went into the wilderness—a wild desert country beyond the Dead Sea—not even wishing to talk with John, whose home was in the wilderness. Perhaps John looked after Him and longed to see and talk with Him, but Jesus had one great desire, to know Himself, and what His work was to be. He felt two natures within Him, the human and the divine, and before He began to teach He wanted to hear the voice of the Divine within Him as clear and strong as He had heard it that day from the skies.

The desert to which He went was not a waste of flat sand, like the African desert, but masses of rock with sand and dry grasses between, great cliffs of chalk and limestone rise a thousand feet above the gloomy gulfs of rock through which torrents run in the rainy season, but which are dry and oven-like in summer. One great cliff called Quarantana is now full of caves cut out of the face of the rock by men who have hoped to win heaven by suffering as Jesus did.

Jesus was thinking—thinking, His human nature being full of hopes, fears, and prayers; His divine nature being full of strength, promise, comfort. He did not think of food when He came, and there was none to be found. So resting at night in a cave, and wandering farther among the mountains by day, Jesus spent forty days in the wilderness of Judea. While there He was tried by the spirit of evil in every way known to human nature, and when all was over, and He had not yielded to sin, His mind was calm and ready for His work, for He knew He was the Son of God.

When He was hungry the tempter said, "If thou be the Son of God command this stone that it be made bread."

It would have been easy for Him to try His power, but He knew that He did not come into the world to use it for Himself, but for others, and so He answered in the words of the Bible,

"Thou shalt not live by bread alone, but by every word of God."

Then in a vision He seemed to be in the Holy City upon a tower of the Temple that stood over a deep valley, and the tempter speaking within Him, said,

"If Thou be the Son of God cast Thyself down, for it is written, 'He shall give His angels charge concerning thee, and in their hands they shall bear thee up, lest thou dash thy foot against a stone.' "

But Jesus knew that though the words were the words of God, the voice was the voice of the tempter, and He answered,

"Thou shalt not tempt the Lord thy God."

Then in a vision again He seemed to see, from the top of a very high mountain, all the kingdoms of the world spread out before Him with their kings, and armies, and cities; their beautiful homes and lovely women, and

9

great men with their gold, and jewels, and precious works of art, and the tempter said,

"All these things will I give Thee if Thou wilt fall down and worship me."

Then all the Divine power in Jesus rose up against this evil whisper, and He said,

"Get thee hence, Satan ; for it is written, 'Thou shalt worship the Lord thy God, and Him only shalt thou serve.' "

We shall never know all that Jesus suffered during this long time when He was away from His home in Nazareth, and away from every human being, tempted by evil, surrounded by wild beasts, and faint from hunger, but we know He won a great victory over evil for us. So he became the Elder Brother and Friend of all who are tempted.

After His long fast and struggle with the powers of evil, angels came and cared for Him, bringing heavenly strength and comfort, and He rose in that strength and came again into the valley of Jordan, and found that spring had come while he had been in the desert, and the willows were green by the river side. John was still preaching and baptizing, but was a little farther up the river at Bethabara.

As Jesus came near John pointed to Him and said to the people,

"Behold the Lamb of God, which taketh away the sin of the world. This is He. . . . And I knew Him not, but He that sent me to baptize with water, the same said to me, 'Upon whom thou shalt see the spirit descending and remaining on Him, the same is He which baptizeth with the Holy Ghost.' "

CHAPTER VIII.

THE FIRST DISCIPLES.

The next day while two men named John and Andrew were talking with John the Baptist, Jesus passed by, and again John said, "Behold the Lamb of God." These two men had been priests and disciples of John, but they turned and followed Jesus, and John was content to have them do so, for he sought no honor for himself. Jesus when he saw them following said,

"What seek ye ?"

And they, hardly knowing what to say, and wishing very much to know Him, said,

"Rabbi, where dwellest thou?"

He did not reprove them for giving Him the honored name of *Master*, but said,

"Come and see."

How gladly they went! No one knows where or how He lived, but whether in a house, or in such a little tent as the people of that region now carry with them when they travel, it was a quiet place where these two men who were looking eagerly for the Kingdom of God could sit at the feet of Jesus and talk with Him. He was a young man like themselves, but there was a wonderful spirit in Him that made them feel like worshipping Him.

The first thing that Andrew did was to go and find his brother, Simon Peter. They were both fishermen from Bethsaida on Lake Galilee, and had come down to hear the new prophet John.

"We have found the Messiah!" said Andrew, and they both went back to Jesus.

When the Lord—for this He had been always—saw Simon Peter He saw his heart, and knew that he would be one of the founders of the kingdom with Him, and so He, looking straight through him, said,

"Thou art Simon, the son of Jona; thou shalt be called Cephas, which is by interpretation Peter." (A stone.)

So John, the loving; Andrew, the obedient, and Peter, the believing began to follow Jesus. And Peter's strong faith was like a foundation of stone in the beginning of the building of the kingdom.

There was another man from Bethsaida who had come down to hear John. His name was Philip. Jesus found him and said, "Follow Me." And he not only followed Jesus, but he went joyfully to find his friend, Nathanael, and tell him that they had found the Messiah, Jesus of Nazareth, the son of Joseph.

Nathanael could not believe that the Messiah would be a man of Nazareth, because the prophets had said that He would come from Bethlehem.

So he said, "Can any good thing come out of Nazareth?"

"Come and see," said Philip, urgently, and he went.

As he came to Jesus he met the deep, kind look that had searched Peter's heart and heard Jesus say,

"Behold an Israelite indeed, in whom there is no guile!" He saw innocence in the heart of Nathanael, but Nathanael wondered how Jesus could know him.

"Before that Philip called thee when thou wast under the fig-tree, I saw thee, said Jesus.

Then Nathanael's whole heart went over to Jesus, and he cried,

"Rabbi, Thou art the Son of God ; Thou art the King of Israel !"

He needed nothing more to prove that Jesus was the Christ, but Jesus told him that he should see greater things, angels out of the open heaven ascending and descending upon Him.

Nathanael became the fifth disciple. His name was afterward called Bartholomew.

CHAPTER IX.

THE FIRST MIRACLE.

Jesus and the five who had become His constant friends and disciples, turned their faces toward home, for they were all from Galilee. It was Spring, and the land was beautiful with the fresh green of the trees and the breaking forth of wild flowers among the grass. On the Journey the disciples scarcely saw the beauty around them, or felt weary from the journey, for they were hearing the gracious words of their new Friend concerning the coming in of the kingdom.

There was to be a marriage feast near Nazareth in the home of a friend. Mary and her family were invited, and also the friends who had come with Jesus. It was at Cana, a village between Nazareth and the lake, and they walked over the hills early to see the bride, crowned with flowers and a white veil, married to the man to whom she had given herself. Then followed a feast at the house of the father of the bridegroom. There were joyful greetings, and garlands of flowers, and wine—for Palestine was the land of vineyards, and they knew how to prepare a harmless wine. Before the feast was over they found that the wine had given out, and those who served the feast were distressed. It was thought a disgrace to fail in hospitality at a wedding feast, and so Mary came to Jesus for advice, saying,

"They have no wine."

"Woman," He said—and among the Jews this was a respectful manner of speaking to a woman—"what have I to do with thee? Mine hour is not yet come."

THE MARRIAGE AT CANA.

He meant that He must act from the Divine Nature, and not from the human nature that He had received from His mother.

"Whatsoever He saith unto you, do it," said Mary to the servants.

He told them to fill with water the six large water-pots of stone that stood near, and they filled them to the brim.

"Draw out now, and bear to the governor of the feast," He said, and it was served at the table, and the master of the feast called to the bridegroom,

"Thou hast saved the good wine until now."

This was the beginning of miracles.

These were happy days for Mary, for she had her Son back again. From the wedding Jesus and His mother, and His brothers, and His disciples went down to Capernaum by the lake for a few days.

Here Peter lived by the blue, beautiful lake that is walled by high hills on one side, while on the other lies what once was the "garden of Gennesaret" watered by streams, and rich with fruits, and grains, and flowers.

CHAPTER X.

IN HIS FATHER'S HOUSE.

The feeling that Jesus had when a boy, that He must be about His Father's business was now satisfied. He had begun the work of His ministry, though He had been doing all those silent years the tremendous work of overcoming evil for us. He met it in His own human nature, and overcame it step by step without yielding to sin. He was to do this work until it should be finished upon the cross, but for three years He was to teach the people the truths of the new kingdom, and show by His life, and at last by the laying down of His life, that love had come into the world to fill the old forms of the law full of the new Spirit of Life. He was to take away the sins of the world, and in place of them give to the world eternal life.

It was time for the Passover Feast again, and Jesus with his disciples joined the Capernaum company and started on the pleasant journey to Jerusalem. They sang the songs of Zion, and rejoiced when the towers of Jerusalem and the Golden Temple came into view, and as they came down the road over Olivet they probably made their camp there where they could look across the valley to the Temple. Everything was moving. Flocks of sheep and herds of oxen were being driven toward the Temple, and crowds of people from near and far were filling the streets, and also moving toward the Holy House.

When Jesus came into the Temple Court He saw something that stirred his whole soul with sorrow and wrath. The sellers of sheep, and oxen, and doves, and the money-changers had brought their things into the great court inside the marble pillars, and on the pavement of many-colored marbles, and were buying and selling noisily, and turning the courts of the Lord into a market. The voices of men and animals must have disturbed those who worshipped in the inner courts. The priests allowed it, perhaps they were paid for doing so, and Jesus, as a Son in His Father's house where the servants had been unfaithful, began clearing the court of all these things, and finding some cord on the pavement He folded it into a short scourge of many strands and used it to drive the cattle and sheep and their keepers out of court. The money-changers would not easily yield, but he poured out their money and overturned their tables, and to those who sold doves he said,

"Take these things hence ; make not my Father's house a house of merchandise."

And the people wondered why they should obey this strange young man, but they did.

It was the Divine light in the face of Jesus, and not the bit of cord that drove them out. They saw that He had a right to clear the Temple courts.

Then the Jews wondered who had given Him this right, and they said to Him,

"What sign showest Thou unto us, seeing Thou doest these things ? "

And this was the sign He gave them : "Destroy this Temple, and in three days I will raise it up."

He knew that they would not understand this, but they would remember it after they had crucified Him and He had risen from the dead, for He spoke of His body.

The Jews turned scornfully away. The Temple had been forty-six years in building, and they thought His promise an idle boast, but they did not forget it. Three years after they helped to bring Him to the cross, accusing Him in the High priests palace of saying these things.

CHAPTER XI.

A TALK ABOUT THE BREATH OF GOD.

Jesus was in the Temple most of the time during the Passover Feast. He taught the people standing among the marble pillars of the outer court. He also did miracles among them, and many believed on Him because of the miracles, but He, knowing their hearts, saw not one among them whom He would call to be with Him in His work, for He could not wholly trust them. The Pharisees and Doctors of the Law also stood and listened to Him, and among them was one whose heart turned toward Jesus. He was one of the highest of the Pharisees, but his heart was not so proud and full of self-love as the hearts of most of the Pharisees. His name was Nicodemus. He longed to talk with Jesus, but he was afraid of what the other Pharisees would say.

He found out where the camp of the Galilean company was, and one night went out of the city gate, across the Kedron bridge and up the slope of the Mount of Olives and found Jesus. There was no place to talk quietly in the crowded tents, so they must have gone out under the shadowy olive trees to talk.

"Master," he said—and it was much for the wise Pharisee to speak so humbly to the young carpenter of Galilee—"Master, we know that Thou art a teacher come from God, for no man can do these miracles that Thou doest except God be with him."

Jesus looked through the heart of Nicodemus, though it was night, and saw what he needed most, and so He made no reply about Himself or His miracles, but said,

"Verily, I say unto you, except a man be born again he cannot see the Kingdom of God."

Nicodemus could not understand how a man could be born when he is old, so Jesus explained that it was a spiritual birth. "That which is born of the flesh is flesh, and that which is born of the spirit is spirit." And as the wind softly stirred the leaves of the olive trees above their heads He said,

"The wind bloweth where it listeth, and thou hearest the sound thereof, but canst not tell whence it cometh and whither it bloweth. So is every one that is born of the Spirit."

(160)

AT JACOB'S WELL.

Nicodemus had always thought that religion was the keeping of the law
as all Jews were taught by the priests, so he was astonished, and said,

"How can these things be?"

"Art thou a master in Israel and knowest not these things?" said Jesus,
and then He spoke to the soul of Nicodemus of the things of the Spirit of
Heaven—The Heaven in which He already lived,—and of the new kingdom
that had begun on earth.

If you will find what Jesus said to Nicodemus in the third chapter of John's
Gospel you will find among other things these beautiful words,—

"For God so loved the world that he gave His only begotten Son, that
whosoever believeth in Him should not perish, but have everlasting life."

Nicodemus found out that life was the breath of God in man, and that by
it man lives. Perhaps he felt it within him as he went down the valley under
the trees and heard the wind among the leaves; and as he came up the steep
way and through the city gate in the silence of the night, perhaps he resolved
to be a disciple of Jesus.

CHAPTER XII.

A TALK ABOUT THE WATER OF LIFE.

After the Passover there were many who had believed in Jesus who
wished to be baptized, and so they went down to Jordan with Jesus and the
disciples, and then the disciples baptized them.

John, who was also baptizing at another point by the river, was told that
Jesus was baptizing and that all men were going to Him. John was rejoiced
at this.

"This my joy therefore is fulfilled," he said. "He must increase, but I
must decrease. He that cometh from heaven is above all."

After this Jesus went back to Galilee, and as He and His disciples went
through the country of Samaria, which lay between Judea and Galilee, they
came at noon near to the little village of Sychar among the hills. It was the
most difficult road to Galilee, and most persons followed the Jordan road
when going back and forth, for the Judeans and Samaritans were not friendly,
but it is written that Jesus "must needs go through Samaria."

While the disciples went up into the village to buy some bread, Jesus sat down by a deep well in the valley. It was built round with stone, and covered from the sun, for the people prized the well not only for the clear, cold water, but because Jacob, the father of all the tribes of Israel dug the well for his family and cattle and flocks hundreds of years before.

While Jesus rested by the well a woman came down the path from the town to draw water. She drew the water with a strong cord that she fastened around her earthen water-jar and was going to put it on her shoulder and carry it away when Jesus asked her for a drink of water. She had not offered Him any for she thought a Jew would not ask even a drink of water from a Samaritan, but Jesus said,

"If thou knewest the gift of God, and who it is that saith to thee 'Give me to drink' thou wouldst have asked of Him and he would have given thee living water."

The woman did not understand His words about water any more than Nicodemus did about the blowing of the wind. Jesus was talking about *life* always and everwhere, but the people were slow to understand Him.

The woman wondered where Jesus could get better water than this from Jacob's well.

"Whosoever shall drink of this water," He said, "shall thirst again, but whosoever drinketh of the water that I shall give him shall never thirst. But the water that I shall give him shall be in him a well of water springing up into everlasting life."

When the woman heard this she asked for it, that she might not be thirsty and come to the well for water, but Jesus, seeing that she could not understand His words began to speak of her life, and so truly that she was amazed and said,

"Sir, I perceive that thou art a prophet." She talked of the mountain near by which had been the place of worship of the Samaritans, and of the Temple at Jerusalem where the Jews worshipped, for she did not want to talk of her own life, which was not good.

Jesus then showed her that "God is a Spirit, and they that worship Him must worship Him in spirit and in truth," and that the hour had come when He wished people to worship him so in every place.

. "I know that Messias cometh, which is called Christ," she said,

"I that speak unto thee am He," He said. Then the woman left her water-jar and hurried away without a word to tell the people of the town.

While she was away His disciples came and begged Jesus to eat, but His spirit was filled with the thought of life, and he said,

"I have meat to eat that ye know not of."

And when they did not understand He said,

"My meat is to do the will of Him that sent me, and finish His work," and when he thought how great the work was that was before Him, it was as if the harvest-time of gathering the people into the kingdom had come.

As they looked out along the valley men were ploughing the fields to sow wheat.

"Say ye not there are four months," He said, "and then cometh harvest? Behold I say unto you, 'Lift up your eyes and look on the fields ; for they are white already to harvest.'"

While He stayed two days in Sychar many believed on him there.

"Now we believe," they said to the woman, not because of thy saying for we have heard Him ourselves, and know that this is indeed the Christ, the Saviour of the world."

CHAPTER XIII.

JESUS IN THE SYNAGOGUE.

Jesus came back to Galilee through the Valley of Jenin and across the plain of Jezreel to Cana, where His disciple Nathanael lived, and where He had wrought His first miracle. While He was in Cana a nobleman who lived at Capernaum came riding into the little town in great haste to asked Jesus to come down and heal his son who was near death. To try him, Jesus said,

"Except ye see signs and wonders ye will not believe."

The nobleman would not stop to talk of this, but besought Jesus, saying,

"Sir, come down ere my child die."

Jesus was glad to see his faith, and ready to meet it.

"Go thy way," He said, "thy son liveth." and the man went away believing what Jesus had said. On the way down to Capernaum by the Lake, some glad-faced servants came hastening to meet him.

"Thy son liveth!" They cried—the very words that Jesus had used. When he asked them when the boy had taken a turn for the better they said,

"Yesterday at the seventh hour the fever left him."

JESUS IN THE SYNAGOGUE.

Then the happy father knew that it was at the seventh hour—one o'clock —that Jesus had said, "Thy son liveth."

There was joy in the house of the nobleman when the father and mother and all the household gathered around the boy who had been healed, and talked of the wonderful power of Jesus in speaking the word of healing.

From Cana Jesus went to Nazareth. John the Baptist had been thrown into a gloomy prison down by the Dead Sea by Herod Antipas because he had rebuked the wickedness of that king, and Jesus knew that His own work was now fully begun, since the prophet, who had come to prepare His way, was laid aside.

While Jesus was at home with His mother and brothers and sisters He went one Sabbath to the village church or synagogue, as He had always done through His childhood and youth. Perhaps His brothers and some of His disciples were with Him, while His mother and sisters parted from Him and entered by another door, as was the Jewish custom. There were many there who hoped that the young carpenter, who had become a teacher, and as many believed, a prophet, would read from the Book of the Law.

After the singing, and the prayers, and the reciting of the creeds, the time came for the reading and teaching. The first lesson had been read, and the ruler of the synagogue took from the sacred place where it was kept another parchment roll, and coming down the steps he handed it to Jesus. It was the roll of Isaiah, and as Jesus went up to the reader's desk He opened and unrolled it until He came to these words,

"The spirit of the Lord is upon me, because he hath annointed me to preach the gospel to the poor ; He hath sent me to heal the broken-hearted, to preach deliverance to the captives, and recovering of sight to the blind, to set at liberty them that are bruised, to preach the acceptable year of the Lord."

When he had finished he rolled the book again and handed it to the minister and sat down. It was the custom of those who were teachers of the people to sit down to teach, while the people all rose and stood until he had finished.

"This day," said Jesus " is this scripture fulfilled in your ears."

The people were looking and listening so earnestly that it was very still, and as Jesus told them simply that He was the very One whom Isaiah had spoken of seven hundred years before, that He had brought the good tidings, and had come to do the work the prophet had spoken of, they looked at each other in amazement. To be sure they had never heard such words of grace and wisdom, but how could this be true?

"Is not this Joseph's son?" they asked each other. Joseph had been their neighbor and Jesus had grown up among them and played with their children. They thought some evil thing had entered into Him disturbing His mind. But when He began to tell them that no prophet was accepted in his own country, and that the Lord was obliged to send them to strangers, as He sent Elijah and Elisha, they were angry with Him. Some of the men wished to teach Him a lesson, and they took Him by force to the edge of a cliff, for Nazareth was built high up among the hills, and were about to cast Him over among the limestone rocks below, but turning away from them, Jesus walked quietly down the hill to the path that led into the valley—and no one was able to lay a hand upon Him to harm Him. "He came unto His own, and His own received Him not," and He went away to preach the good tidings in other towns. The heart of Mary must have been full of sorrow when she saw her Son "despised and rejected of men" as Isaiah prophesied, but she hid her sorrow, and remembered the words of the Lord brought to her by the angel before her Son was born.

And so Jesus went down to Capernaum where he had friends and disciples, and afterward His mother and His brothers went to Him there, but Nazareth knew him no more.

It was about this time that it is supposed that Jesus went alone to a religious feast at Jerusalem, and while there cured a poor man who could not walk. He lay on his mat near a spring called Bethesda. It was covered by a roof, and had five porches. Here the sick were brought by their friends that they might, when they saw the waters bubble up, step in and be cured. They believed then an angel came down and made the moving of the waters, but it was probably one of the kind called intermittent springs. There is one at Jerusalem now called the "Fountain of the Virgin" which rises at certain times.

Jesus saw the poor friendless man who had waited for thirty-eight years for the chance of stepping into the waters when they were moving, and had been disappointed for others stepped in before him. Looking at him, He said,

"Wilt thou be made whole?"

The man explained why he could not be cured, for there was no man to help him. Then Jesus said,

"Rise, take up thy bed, and walk."

He rose at once, and walked, carrying the mat on which he lay.

The Jews were angry when they heard of it for the man had been cured on the Sabbath, but Jesus told them that they were all refusing eternal life because of their unbelief, saying,

"Ye will not come unto Me that yet might have life."

CHAPTER XIV.

AMONG THE FISHERMEN.

Capernaum was on the shore of the beautiful lake of Galilee. There were villages clustered around the lake then and all Galilee was swarming with busy life, but now there are few inhabitants, and Capernaum is only a heap of stones. Some of these stones, which may now be seen, are carved in such a way that we may know that they are a part of an ancient synagogue. This was the synagogue, perhaps, that a good Centurion built whose servant Jesus cured when he was near death, and here in Capernaum lived the nobleman whose son Jesus cured by a word, and here lived His first disciples, Peter and Andrew, and James and John, and here Matthew, who sat in his little office taking the taxes that the people had to pay, may have seen Jesus pass, and may have heard him speak before he became a disciple.

The beautiful plain of Gennesaret spreads out from one end of the lake, and there is a white beach of shells there, while at other points on the lake there are hills and great rocks close to the water.

On this white beach Jesus stood one spring morning teaching the people. As the fisher-folks and others gathered close around to hear Him, He was pushed so near the water that He stepped into Peter's boat, which was near the shore, and asked him to push it out a litle way into the water, and there in the stern of the boat Jesus sat and taught the people who stood thick upon the shore.

The boat of Zebedee, the father of James and John was near by, for they were the partners of Peter and Andrew. They had washed their nets and had given up fishing until night again, for morning was not a good time for fishing, but Jesus said to Peter and Andrew,—

"Launch out into the deep, and let down your nets for a draught."

The disciples were surprised at this, for it was not the hour for fishing, and Peter said,

"Master, we have toiled all night and have taken nothing ; nevertheless at thy word I will let down the net."

When they had done this they found that their nets were filled with fishes, so that they called to James and John to come and help them, for their nets were breaking. When they had emptied the nets into the two boats they were filled so full that they began to sink.

Then Peter fell down at Jesus's knees and cried out,—

"Depart from me, for I am a sinful man, O Lord !" so wonderful did the miracle seem to him.

But to Peter Jesus said,—

"Fear not ; from henceforth thou shalt catch men." James and John He also called, and showed them that the time had now come for them to help Him in founding the Kingdom.

They did not wait to sell the great draught of fishes that they had brought to land ; and they did not wait to sell their fishing boats and nets, but they forsook all and followed Jesus. They did not know that their names would be known forever as the founders of the Christian Church with Him who was its divine Head.

CHAPTER XV.

THE HEALING HAND OF JESUS.

The Jewish church, or synagogue at Capernaum was very beautiful. It was of white marble, and richly carved, and was the gift of a Roman officer to the Jews.

One Sabbath morning Jesus went in and sat among the learned Rabbis, for He wished to speak to the people as He had near Nazareth. The people knew and loved him, and the place was crowded to hear Him speak. He sat there through the singing, and the prayers, and the reading.

The parchment rolls of the law and the prophets were in a case behind Him ; and there was the curtain, and the branched candlesticks. Then He went to the Teacher's seat, and while all the people stood He sat and taught them. People wondered, as they always did, at his words, for they were not like the words of the Rabbis,—they were as if God Himself were speaking through a man.

In the midst of it there was a loud cry from a man who looked like a maniac. He had followed the people in, and the words of Jesus had disturbed the evil spirit that was in Him,

"Let us alone," it cried, "what have we to do with thee, thou Jesus of Nazareth. Art thou come to destroy us? I know thee who Thou art,—the Holy One of God."

"Hold thy peace, and come out of Him," said Jesus, and the poor man fell headlong on the marble floor, but in a moment he was free, for the evil spirit had obeyed the word of Jesus, and this astonished the people so much that they told it through all the town and the country round about.

When He went home from the synagogue, for Peter's house was one of His homes, He found the mother of Peter's wife very ill of fever, and they brought Jesus to her bed. He bent over her and said some words to that which had caused the fever, and at once it was gone.

She seemed to be quite well again, and her first wish was to do something for this wonderful man whom Peter had been following, and she rose and helped to prepare food for Him.

The people did not dare to come to Jesus for healing while it was yet the Sabbath, for the Rabbis said it was wrong to cure people on the Sabbath day, but as soon as the sun had set the Sabbath ended, and then the streets were filled with people who came for themselves, or bringing their sick friends to be touched by the hand of Jesus. All around the little house of Peter they crowded, while He walked among them looking at them with pitying love, and "He laid his hands on every one of them, and healed them."

CHAPTER XVI.

FOLLOWING JESUS.

The next morning Jesus went out among the hills alone. All day He was pressed upon by the poor, the sick, the blind, and the lame, or those who were hungry for the word, and so at night or early morning He went out to be alone, to think of the great work he had come to do, and to pray or talk to the Father, for Jesus and the Father were one. But the people followed Him, and begged him not to leave them.

THE NET FULL OF FISHES.

"I must preach the kingdom of God to other cities also," He said, "for therefore am I sent." And He took his disciples and started on a journey from village to village through Galilee. There were about two hundred of these towns, and they were near together. It was the springtime, and the fields and hills between the villages were beautiful with flowers and growing grain. Sometimes He taught in their churches, and sometimes under their trees or trellises, and wherever He went the common people heard him gladly.

Once as He drew near a town a leper followed Him. He followed Him into the town, which was against the law, for the leper was not allowed to live inside a town, or to come near the people, as the touch of a leper would give the disease to another. But so earnest was he to see Jesus that he came through the crowd and fell on his face before Jesus, saying,

"Lord if Thou wilt, Thou canst make me clean."

Jesus put forth His hand and touched him, saying, "I will ; be thou clean."

Suddenly the leprosy left the man, and his dead and filthy skin became as healthy as a child's, and Jesus sent him to the priest to offer that which the law commanded for the cleansing of lepers. It was a long, and often costly process that a leper must pass through to be cleansed from his disease, but the word of Jesus was with power, and brought divine life to take the place of death, for leprosy was a slow death.

When the Lord came back to Capernaum the people thronged Him, and when He rested in the shaded court of a friend's house it was soon filled with the eager people who longed to hear His word, or be healed by His touch.

Once it was so crowded in the court that some men, who were bringing a friend to Jesus who was helpless with palsy, took him up by the outside stairs to the housetop. There, by taking up a few tiles, they made an opening just over the place where Jesus sat, and the people soon saw the man lying on his mat before Jesus, for they had let it down by cords through the opening.

Jesus saw the faith of the four men who had let their sick friend down at His feet, and it touched His heart. He also saw the longing in the soul of the sick man to be good and pure, and He said,

"Son, be of good cheer, thy sins be forgiven thee."

The Scribes, who were always copying the Scriptures—for there was no printing done in those days—were always watching to hear Jesus say something contrary to the Law of Moses, that they might tell it to the priests,

JESUS HEALING THE SICK.

and some who were sitting there looked at each other and said in their hearts,
"Who can forgive sins but God only?"

Jesus heard their thoughts and asked them why they reasoned in this
way with themselves, and which seemed to them the easier, to forgive sins
or to heal the body.

But that they might know that He had power over the body as well 'as
the soul He said to the sick man,

"Arise; take up thy bed, and go thy way into thine house."

The man rose and rolled up his mat and carried it out, the people
falling back astonished to let him pass, for his palsy had left him and he
walked out strong and well.

"We have seen strange things to-day," the people said among themselves
for they could not understand how a man could forgive sins or heal disease.

When Jesus left the house to go down to the sea-shore He passed the
Custom-house, where the tax-gatherers, or "publicans," gathered money from
the Jewish people to pay to their conquerors, the Romans.

The Romans were very hard in their dealings with the Jews, and made
themselves rich by taking money from the poor of their provinces.

The people did not like the tax-gatherer, and his was not a pleasant office.

Levi, also called Matthew, was a rich tax-gatherer at Capernaum, and as
he sat in his office looking out upon the market-place he saw Jesus passing
by.   Perhaps he had often heard Jesus teach by the shore and in the market-
place, and longed to follow Him.   He saw the Teacher stop at his open
door, and heard Him say,

"Follow Me."

That was enough; Matthew left all, rose up and followed Jesus. He had
a business that made him rich, but he was ready to leave it all to be a disciple
of Jesus.

He wanted all to know that he had chosen a new life, and so he gave a
great dinner to his friends, and invited Jesus and His five disciples that he
might confess before them all his faith in Jesus.

The Pharisees looked down upon the publicans and thought them a people
unfit to associate with, and when they passed by and saw Jesus sitting in
Matthew's house at the feast they asked His disciples as they went in and out
why their Master ate with "publicans and sinners," a thing they felt themselves too good to do.

Jesus Himself answered them in words that have helped many sinful
people to come to Him since.

"They that are whole need not a physician, but they that are sick. I
came not to call the righteous but sinners to repentance."

And then He turned to talk with Matthew and his friends, who listened
to every word that fell from His lips, and did not try to find fault with Him
as the Pharisees did.

Matthew had made a rich feast, and his table was no doubt piled with
the beautiful fruits of the plain of Gennesaret, but the eyes of all and the
thoughts of all were fixed upon the wonderful Teacher, and Matthew, the
publican, who had become His disciple.

CHAPTER XVII.

FRIENDS OF JESUS.

Jesus had a good and true reason for choosing just twelve men to help
Him to begin to build the first Christian Church, or the Kingdom of Heaven
on the earth. We cannot yet understand the reason for everything He did,
but quite enough to help us to believe in Him, and to give us a place in His
kingdom. He had called half that number and soon He called six more to
join them, and named them apostles.

Before He called them He went up into a mountain to be alone. He
left Capernaum and went up through a rocky vale to a high plain where the
grass lay thick and the wild flowers were coming up among it, for it was
spring-time. Two hills, or peaks rose out of this plain, and there was a grassy
hollow between. They were called the "Horns of Hattin." From one of
these hills Jesus could see the lake with its cities, and the plain dotted with
villages below, and beyond them the great Mount Hermon crowned with
snow. Here Jesus stayed all night, and the next morning came down into
the grassy dale between the peaks where the people were gathering. The
disciples went to meet Him, and He told them that He had chosen twelve of
them to be with Him in His work, and to preach the Good Tidings to the
people.

He called to His side Peter and Andrew, and James and John—the two
pairs of brothers who were His first friends; then Philip, of Bethsaida, Bartholo-
men, from Cana, and Matthew, the tax-gatherer of Capernaum, who afterward

wrote the first gospel.   He also chose Thomas, of Galilee ; James and Jude, two brothers from Capernaum; Simon, of Galilee, and Judas Iscariot, who came from the country near Jerusalem.   Five of these, it is said, were His cousins. More than half of them were fisherman, and none of them were learned men, unless Bartholomew might be called one.   How wonderful it must have been to see these twelve earnest young men gathered around Jesus, ready to go where He should send them, or follow Him to death.   No kings or emperors on earth ever had so great honor given them as that which Jesus gave to these men, for they became the Lord's spiritual brothers, and princes in His spiritual kingdom.

Then Jesus came down among the people.   Some had brought sick friends up the rocky gorge for Jesus to touch ; or they had brought poor souls possessed by devils for Him to set free, and He healed them all.

Then He sat down and taught the people.   The sayings of that wonderful day are kept in the gospels, and are called the "Sermon on the Mount." There was no choir, no organ, no church made with hands, but the words are now read in every Christian church in the world.   The preacher sat on a green hillock, His dark cloak thrown back showing His white tunic, and the spring sunshine lay on His holy, beautiful face and flowing hair.   All this the people saw, but they saw much more than this.   They saw something divine in His face.   His form, and the light around Him, and what they heard seemed to them to be the words of a Divine Man.   He looked lovingly on the little group of disciples near Him, and blessed them in beautiful words that we call the Beatitudes, or the Ten Blessings.   He said to them and to us that the "blessed" (happy) are the good, humble, pure souls who have little of this world's wealth and friendship, but much faith and love.

If you will read the fifth, sixth and seventh chapters of Matthew you will know much that Jesus taught that heavenly day on Hattin Mount. He taught them the law of love and forgiveness ; the law of purity and truth. He taught them to be humble and simple, especially in prayer, and not like the Pharisees. He gave them a wonderful prayer that we call "the Lord's Prayer," though it is a prayer to the Lord, for all Christians in all ages to bring to Him.   He told them that if they were children of God they could not be worldly, loving themselves and the world best ; neither could they serve two masters. Then He taught them a beautiful lesson of trust in the Heavenly Father by pointing to the birds that flew above them, and reminding them how they were fed and cared for ; and also by pointing to the wild field lilies that grew near by, their scarlet petals shining in the sun.

SERMON ON THE MOUNT.

"Consider the lilies of the field how they grow," he said, "they toil not, neither do they spin, and yet I say unto you that even Solomon in all his glory was not arrayed like one of these," and then He asked them if God, who clothed the lilies, would not clothe His own children, and told them to have no fear for the future, but to seek the Kingdom of God first and always, and all needed things would be given to them.

Then He looked away from the birds and the lilies into the eyes of the people and saw their need of love and truth, for he could read their hearts. He told them that they should not judge each other, or look long upon each other's faults, but rather upon their own, and showed them how they might ask God for love and truth, and it would surely be given them, because the Heavenly Father is more just, and kind, and loving than an earthly father can be.

And here is the Golden Rule of Christ, which, if we live by it, will bring heaven down to earth.

"Whatsoever ye would that men should do to you, do ye even so to them."

He told them that the way of the world was wide, and many were crowding into it, while the heavenly way was narrow in this life, and few were finding it, though many talked much about it, and seemed to have found it. He said that it would be shown in the day when we all appear before God who has truly followed Him. He said that the true men were like the wise man who built his house upon a rock, and when the winds, the rain, and the flood came it stood fast, because it was founded on the rock; and the false were like the foolish man who built his house upon the sand, and when the winds, and the rain, and the floods came it fell, and great was the fall of it.

The people went away from this great meeting among the hills to think it over. It was so new and so wonderful, not at all like the teaching of the scribes, for the young carpenter of Nazareth spoke like a Teacher of teachers. Ever since that day when the Lord sat and taught the truths of the Kingdom of Heaven, and the people stood upon the grassy plain among the spring flowers and the wild thyme to hear his words, the Sermon on the Mount has been known as the greatest sermon the world has ever known.

CHAPTER XVIII.

THE LORD OF LIFE.

Jesus came down to Capernaum again and found the same crowds of needy people, who were like sheep having no shepherd. The rich as well as the poor had their wants and their troubles.

A good Roman officer, called a Centurion, because he was captain over a hundred men, had a servant who was so faithful to him that he was very fond of him. The servant was very sick, and when the Centurion heard that Jesus was again in Capernaum he went to the chief men of the city and asked them to get Jesus to come and cure his servant. He feared to ask the favor himself, for he thought Jesus was a Jew who would not like to have dealings with the Romans. So the Jews spoke to Jesus about it saying that the Centurion was the good man who had built a beautiful synagogue for them. Jesus did not need to be urged to be kind to a Roman for He loved all the people of the earth alike.

While He was on His way some friends of the Centurion came to meet Him with a message.

"Lord, trouble not Thyself," he said, "for I am not worthy that Thou shouldst enter under my roof; Wherefore neither thought I myself worthy to come unto Thee; but say in a word and my servant shall be healed."

Jesus told the people who followed Him that He had not found such faith as this among their own people. And when the men returned to the Centurion's house they found the servant cured of his sickness.

But some of the Jews were offended because Jesus had said that a pagan Roman could have more faith than a Jew, and that they would enter the Kingdom of Heaven while the Jews would be left out.

The next day Jesus and His disciples went to a little city called Nain, set up among the hills, more than twenty miles away. When they were near the city gate they met a funeral procession coming out. They were going to the burying ground on a hillside not far away. There were hired mourners, as is the custom in that country, who made many doleful noises, and behind them came a weeping woman—the mother of the young man who had died.

His body was borne by friends and followed by many more, for all felt sorry for the poor woman who had lost her only son.

(179)

As the procession passed Jesus said two little words to the woman—
"Weep not," and then He put forth His hand and touched the bier. The men
who bore it set it down before Jesus who looked down into the face of the
dead, saying,

"Young man, I say unto thee, arise!"

In a moment the young man opened his eyes, sat up, and began to speak,
and Jesus gave him back from the grave to his happy mother.

While Jesus was near Nain some of the disciples of John the Baptist
came to see Him. John was in prison still, down in the low, hot country by
the Dead Sea. He had heard strange stories about Jesus from the disciples
who came to see him, and because they were not settled in their mind about
Him, John sent them to find Him and to say,

"Art thou He that should come, or do we look for another?"

Jesus told them to go and tell John what they saw.

"The blind receive their sight and the lame walk, the lepers are cleansed,
and the deaf hear, the dead are raised up, and the poor have the gospel
preached to them, and blessed is he whosoever shall not be offended in me."

Then Jesus taught the people who stood by, and the lesson ended with
these words which he speaks to the whole world,

"Come unto me, all ye that labor and are heavy laden, and I will give
you rest; take my yoke upon you and learn of me, for I am meek and lowly
of heart, and ye shall find rest unto your souls; for my yoke is easy and my
burden is light."

This is the loving invitation of Jesus to every one of us to enter the
Kingdom of Heaven, and it is the King Himself who invites us.

CHAPTER XIX.

MARY OF MAGDALA.

There was a Pharisee named Simon, who was very curious to know what
Jesus taught, although he had no wish to be His disciple. He was a rich man
and lived in a beautiful house with a court. Beyond the court was a banqueting
room with couches on which guests sat leaning upon the tables in the Eastern
fashion. There were other guests invited to hear Jesus talk, the friends of

JESUS IN THE STORM.

Simon, and it is quite probable that when they came the servants of Simon met them and took their sandals and washed their feet and arranged their hair as was the custom, and were also heartily welcomed by Simon. When Jesus came He had no such service or welcome given Him, for Simon did not love Him ; he was only curious about Him.

While they were at the tables a beautiful young woman came in through the open door and passed swiftly by the couches on which the guests were reclining until she came to the place where Jesus was. No one spoke to her or about her, for they all knew that she had been a sinful woman. But soon they saw that she bent weeping over the feet of Jesus where He lay upon the couch, and soon they knew by the odor of costly perfume that she was anointing His feet. As her tears fell she wiped His feet with her long hair, and kissed them again and again.

Simon looked at her severely, but said nothing, though he wondered in his heart why Jesus did not know that a sinful woman was touching Him. Then said Jesus,

"Simon, I have somewhat to say to thee." And Simon replied, "Master, say on."

Then Jesus told a little story of a man who had two debtors ; one owed him five hundred pence, and the other fifty ; and when they had nothing to pay he frankly forgave them both. Then he asked which of them will love Him most ?"

"I suppose that he to whom he forgave most," said Simon, and Jesus told him that he was right.

Then He turned and pointed to the woman, saying,

"See'st thou this woman ?" and the eyes of all were fixed on the weeping Mary of Magdala.

When Jesus had told Simon that he had failed to bring water for His feet, though she had washed them with her tears, and wiped them with her hair ; that he had given Him no kiss of welcome, and she had not ceased to kiss His feet ; that he had not anointed His head with oil, but she had anointed His feet with costly ointment, He added,

"Her sins which are many are forgiven ; for she loved much ; but to whom little is forgiven the same loveth little." And turning to the woman He said,

"Thy sins are forgiven ; thy faith hath saved thee ; go in peace."

As Jesus went through the villages of Galilee He found many friends and many enemies. The twelve were with Him, learning daily the wonderful lessons He taught, and preparing to be preachers of the glad tidings also.

Not only Mary of Magdala, but Susanna, and Joanna, the wife of King Herod's steward who had been cured by Him, were His grateful friends. Some priests came down from Jerusalem to watch Him, and to tell the people that He was not a true teacher, and this pleased the Pharisees. They saw that He did wonderful things that no man could do, but they said that He did it by the power of the spirit of evil, and they asked Him to show them a sign that he was from God.

The Lord spoke words to the Pharisees that must have burned like coals of fire, for it showed how false and wicked their hearts were while their outward life seemed to be very religious.

He told them that no sign should be given them except that of Jonah ; as he was three days and three nights in the great fish, so should the Son of Man be three days and three nights in the heart of the earth, and though the men of Nineveh were wicked, yet they repented at the preaching of Jonah, but the men of Jerusalem did not repent, though a greater than Jonah was among them.

Mary and her sons had come from Nazareth hoping to take Jesus away from the crowds, perhaps, for a rest among the hills, for the summer heat was great down by the lake and along the Jordan. Some one sent word to Jesus, as He sat teaching within the court of a house, that His mother and brothers were outside, and wished to speak with Him. The crowd was too great for them to enter. Before Jesus rose to go out to his mother, He paused a moment to teach the great lesson He had come to bring to the world. Looking at His disciples He said,

" My mother and my brethren are these which hear the Word of God and do it."

CHAPTER XX.

STORIES TOLD BY THE LAKE.

Jesus was glad to go among the fishermen and teach the people by the Lake, for their hearts were like the good ground into which the farmer loves to drop his seed, while the hearts of the rich, proud Pharisees were like the rock on which seed cannot grow. Perhaps he was thinking of this as He walked out one morning from Peter's house along the pebbly shore and sat down to talk with the people. The crowd always grew large around him there, and He had to again enter a fishing boat and sit a little out from the shore that the people might see and hear Him more easily. He taught them as no man had ever done before. He told them short stories, often taking the subject from something the people could see. Perhaps this morning as He looked over the lovely plain of Gennesaret, He saw a sower casting seed into a brown and furrowed field, for it was the time of the year for sowing the winter wheat. This is the story of "The Sower :"

"A sower went out to sow his seed," said Jesus, "and as he sowed, some fell by the wayside, and it was trodden down, and the fowls of the air devoured it.

"And some fell upon a rock; and as soon as it was sprung up it withered away, because it lacked moisture.

"And some fell among thorns, and the thorns sprang up with it and choked it.

"And other fell on good ground, and sprang up and bore fruit an hundred fold."

And then He said, "He that hath ears to hear let him hear," for He knew that some could understand with the heart that He was talking of the Word of God, but there were many who could not.

His disciples asked Him to make the story plain to all, and so He said, "The seed is the Word of God. Those by the wayside are they that hear; then cometh the devil and taketh away the Word out of their hearts lest they should believe and be saved.

"They on the rock are they which, when they hear, receive the Word with joy, and these have no root, which for a while believe, and in time of temptation fall away.

"And that which fell among thorns are they which, when they have heard, go forth, and are choked with cares and riches and pleasures of this life, and bring no fruit to perfection.

"But that on the good ground are they which in an honest and good heart, having heard the Word, keep it, and bring forth fruit with patience."

He also told them a story called "The Wheat and the Tares," of a man who sowed good seed in a field, but when it sprung up and bore grain there were weeds growing among it called tares, for an enemy had sowed the seed at night and it had grown up with the wheat. The man's servants wished to pull out the tares, but the master of the field said both should grow together

JESUS TEACHING BY THE SEA.

until the harvest, that the wheat might not be uprooted with the tares. At the end of the harvest the tares would be burned and the wheat gathered into the barn. In this way he taught them why good and evil are allowed to grow together in this world.

He also taught them in the story of "The Mustard Seed," that the growth of the Lord's Kingdom in the heart is like a mustard seed sowed in a field—which is the least of seeds—but which becomes a great plant, so large that birds light on its branches. He told them other stories also that were to show them that the Kingdom of Heaven was life, and not a written law, and that it grows in the hearts of people as a seed grows in a field, one seed bearing many seeds, until the time when the Lord's Kingdom shall fill the earth as the ripe wheat fills the field in harvest.

One of the stories told that day was about "The Treasure." He told them of a man who, when digging in a field, found a treasure, a mine of gold, perhaps, and went and sold all that he had to get money enough to buy that field. Another one was the story of "The Pearl," which a pearl-hunter found. It was so large and beautiful that he sold all he had to be able to buy it. Both these stories were to teach that heaven in the heart is worth more to us, when once we find it, than all the treasures or pleasures of this world.

He also told a story of a "Fishing Net," which caught fish of every kind, but when it was drawn to shore the fishermen gathered the good fish into baskets, but threw the bad away. This story was something like that of the "Wheat and the Tares," showing how good and evil are at last separated.

This was a wonderful day by the blue waters of the Lake of Galilee. The people went home thinking much about the new Teacher and His stories of the Kingdom of Heaven.

The great Sower of the Seed had been dropping it into their hearts, and He alone knew which hearts were "good ground."

CHAPTER XXI.

STILLING THE STORMS.

When Jesus was very tired from teaching the people and healing the sick He used to cross the lake and go up among the rocks of Gadara, a wild region where there were few villages. After the last long day of teaching by the shore Jesus needed rest, but neither at Peter's house, nor any where on that side of the Lake could He get away from the crowds that followed Him to hear Him, or to be healed by Him.

In the evening, when the people came back to Him, He took the large fishing-boat with His disciples, and set out for the other side. Several beside His disciples wished to go with Him. A scribe wished to follow Him, but Jesus told him that He had no home, no place to lay his head, though the foxes had holes and the birds of the air had nests. Perhaps Jesus saw that the scribe was not ready to leave all and follow Him. Another wished to go, but thought he ought first to bury his father, but Jesus said to him,

"Follow me, and let the dead bury their dead." This He said of the Jews who were spiritually dead.

After they had gone far out upon the Lake a great wind storm rose. It came sweeping down upon them from the hills, rattling the ropes and swelling the sails so that they had to bring them down and fasten them, and and then take the oars. Every part of the little ship was covered with spray from the rising waves, and the disciples began to feel afraid.

Where was Jesus? He was asleep. They had brought a cushion for His head, and He had fallen asleep in the stern of the ship. As a wave fell upon them and they were in danger of sinking they woke Jesus saying,

"Master, Master, we perish!"

Then He rose and spoke to the winds and waters, and the storm ceased, and there was a great calm.

The fishermen had never seen anything so wonderful as this, and they looked at each other, almost more afraid of Jesus than they had been of the storm.

"What manner of man is this," they said, "that even the wind and the sea obey Him!"

Jesus also wondered, and said,

"Why are ye so fearful? How is it that ye have no faith?"

As soon as they had landed in Gadara a strange man came out of the rock tombs to meet them. He was naked and wounded, for he was always wandering in the mountains and among the tombs, crying and cutting himself. Jesus was sorry for him for He knew that it was the evil spirits within him that made him so unhappy. The poor man tried to worship Jesus, and the evil spirits only cried out the more, begging to be let alone.

When Jesus asked "What is thy name," he answered, "My name is Legion, for we are many."

Jesus made the poor man free by commanding the evil spirits to come out of him. They entered into a herd of swine near by, and the frightened creatures ran down a steep place into the lake and were drowned. The men who kept them were afraid and ran away, telling all whom they met of the thing that had happened. Some people came to see for themselves, and they found the wild man of the tombs clothed and quietly sitting at the feet of Jesus listening to His word. They were afraid of Jesus and begged Him to go away. They did not understand that He wished to bless and not to harm them.

As He went back to the ship the man who had been cured of his insanity begged to go with Him, but Jesus told him to go instead to his friends at home and tell them what the Lord had done for him.

The next morning the people of Decapolis heard a strange story from the wild man of the tombs, but was now a reasoning man again.

And so Jesus stilled the storm of wind on the Lake and the storm of evil in a soul.

CHAPTER XXII.

CALLED BACK.

When Jesus came back to Capernaum He found the crowd of friends at the little wharf full of concern about Him, and glad that no harm had come to Him during the storm. Among them was one who had watched anxiously for the boat, for he had a little daughter at home very ill indeed, so ill that she was "at the last breath." His name was Jairus, and he was a ruler of the synagogue. He was so troubled that he fell at the feet of Jesus, begging Him to come and lay His hand on his child that she might live.

Jeuss went with him, a throng of people with them, hoping to see Him do a great work.

While He was on the way a woman who had been sick twelve years followed close behind Him, and put forth her hand timidly toward Him.

"If I may touch but His clothes I shall be whole," she said to herself, and she touched them with faith in her heart.

Jesus, who knew all hearts, turned straight around and said:

"Who touched My clothes?"

THE LITTLE GIRL WHO WAS CALLED BACK.

How the woman shrank back and trembled when she heard that, for she was afraid she had done wrong.

The disciples thought it strange that He should ask this, as the people thronged so close that they could not help touching Jesus. But the woman knew what He meant and she came and fell down before Him, fearing and trembling, and told Him all the truth.

Jesus did not look sternly at her as she thought He would do, but He said gently,

"Daughter, thy faith hath made thee whole ; go in peace, and be whole of thy plague."

While the woman was still at His feet full of gratitude and love because she felt herself cured, some friends came from the ruler's house to bring sad news.

"Thy daughter is dead," they said, "why troublest thou the Master any further?"

Jesus saw the looks of grief on the father's face and said quickly,

"Be not afraid, only believe."

So they went to the ruler's house, and into the inner room where the little maid lay. Many wished to press in after them to see what Jesus would do, but he took only Peter and James and John with the father and mother of the maiden into the quiet, darkened room. As He went in He said to some who were mourning noisily in the outer room,

"Weep not ; she is not dead, but sleepeth." Jesus loved to call death a "sleep," for He knew that we never die. Then He took the little maid by the hand and called her. She had not gone so far into the country we cannot see that she could not hear a divine Voice calling to her,

"*Talitha cumi!*" ("Maiden, arise !") At once she rose and walked. She was a little girl of twelve, and very dear to her father and mother, and there was no doubt great joy as well as wonder in the house of the ruler that bright morning after the storm. In their joy and wonder there was danger of forgetting to give her the food she was in need of, and so Jesus gently reminded them, commanding that something should be given her to eat, but he charged them not to talk about the return of their little daughter.

CHAPTER XXIII.

TWO BY TWO.

Jesus had a desire to once more speak to the people of His own little town of Nazareth, and so He came again to His own, but His own received Him not. Once more he went into the Nazareth Synagogue where He had listened to the reading of the law all through His childhood, and to teach as He had done nine or ten months before. They did not rise up and thrust Him out as they did then, but they cast cold looks and scornful words upon Him. They could not understand His great power and wisdom, but they would not believe in Him.

"Is not this the carpenter, the Son of Mary," they said, "the brother of James and Joses, and of Juda and Simon? And are not His sisters here with us?" They were offended with Him. Jesus, knowing their faults said,

"A prophet is not without honor, but in his own country, and among his own kin, and in his own house."

He wondered why they were so unbelieving, when in His great love for them He was ready to do works of mercy among them, and to tell them the glad tidings of the Kingdom of Heaven, but He laid His hands on a few sick folk and healed them, and that was all.

As He went away to come back no more, His heart turned toward the many who were waiting for the tidings that His old friends had rejected, and He called the twelve together to send them out, two by two, into the world around them. He gave them power to cast out evil spirits, and to heal the sick ; and He put the preaching power within them so that they could tell to others the wonderful truths of the Kingdom of Heaven. He told them that they must take nothing for their journey, except a staff, with which to walk over the steep mountain paths. He told them also to bless the house that sheltered them, and to leave the house or the city that would not receive them. He said that they would have many trials, and that their lives would be sought by wicked men, but that they need not fear, for the very hairs of their head were numbered, and that even a sparrow could not fall to the ground without their Father, and they were of more value than many sparrows.

He said many other words to them that gave them comfort and strength. They had left all to follow Him, and He showed them how, in losing their all in this life they were finding much more than that—even eternal life.

So, two by two, they went forth and left Jesus alone.

That great and good man, John the Baptist, was still in the prision of King Herold Antipas, down by the Dead Sea. He had been there more than a year, but no word came from the king saying that he was free. Queen Herodias wanted him to be put to death for he had spoken against her marriage with King Herod. She was a wicked woman, and the evil hate the good. Herod believed in his heart that John should go free, but for the Queen's sake he kept him in prison, but allowed his friends to see him, and sometimes sent for him secretly to hear him talk of the Kingdom of Heaven.

On the king's birthday he gave a great feast to his lords and captains, and when they had been served with dainty food in dishes of silver and gold, and had tasted the rare fruits and the costly wines, the dancing girls came in to flit over the polished marble floor, and wave their airy scarfs to please the king and his guests.

At last a young girl came in and danced alone. She was dressed like a princess, and she was a princess.

Queen Herodias had sent her young daughter, Salome, where an innocent girl and a queen's daughter should not have gone.

She pleased the king and his lords greatly, and when she had finished, and had knelt before the king to hear what he had to say to her, he cried,

"Ask of me whatsoever thou wilt, and I will give it thee," and with an oath he declared that he would certainly do it if she should ask the half of his kingdom.

She did not decide for herself, but ran to her mother, saying,

"What shall I ask?" And the cruel mother said,

"The head of John the Baptist."

King Herod did not expect this. He thought she might ask for some jewel of great price, or perhaps a royal palace for her very own, and when he heard her request he was very sorry. But an oath made before his lords could not be broken.

He sent men to the prison, and the good prophet, who had never known fear, went home to God, and they brought his head to the princess who gave it to her mother. The king's feast ended in gloom, and the poor girl, who only obeyed her wicked mother, had nothing but a dreadful memory to keep forever as the king's gift.

And the king himself—what trouble followed him during the rest of his life! Riches and honors were all taken from him, and he was sent out of his own country, while John had gone to his Father's house in the Heavenly Country to suffer no more forever.

John's disciples buried the body of their beloved master, and then went and told Jesus. Only Jesus can give real comfort in trouble.

The disciples—now called apostles, or teachers—who had been out teaching among the villages, heard, perhaps, of the death of John the Baptist, and came back to Jesus two by two, as they had gone out. They had been preaching, healing the sick, and casting out evil spirits. They often said "The Kingdom of Heaven is at hand," and the people wondered if it would not be best to rise up and make Jesus their king.

Herod heard of the work of Jesus and the apostles, and was afraid. He half believed that John whom he had killed had risen from the dead. He tried to see Jesus, but the One who had come to preach the gospel to the poor had no time to give to Herod.

As Peter, and John, and Andrew and all the rest came back they were full of stories of the wonderful things that had been done through the power that the Lord had given them. Many came with them to find Jesus. He saw that they needed to come away from the crowds that were always around them so that He could speak to them of their work, and so that they could rest, and think, and pray.

They took a boat and crossed the Lake. The shore was crowded with people who wished to be with Jesus, and when they knew that He was going to Bethsaida-Julias at the northern end of the Lake they resolved to follow Him, for it was only a few miles away.

At the end of the Lake they entered the Jordan river, and sailing up a little way to the landing-place they saw the people coming, some in boats, and more in groups along the shore—men, women and children—and Jesus, filled with love and pity for them, led them to a green hillside where He sat down to teach them as He had often done before.

It was spring, and the grass was like a great green carpet sprinkled with bright wild-flowers, while the river, lined with bushes flowed below, and beyond lay the beautiful blue Lake. The disciples stood around their Master while He taught the people in simple language that they could understand the greatest truths the world has ever heard. All the afternoon He spoke to them, and when the sun was slowly going down over the hills of Galilee they still wished to stay. They were as sheep having no shepherd. The disciples

11

were troubled about them, for they were far from the villages where bread could be bought, and they had nothing to eat. They begged Jesus to send them away.

"Give ye them to eat," said Jesus. Then the disciples were astonished, for there were about five thousand men, beside the women and children. "Shall we go and buy two hundred pennyworth of bread, and give them to eat?" said Philip. Then Jesus, who knew what He would do, said, "How many loaves have ye? Go and see."

They went among the people, and Andrew came back, saying,

"There is a lad here which hath five barley loaves, and two small fishes; but what are they among so many?"

Then Jesus told His disciples to seat all the people in order upon the green grass, and soon there were little companies of fifty, and larger ones of an hundred sitting all over the hillside with their faces turned toward Jesus, who stood looking out upon them as a father would look upon his children. What were they waiting for? No one knew, but they saw Him take the little lad's basket of bread and the two little fishes and look up to heaven, blessing them as He did so. Then He began to break the bread and divide the fishes. As He broke the bread and gave to the disciples they took it away to the people sitting on the grass, and when they came back to Jesus there was still more waiting for them. In this way all the people were fed.

When they were satisfied Jesus said to His disciples,

"Gather up the fragments that remain, that nothing be lost."

And they filled twelve baskets with the pieces of the barley loaves that were left.

What a silent and wonderful supper of bread fresh from the hand of its Creator!

At last they began saying to each other in a low voice,

"This is of a truth that Prophet that should come into the world!" and they began to ask each other if it would not be best to take Him at once and make Him king whether he would or would not consent, but when He saw what they wished to do, He slipped away and went farther up among the hills to rest.

Evening had now come, and the people not finding Jesus, went away to their homes, and the disciples in their little ship returned to Capernaum. The people could not understand, nor could His disciples, that Jesus did not come to be an earthly king over the little nation of the Jews. Not until

FEEDING THE FIVE THOUSAND.

the Holy Spirit came to make all things clear did they understand that He was to be the Spiritual King of all the world.

CHAPTER XXIV.

WALKING THE WAVES—THE TWO KINGDOMS.

While Jesus was alone on the mountain side the disciples were trying to reach Capernaum in their fishing boat. It was not a long sail, but a contrary wind had risen and was blowing them out into the Lake away from the landing place.

They had taken down their sail and were rowing, but by three o'clock in the morning they were still out upon the Lake.

Jesus, who knew all things, saw them struggling with the oars, and coming swiftly down the mountain side He went to them walking upon the water.

The disciples saw a form through the darkness drawing near to them, and strangely enough they did not think of Jesus, but cried out in terror, saying,

"It is a spirit." Then the clear sweet voice of their Master rose over the sound of the wind and the waves, "Be of good cheer, it is I, be not afraid." And Peter, full of glad faith, cried out, "Lord, if it be Thou, bid me come unto Thee on the water."

When Jesus said "Come," Peter climbed over the side of the boat and began to walk toward Jesus, but when a strong wind drove the waves upon him he lost sight of the Lord for a moment, and he was afraid.

"Lord, save me!" he cried, and began to sink.

Then Jesus stretched out His hand and caught Peter, saying, "O thou of little faith, wherefore didst thou doubt?"

When they both entered the ship the wind ceased, and while the disciples wondered and worshipped, saying, "Of a truth Thou art the Son of God," they found themselves at the land not far from Capernaum.

It was on the white beach of pebbles and shells that bordered the plain of Gennesaret where they moored the boat in the early morning, and as soon as the people saw them they began bringing their sick friends to Jesus. Many were too ill to walk, and were brought on little beds or mattresses and laid at Jesus's feet, and there they were healed if they but touched the hem of His garment.

Many of those who brought the sick to Jesus had been with Him on the mountain side, and had eaten of the wonderful bread of heaven that He had broken for them. They believed that He could do anything that He would.

The people whose hearts were set upon making Jesus their king followed Him wherever He went. Some who had been with Him when He made bread for the great company on the hillside at Bethsaida-Julias found Him teaching in the synagogue at Capernaum.

"Teacher, when camest thou hither?" they said. Jesus, knowing that they cared more for His gifts than for His teaching, said, "Ye seek me, not because ye saw the miracles, but because ye did eat of the loaves and were filled," and told them that they should not labor for the food that perishes, but for that which endures forever.

They still wished Him to do some wonder, or show them how to work wonders, for they asked Him what they should do to work the works of God

"This is the work of God," He said, "That ye believe on Him whom He hath sent." Still they remembered the miracle of the bread.

"What sign showest Thou?" they said, "Our fathers did eat manna in the desert." Then He spoke plainly to them of Himself.

"The bread of God is He which cometh down from heaven, and giveth life unto the world." One more spiritual than the rest said reverently, "Lord, evermore give us this bread."

Then Jesus spoke those words about Himself that turned many away from Him. He showed them that He could never be what they expected Him to be—an earthly king. He had only the things of the Spirit to give them, and He called them to a kingdom that could be seen only with spiritual sight.

"I am the bread of life," He said, "He that cometh to me shall never hunger; and he that believeth on me shall never thirst. All that the Father giveth me shall come to me, and him that cometh to me I will in no wise cast out."

The Jews were offended with Him because He had said, "I came down from heaven." "I am the living bread which came down from heaven," He said. "If any man eat of this bread he shall live forever; and the bread that I will give is my flesh which I will give for the life of the world."

Then the Jews were vexed and turned to talk among themselves. They could not understand what He meant, but they saw plainly that He was not going to agree with their plan to make Him the King of the Jews, who would lead them out of their bondage to the Romans, and establish them forever as a nation.

They did not want to follow Him, but they wanted Him to follow their plan. And as for His talk about being the "bread of life,"—"This is an hard saying," they said, "who can hear it?"

While they murmured Jesus said,

"Doth this offend you? What and if you shall see the Son of Man ascending where He was before?"

"*It is the Spirit that quickeneth; the flesh profiteth nothing; the words that I speak unto you, they are Spirit, and they are life.*"

Then they knew that He meant something above what they could see, or what they wanted, and many turned away from Him and went to their homes disappointed. He had said, "there are some of you that believe not," and it was true. Jesus turned to the twelve who stood in silence near Him,

"Will ye also go away?" He said.

Loving, impulsive Peter cried out,

"Lord, to whom shall we go? Thou hast the words of eternal life, and we believe and are sure that Thou art that Christ, the Son of the living God."

"Did I not choose you twelve," said Jesus, "and one of you is a devil."

Already evil spirits had tried to turn Judas away from the Lord by tempting him, and he had let them into his heart. And Jesus, who knew all men, saw them there.

CHAPTER XXV.

A JOURNEY WITH JESUS.

Jesus went away with His disciples into the "borders of Tyre and Sidon." He did not go to the Passover feast, for the anger of the Jews had been growing more violent toward Him and His disciples, and he took the twelve away from the crowded towns around the Lake into the parts that bordered upon a heathen country. He could do far more for the simple-hearted heathen than for Jews who believed themselves to be wise and religious.

When it was known that the young teacher of Nazareth was among them some came to Him who were not Jews. One was a Syrian woman whose

JESUS IN THE WHEAT FIELDS.

daughter was troubled by an evil spirit, and she begged Jesus to have mercy upon her. The disciples were not pleased to have her follow them with strange cries in another language. They believed that the works of Jesus were for the Jews only, and so they begged Him to send her away. Jesus was silent, for He knew all hearts, and saw faith growing in the heart of the poor woman.

He said, trying her faith,

"It is not meet to take the children's bread and cast it to dogs."

"Truth, Lord," she said, "yet the dogs eat of the crumbs which fall from their master's table."

Then Jesus hid Himself no longer from her faith, but said.

"O woman, great is thy faith! be it unto thee even as thou wilt." And her daughter was cured that very hour.

Jesus did not go down by the great sea, though He could see it lying like blue and silver across the west whenever He came to a hilltop as they journeyed, but He went northward to the hills that lie around the mountains of Lebanon. Upon these mountains grew the cedars that Solomon's servants cut down and carried to Jerusalem for the building of the Holy House. They stopped in the Lebanon villages, and came at length to the foot of Mount Hermon, and to the Jordan, crossing over and passing near the place where the great company who followed Jesus had been fed. As they came into Decapolis on the east side of the lake of Gennesaret the people came to Him in crowds again for healing. There He healed a man who could neither hear nor speak.

Coming to Gadara He found crowds coming with their sick for healing. Eight months before He had healed a poor man in whom was a legion of devils, casting them out into a herd of swine, and they had begged Him to leave their coast for they were afraid of Him, but now they were glad to come to Him for healing. No doubt the man who had been healed had told them of the gentleness of Jesus, and of His wonderful words, and had brought many to Him.

It was in Bethsaida-Julias that Jesus once opened the eyes of a blind man. He did not see clearly at first, but when Jesus laid His hand a second time upon his eyes he saw quite well, and was so grateful that he wanted to go and tell all his friends about it, but Jesus told him to go quietly home.

Two blind men followed Him also, crying, "Thou Son of David, have mercy on us!" They followed Him into a house and there Jesus asked, "Believe ye that I am able to do this?" "Yea, Lord," they said.

JESUS WALKING ON THE WAVES.

"According to your faith be it unto you," He said, touching their eyes, and their eyes were opened at once.

Though Jesus had said, "See that no man know it," yet they told it through all that country.

CHAPTER XXVI.

THE CHRISTIAN SABBATH—PETER'S CONFESSION OF FAITH.

Jesus was walking with His disciples one Sabbath day and talking of the Kingdom of Heaven when they came to a field of ripe grain. They had been gathering food for their souls from the teachings of Jesus, and had forgotten to take food for their bodies until they saw the ripe grain and knew that they were hungry. Some of them began to take the heads of wheat (or barley), to rub them in their hands to separate the grain from the chaff, and eat the kernels of wheat.

Following close after them were some men who had been told to watch Jesus and His disciples, and see if anything could be brought against them.

They held very strict views about keeping the Sabbath, as all Pharisees did, and here they saw something that might be called breaking the Sabbath, for were they not really reaping the wheat, and sifting it through their hands?

"Behold thy disciples do that which is not lawful to do upon the Sabbath day," they said. "The Son of Man," said Jesus, "is Lord even of the Sabbath day."

Another Sabbath He entered into a synagogue and taught. Among the people stood a man who had a helpless and withered hand. The same Pharisees who had followed Jesus as spies when He walked through the grain-fields were watching Him in the Synagogue to see if He would heal on the Sabbath. He knew their thoughts, and called the man, saying, "Rise up and stand forth in the midst."

The man rose, and while he stood waiting, Jesus turned to the Pharisees who were eagerly watching to see if Jesus would do something that was forbidden in their law, and said,

"Is it lawful on the Sabbath days to do good, or to do evil? To save life or to destroy it?" The Pharisees dared not answer, and Jesus, looking round upon them all, said to the man, "Stretch forth thy hand."

The man obeyed. Although he had not been able to raise his hand, he stretched it forth, and it became as whole and as strong as the other.

The Pharisees went away very angry, and tried to make a plan among themselves for bringing Jesus into trouble.

Jesus came to fill the law about the Sabbath full of the spirit of heaven ; to teach love and service to the neighbor, as well as the love and worship of God, but they could not understand Him.

Jesus was near the end of His ministry to the people east of the Jordan in the country called Decapolis. They were not like the Galilean Jews, they were half heathen people who lived among the wild, rocky hills of that region. They were poor and ignorant, yet they were more ready to accept the gospel than the wise and wicked Pharisees had been.

He had been kind to them in their sickness and poverty, and they followed Him with their sick, and lame, and deaf, and blind, leaving them at His feet until they arose praising God that they had been saved from their sufferings.

Jesus had been teaching in the wild mountain country, and the people would not leave Him to go away to their homes. After three days Jesus said to His disciples, "I have compassion on the multitude because they continue with me now three days and have nothing to eat, and I will not send them away fasting lest they faint by the way."

The disciples did not remember the Lord's power to create bread, and wondered where they should find it in the wilderness to feed such a great multitude.

But when Jesus knew that they had seven loves of barley bread and a few little fishes He told the people to sit down on the ground, and after giving thanks over the loaves and the fishes, He divided them and gave to His disciples, and the disciples gave to the people. There were four thousand men beside women and children who took the bread that came from the Lord's hands. After all had eaten and were filled they took up seven baskets of the food that was left.

Jesus, though He could create food for the people, taught them to use it wisely and waste nothing.

When the people had been sent to their homes, Jesus, with His disciples, took a fishing boat and crossed the Lake only to find the Pharisees there ready to question Him, and to tempt Him to show them some great sign from heaven.

He told them that they could read the signs of the coming weather in the sky, but they could not see the signs of the times.

Only a wicked people look for a sign, He said, and no sign should be given except the sign that Jonah gave to the Ninevites—a call to repentance.

Then He left them, for He saw the hardness of their hearts.

Again they took their journey in the little ship to the northern end of the Lake, and after landing, followed the east side of Jordan until they passed near the place where the five thousand had been fed by a miracle as they sat on the green hillside.

The disciples found that they had forgotten to bring bread with them. They remembered, perhaps, that they had here eaten the bread that the Lord had created ; but the heart of Jesus was heavy with the thought of the unbelief of the people He had come to save, and He said,

"Take heed and beware of the leaven of the Pharisees and the Sadducees."

The disciples did not understand Him, and wondered if He spoke thus because they had not brought bread.

Then Jesus, seeing that they had but little faith, reminded them of the supper on the hillside, when more than five thousand were fed, and of that later meal among the rocky hills of Decapolis, when four thousand and more were fed, and that they did not need to be concerned about food for the body so much as to beware of the false teaching of the Pharisees and of the Sadducees.

They walked still further north, directly toward that beautiful mountain that lifts its head, white with the glistening snow, high above the hills that lead up to it, so that it may be seen over the larger part of Palestine.

They came to Cæsarea Philippi, one of the most beautiful places in the world. It lay in the green lap of Mount Hermon high above the sea, and shut in by cliffs and forests. The upper springs of the Jordan are here. They leap out of a great cavern in the side of the mountain—a river of clear, cold water.

The old Greeks loved the place, and built there a temple to the god of nature, but after the Romans came it was named for the Emperor and Philip the Tetrarch. Here there were more Gentiles than Jews, for it was a gay town in the summer, and people from other towns came to this city of palaces, temples, baths, theatres, and statues. These people did not wish to hear the words of Jesus, but the coolness and beauty of the country around this birthplace of the Jordan made it a fit place to bring His disciples where they could talk over the things of the kingdom without being disturbed by the Pharisees.

Here He was able to pray alone, and once, after prayer, He questioned His disciples about Himself.

"Whom say the people that I am?" He asked.   They remembered their talks with the people and said,   "John the Baptist, but some say Elias, and others say that one of the old prophets is risen again."   "But whom say ye that I am?" He asked.   Then Peter, the believing disciple, made his confession of faith,—

"Thou art the Christ, the Son of the living God."   Jesus was glad to hear this, for many had come to doubt Him, and many had gone away from Him since they knew that He would not be an earthly king.

"Blessed art thou Simon, son of Jonas," He said, "for flesh and blood hath not revealed it unto thee, but my Father which is in Heaven."

He saw that Peter's faith in the truth was like his name, which means "a rock," and so He said,

"Thou art Peter, and on this rock will I build my church, and the gates of hell shall not prevail against it."

Peter's faith in the truth was also in the hearts of the other disciples for whom He spoke, and Jesus saw that they could now bear what he had to say to them without going away.

He told them that He must soon go to Jerusalem and suffer many things from the chief priests and the scribes and the elders, and that He should be killed by them, and rise again from the dead the third day.

Even Peter's faith was shaken by this.   How could the Son of God be killed?   He could not believe His Master meant it so.

"Be it far from thee, Lord," he said, "this shall not be unto thee."

Jesus saw the spirit of fear and unbelief rising up in Peter, and to this— not to Peter himself—Jesus said,

"Get thee behind me, Satan; thou art an offence unto me; for thou savourest not the things that be of God, but those that be of men."

Then He plainly told them what they must be ready to meet if they followed Him.   They must not hope for any earthly honors or riches, and they must put aside their own wishes and obey the Lord alone.

He told them that whoever wished to live for this world alone would lose all, but whoever was willing to lose all for His sake should find eternal life.

"For what is a man profited," He said, "if he shall gain the whole world and lose his own soul, or what shall a man give in exchange for his soul?"

CHAPTER XXVII.

"AND WE BEHELD HIS GLORY"—A FATHER'S FAITH.

Jesus stayed near Cæsarea Philippi with His disciples for a week. The villagers were cutting the ripe grain, the vineyards were rich with clusters of the rich grapes that grew on the Lebanon hills, and the olives were ripening for the time when they would be put in the presses to make the delicious "oil olive." In that week He must have had many wonderful talks with the villagers.

One evening, as they had come over the lower hills of Hermon, Jesus left the disciples to wait for Him below, taking only Peter and the brothers James and John with Him up the mount. They did not go to the very top but rested on one of the lower peaks. While Jesus went a little distance from them to pray, the three disciples, wrapped in their thick mantles, lay down to wait for Him. In that high clear air they seemed very near heaven. The stars seemed almost as near as the lights in the villages below. They were tired, and watching their Master in prayer, they fell asleep. While they slept they seemed to see a change in the face of Jesus as He prayed. It grew light with a strange inward glory, and all His garments became white and glistening like the snows of Hermon in the sun. They also saw two men with Him whom they seemed to know were Moses and Elias, who had gone to heaven centuries before.

They also heard them talking with Jesus, and they spoke of the same thing that had troubled Peter when Jesus had spoken of it—that He should die at Jerusalem.

They awoke out of sleep, but the vision did not pass away like a dream, they still saw it all.

But as it began to melt away, Peter said, hardly knowing what he said,

" Master, it is good for us to be here, and let us make three tabernacles, one for Thee, and one for Moses, and one for Elias."

Then the glory around Jesus grew until it seemed like a bright cloud at sunset, and it came and wrapt them around in its soft brightness, and they were afraid.

In the silence they heard a Divine voice, saying,

" This is My beloved Son ; hear Him."

(206)

When the voice was passed they looked up and saw Jesus there alone. He was bending over them, touching them tenderly, and saying,

"Arise, and be not afraid."

As they came down the mountain He told them to tell no one of the vision until after He had risen from the dead.

It seemed to the disciples, no doubt, like coming down from heaven to earth when after a long walk and talk with Jesus in the summer morning they came near the village they had left, and found the people—among them some Jewish lawyers—disputing with the group of disciples there. As soon as they saw Jesus they all ran to Him, and greeted Him.

One of the men explained what they were disputing about.

" Master," he said, " I have brought unto thee my son which hath a dumb spirit," and he described the frightful state into which it had brought his boy, and added that the disciples could not cast it out.

" Bring him to me," said Jesus, and they brought him, the evil spirit within him throwing him into convulsions as they laid him at Jesus' feet.

"How long is it ago since this came to him ?" said Jesus.

"Of a child," said the father, "and ofttimes it hath cast him into the fire and into the waters to destroy him, but if thou canst do anything, have compassion on us, and help us." Jesus said,

" If thou canst believe, all things are possible to him that believeth."

Then the poor father cried out with tears, "Lord, I believe ; help thou mine unbelief ! "

The Lord did not wait for greater faith than this. He charged the evil spirit to come out of the boy, and after a great struggle it left him as one dead, but Jesus took him by the hand and he arose.

" Why could not we cast him out ? " said the disciples afterward.

" This kind," said Jesus, can come forth by nothing but by prayer and fasting."

As they turned their steps toward home—the Lake side in Galilee—Jesus again spoke of the work that lay before Him. The disciples listened sadly, but could not understand why He should speak of being killed, and of rising again from the dead, and they dared not ask Him questions about it.

CHAPTER XXVIII.

THE LORD AND THE LITTLE ONES—LEAVING GALILEE.

As the Lord and His disciples walked over the hills into Galilee some of them fell behind wondering among themselves what He could mean when He spoke of being killed and of rising again. Perhaps they thought it only a sadness that would pass away, and so full of faith in His power were they that they could not believe that One who could raise the dead could Himself die.

"He will be a King," they thought, and began to wonder who among them would be chosen to be greatest in His Kingdom, and even to quarrel about it.

After they had reached Capernaum, and were at home again—probably in Peter's house—Jesus said to them,

"What was it that ye disputed among yourselves by the way?"

There was no word from any one of them, for they were ashamed. Then the Lord sat down, and calling the twelve around Him, said gently,

"If any man desire to be first, the same shall be last of all, and servant of all."

A little child stood near listening, and wishing, perhaps, that he might be a grown man so that he also could be a disciple.

Making room for him in the midst of them all, He called the child, Peter's child, perhaps, who came joyfully to Him. Taking Him tenderly in His arms He said,

"Whosoever shall receive one of such children in my name receiveth me, and whosoever shall receive me, receiveth not me, but Him that sent me."

And He taught His disciples to be humble as a little child in these beautiful words :

"Except ye be converted, and become as little children, ye shall not enter into the Kingdom of Heaven."

"Take heed that ye despise not one of these little ones, for I say unto you that in heaven their angels do always behold the face of my Father which is in heaven."

He also told them of the love of the Father in seeking His lost children. That if a shepherd had but lost one of his hundred sheep, he would leave all the others to go out into the wild mountains to look for the lost sheep. How much more would the Father do for His own, and especially for His little ones.

"Even so," He said, "it is not the will of your Father, which is in heaven, that one of these little ones should perish."

Before going to the Feast at Jerusalem the Lord Jesus said many things to His disciples that would help them to be loving and forgiving toward each other and all the world, for they were very soon going to meet trouble which would try their love and their faith. He told them to deal gently with those who had done wrong, that they might win them back to the right way. He told them that they should have help from heaven when they asked for it, even if there should be only two to ask.

"For where two or three are gathered together in my name," He said, "there am I in the midst of them."

"How oft shall my brother sin against me, and I forgive him?" asked Peter, "till seven times?"

"Until seventy times seven," said Jesus, and He did not mean that we should even count the number of times that we forgive.

Then He told them a story of a forgiving king and an unforgiving servant that you may read in the eighteenth chapter of Matthew.

At the time of the Feast of Tabernacles, the people went up to Jerusalem to offer gifts in the golden Temple for the harvest that the Lord had given them, and to join in a praise service there.

They brought oil, and wine, and wheat, and barley; dates, pomegranates, and figs—something of all they had gathered, and while they marched toward the holy city they sang joyful songs that David had written long before. When they reached Jerusalem they built bowers of branches cut from the trees and lived in them for a week.

Even in the city the people came out of their houses and lived in bowers on the streets and public squares, or upon the flat roofs of the houses, and the hillsides round were covered with the green booths.

The brothers of Jesus came down to Capernaum on their way to the Feast at Jerusalem, and they asked their elder Brother to go also into Judea and show Himself to the world, that His miracles might be seen of all, for they did not believe in Him yet. But Jesus said,

"My time is not yet come, but your time is always ready."

So they went on their journey, and Jesus stayed in Galilee.

After a few days He set His face toward Jerusalem, taking the shortest way through Samaria. The Samaritans were not friendly to the Jews, and the disciples, who had been sent on before to find lodging for the company in a village, were not allowed to bring their Master there.

The gentle John and his brother James were angry that unkindness was shown to Jesus, and wished to call down fire from heaven to destroy the villagers, but Jesus said,

"Ye know not what manner of spirit ye are of, for the Son of Man has not come to destroy men's lives, but to save them."

And they went to another village. On the way they found men who wished to follow Jesus as the disciples did, but while some were ready to leave all, others wished to first bid their friends farewell, or bury their dead, but Jesus saw something in their hearts that showed that they were not fit for the Kingdom of God.

There were many beside the twelve who fully believed in Jesus, and were ready to tell others of the coming kingdom, so He sent them out to all the places where he intended to go, until there were seventy of them preaching the good news. They went, saying, "The Kingdom of God is come unto you," and they healed the sick in Jesus' name. When they returned they were full of joy, saying,

"Lord, even the devils are subject unto us through Thy name." But Jesus said, "Rejoice not that the spirits are subject unto you, but rather rejoice because your names are written in heaven."

CHAPTER XXIX.

AT THE HOUSE OF MARTHA—THE GOOD SHEPHERD.

While Jesus was on His way to Jerusalem a lawyer came and asked Him questions. He did not want to be a disciple, yet he asked what he should do to have eternal life.

Jesus asked him what the commandments said about it, and the lawyer repeated the two great commandments concerning love to the Lord and to the neighbor.

"Thou hast answered right," Jesus replied. "This do and thou shalt live."

"And who is my neighbor?" said the lawyer.

THE MOTHERS OF JERUSALEM.

Then Jesus told a story of a man who went down to Jericho, and was nearly killed by thieves. A priest came that way and when he saw a man who needed help he passed by on the other side of the road. So did a Levite, one of the helpers in the temple worship, but a Samaritan (and the Samaritans were despised by the Jews) came that way, and he stopped in pity for the poor man, dressed his wounds, set him upon his own beast and brought him to an inn and took care of him. When he left the inn he also left money for his care, with the promise of more if it should be needed. Then Jesus asked the lawyer which of these three men was neighbor to him who fell among thieves.

"He that showed mercy on him," said the lawyer. Then said Jesus unto him,

"Go thou and do likewise."

As Jesus came near to Jerusalem He passed through Bethany, a little town at the foot of the Mount of Olives, where perhaps some of His disciples had been preaching the new gospel before Him. There He was gladly received into the house of Martha, who prepared the table with her own hands to offer the best in her house to her honored Guest. She had a brother named Lazarus, who was probably at the feast in Jerusalem, and a younger sister named Mary who loved to listen to every word that Jesus spoke. As every family built a bower of branches during this feast to remind them that for forty years they lived in such houses in the wilderness while coming out of Egypt, there must have been one in the court of Martha's house, and there, perhaps, Jesus rested while Mary sat at His feet and heard His word.

Martha was very busy serving her honored guest, and thought Mary ought to help her in the house, but Jesus said, "Martha, Martha, thou art careful and troubled about many things; but one thing is needful, and Mary hath chosen that good part which shall not be taken away from her."

When the Feast of Tabernacles was at its height Jesus came up to the Temple at Jerusalem. The people had been looking for Him, and as soon as the noble, earnest-faced young Teacher was seen walking in the marble court of the Temple they thronged around Him to hear Him teach, or to see if He would do any miracle.

Some wondered at His wisdom and His doctrine, and asked where it came from, "My doctrine is not mine," He said, "but His that sent me. If any man will do His will he shall know of the doctrine."

He taught them many things that day, and hinted at the same thing that had troubled His disciples, and these were His words,

JESUS IN THE HOUSE AT BETHANY.

"Yet a little while am I with you, and then I go unto Him that sent me. Ye shall seek me and shall not find me, and where I am thither ye cannot come."

The priests, the scribes, and the Pharisees were listening, and He knew that their hearts were too full of pride and self-love to receive His word. They could not go to Him, for they would not let Him come into their hearts.

On the last day, the great day of the Feast, Jesus stood and cried to the people who were about to go back to their homes. His great heart was breaking to bring them into the Kingdom of Heaven, and He knew that they would be scattered as sheep having no shepherd.

"If any man thirst," He cried, "let him come unto me and drink." And He then promised to such as believe the Holy Spirit to dwell in them, and to flow out toward all the world like rivers of living water.

So wonderfully did He preach that many said, "Of a truth this is a prophet," and others said, "This is the Christ," while others were filled with anger and wished to arrest Him. Indeed, when the priests· and Pharisees urged the officers to take Him, they said,

"Never man spake like this man," and they would not lay hands on Him.

But Nicodemus, a learned doctor of the law, was a friend of Jesus. He it was who had a talk with Him one night under the olive trees about the Spirit—the breath of God, and he with wise words turned the hatred of the Jews away from Jesus for the time, and they went to their own houses.

Jesus taught in the Temple again the next day, and all the people came to listen.

It was here, perhaps, that the wicked Scribes and Pharisees brought to Him a poor woman who had sinned. They told Him that according to the law she ought to be stoned, and asked what He would say about it. He did not answer, but seemed to be writing on the ground before Him as though He did not hear them. At last, because they would have an answer He looked at them saying,

"He that is without sin among you, let him cast the first stone," and He wrote again on the ground. No one answered Jesus, but one by one they went away too much ashamed to speak. "Hath no man condemned thee?" asked Jesus of the woman standing sorrowful and alone.

"No man, Lord," she said.

"Neither do I condemn thee," He said, "go and sin no more."

Then Jesus sitting in the Treasury of the Temple said,

THE GOOD SAMARITAN.

"I am the light of the world. He that followeth me shall not walk in darkness but shall have the light of life."

Many other things He said that His enemies tried to turn against Him, and the healing on the Sabbath day of a man who had been born blind stirred the anger of the Jews against Him, so that they sought by much questioning to accuse Jesus of sin, not knowing that they were themselves spiritually blind.

But He turned from them to call to the people again as He did on the last day of the Feast, for in His love and pity He longed to bring the lost children of Israel to Himself that He might bless them, as a shepherd brings back the sheep that stray from the fold.

"I am the Good Shephered; and I know my own, and my own know me," said Jesus, "even as the Father knoweth me, and I know the Father; and I lay down my life for the sheep, and other sheep I have which are not of this fold; them also I must bring, and they shall hear my voice; and they shall become one flock, one Shepherd."

Other beautiful and blessed words He said about the Shepherd and His flock which are written in the tenth chapter of the Gospel of John, but the learned Jews would not listen to Him, and thrice tried to kill Him by stoning Him, but they could not harm Him, for His time had not come.

Then he went away beyond Jordan, where John first baptized, and many believed on Him there.

CHAPTER XXX.

THE LESSON STORIES OF JESUS.

When Jesus was at prayer His disciples stood reverently apart from Him, and one day a disciple came near when he had ceased and said,

"Lord, teach us to pray, as John also taught his disciples."

Then the Lord taught them the beautiful prayer that is now said daily all around the world, and known to every one of us, beginning, "Our Father which art in heaven, Hallowed be Thy name."

And He told them how pleased God is to have His children ask Him for what they need, or come to Him in trouble.

"Ask, and it shall be given you," He said; "seek, and ye shall find; knock and it shall be opened unto you."

THE RETURN OF THE PRODIGAL.

"If a son shall ask bread of any of you that is a father, will he give him a stone? or if he ask a fish, will he for a fish give him a serpent?"

"If ye then, being evil, know how to give good gifts unto your children, how much more shall your Heavenly Father give good gifts to them that ask Him?"

It was while the Lord was teaching in the country called Peræa, east of Jordan, that He told many things that His disciples remembered and wrote in a book afterward, when the Holy Spirit had come to "bring all things to their remembrance," as He had promised.

He had been teaching three years, and was thirty-three years of age.

Some of the people who lived at Bethabara, by Jordan, were present when He was baptized by John, and they were glad to have him stay among them and teach, for they were a kindly people, and though not learned like the men who were often to be found in the Temple courts and in the Synagogues, they were the common people who, hearing the word and loving it, were wiser than the Pharisees.

The Lord told many stories that these people would remember, and afterward understand by the teaching of His Spirit which He said would be given to them. You will read all of them in the Gospels, but here we cannot tell them all.

The story of "The Fig-tree in the Vineyard," "The Great Supper," and "The Foolish Rich Man" were stories of warning to those who were turning away from the things of heaven to the things of the world, and they were meant for all who should read them in the ages of the world.

So were the three stories—they are called "parables" in the Gospels—of the lost things; "The lost sheep," "The lost piece of money," and "The lost son." They were given to us to show the great love of the Heavenly Father for His children, and His constant care in seeking for them when they are wandering away from Him. These stories are the voice of the Father always and everywhere calling His children home, and many a poor soul has turned homeward with tears of repentance after reading them.

One of these stories of lost things will be told here, but it is far more beautiful in the language of the Scriptures.

There was once a rich man who had two sons, and the younger one came to him and said,

"Father, give me the portion of goods that falleth to me."

And so the father divided his property, and gave the younger brother his share. In a few days he had gathered it all together and settled his affairs so that he could go away.   He went into a distant country, and there he spent all that he had among bad people who seemed to be his friends, but were really his worst enemies.

When all that he had was spent there came a time of great trouble. There was very little food in the land, for there was a famine, and he was obliged to go to work for the little he could get.   It was not easy to find work, for the only thing he could do was to hire himself to a man who kept pigs.   His work was to stay in the fields and feed them with husks, the hard pods of the carob tree.   Sometimes he was so hungry that he would have been glad to eat even these, but "no man gave unto him."   Then the young man "came to himself."

"How many hired servants of my father have bread enough and to spare," he said, "and I perish with hunger!

"I will arise and go to my father, and I will say to him, 'Father, I have sinned against heaven and before thee, and am no more worthy to be called thy son : make me as one of thy hired servants.' "

The father must have been watching for his lost boy, for while he was yet a great way off he saw him, and ran to meet him.   He put his arms around him and kissed him without once speaking of his sins, and he called his servants to bring the best robe and put it on him, and a ring for his hand, and shoes for his feet, and then to kill the fatted calf to make a feast for all,

"For," he said "this my son was dead, and is alive again ; he was lost, and is found."

The elder son had been away in the field but when he came home heard music and dancing, and called to a servant to ask what these things meant. When he had heard he was very angry, and would not go in.   His father came out to beg him to come in and greet his brother, but he said,

"Lo, these many years do I serve thee, neither transgressed I at any time thy commandment, and yet thou never gavest me a kid, that I might make merry with my friends."   But the father said,

"Son, thou art ever with me, and all that I have is thine.   It was meet that we should make merry and be glad, for this thy brother was dead, and is alive again, and was lost and is found."

There are other stories told by Jesus while in Peræa, which you will find in the gospel by Luke, the beloved physician.   One is about the "Unjust Steward," and another is the story of the "Unjust Judge."   Still another is called "Dives and Lazarus," or the "Rich man and the Beggar."

The parable of "The Pharisee and the Publican," describes two men who went up into the temple to pray; the one a Pharisee, and the other a publican.

The Pharisee prayed with *himself,* thus, " God, I thank thee that I am not as other men are, or even as this publican. I fast twice a week. I give tithes of all I possess."

And the publican, standing afar off, dared not even lift his eyes to heaven, but smote upon his breast, saying, "God be merciful to me a sinner!"

"This man," said Jesus, "went down to his house justified rather than the other; for every one that exalteth himself shall be abased, and he that humbleth himself shall be exalted."

—

CHAPTER XXXI.

THE VOICE THAT WAKED THE DEAD—THE CHILDREN OF THE KINGDOM.

While Jesus and His disciples were still east of the Jordan trouble fell upon the happy home in Bethany where Jesus had been an honored guest. A messenger was sent to Jesus in great haste, saying,

"Lord, behold, he whom thou lovest is sick."

It was from Mary and Martha concerning their brother Lazarus.

Jesus sent the messenger back with this message,

"This sickness is not unto death, but for the glory of God, that the Son of God might be glorified thereby," and He remained two days longer where He was. Then He said,

"Let us go into Judea again."

The disciples reminded Him that the Jews there had tried to take His life.

"Our friend Lazarus sleepeth," said Jesus, "but I go that I may awaken him out of sleep."

The disciples thought that if he slept he was doing very well, until Jesus told them plainly,

"Lazarus is dead."

Then Thomas was full of sorrow and said,

"Let us also go that we may die with him."

Bethany was not far from Jerusalem, and when they reached the house of Martha, Lazarus had been dead four days, and was placed in a rock tomb.

JESUS WEPT.

Many Jews from Jerusalem had come out to Bethany to comfort Mary and Martha, and to mourn for their friend Lazarus.

When Martha heard that Jesus was coming she ran to meet Him, but Mary sat still in the house. She thought, perhaps, that He had come too late, and the same thought may have been in Martha's mind when she said,

"Lord, if thou hadst been here my brother had not died, but I know that even now whatsoever thou wilt ask of God, God will give it thee."

"Thy brother shall rise again," said Jesus.

I know that he shall rise again in the resurrection at the last day," she said.

Then Jesus spoke those heavenly words that have been the comfort of the sorrowful ever since,

"I am the resurrection and the life : he that believeth in me, though he were dead, yet shall he live : and whosoever liveth and believeth in me shall never die. Believest thou this?"

"Yea, Lord," answered Martha, "I believe that thou art the Christ, the Son of God which should come into the world."

Then she called Mary quietly, so that the people who were noisily wailing should not hear.

"The Master is come and calleth for thee," she said.

Then Mary rose quickly and went to meet Jesus. The people who were trying to comfort her followed her, for they thought she was going to the tomb to weep there ; but they saw her go to meet Jesus and fall at His feet saying, as Martha did,

"Lord, if thou hadst been here, my brother had not died."

When Jesus saw the tears of Mary and her sister and their friends He wept also, not for Lazarus, but His heart was moved for them, and He shared their sorrow.

They brought Him to the tomb—a cave with a stone lying upon it. When He asked them to take away the stone Martha's faith began to fail ; but the stone was rolled away, and when Jesus had prayed He called with a loud voice,

"Lazarus, come forth!"

And all who were bending forward toward the low, dark door of the tomb saw a man wrapped in linen come forth from the darkness and try to ascend the stone steps.

"Loose him and let him go," said Jesus. And then there was a scene

THE PHARISEE AND THE PUBLICAN.

so full of sacred joy that John, the disciple, who tells the story, does not show it to us.

After this many believed in Jesus, but others went and told the Pharisees all about it.

It was spring in Peræa, and the valley of the Jordan was full of the singing of birds and the color of blooming trees and wild flowers, while in the fields the young wheat was growing. The people thronged to Jesus in crowds, for He taught them in the open air. The disciples were busy with the people, explaining to the dull, listening to those who wished to ask something of the Master, or keeping back the curious. This had to be done in every village through which they passed. There were many mothers with their children around them who came out of their low white houses to follow Jesus in the way, and to listen when He sat down to teach.

The mothers loved to have the Rabbi's bless their children, for since the days of Abraham, Isaac and Jacob, the blessing of a good man means much to the Israelite.

One day some mothers brought their little ones to Jesus, and begged Him to bless them. The disciples told the mothers to stand back, and not trouble the Master while he was teaching. Jesus knew what they were saying, and He called them unto Him and said,

"Suffer little children to come unto me, and forbid them not, for of such is the Kingdom of God. Verily I say unto you, whosoever shall not receive the Kingdom of God as a little child shall in no wise enter therein."

In this way he made it clear to His disciples, to the mothers, and to all who have read His word since that day, that every child is a citizen of the Lord's Kingdom, and dear to the heart of the King.

Perhaps the mothers had heard that the Lord was about to leave the country east of Jordan to go up to Jerusalem, and they longed to have their little ones share in the blessing they had received while sitting at the feet of the great Teacher and learning of Him, for soon after He crossed the Jordan, and, teaching as he went, set His face toward Jerusalem.

CHAPTER XXXII.

THE YOUNG MAN THAT JESUS LOVED.

A rich young ruler came running after Jesus one day, saying,
"Good Master, what shall I do to inherit eternal life?"

So eager was he to know that he knelt before Jesus by the road side.

Jesus spoke gently to him telling him that God alone is good, and that
he knew the commandments that God had given.

"All these have I kept from my youth up," said the young man.

As Jesus looked upon him He saw that he was really trying to be good,
and hoping that he could do some great and good act that would give him a
certain entrance into heaven. He had been taught by the Rabbis that men
were saved by keeping the law and doing outward works of righteousness.
He did not know that heaven must begin in his own heart.

Jesus, reading his heart, loved him, and longed to have him know the
truth.

"Yet lackest thou one thing," he said, "sell all that thou hast and dis-
tribute unto the poor, and thou shalt have treasure in heaven; and come,
follow me."

When he heard these words the young man turned away and lost the
eager look with which he had come to the Lord's feet. He was very sorrowful, for he was very rich, and he found that he loved his riches more than he
loved anything else.

"How hardly," said Jesus, "shall they that have riches enter into the
Kingdom of God! For it is easier for a camel to go through a needle's eye
than for a rich man to enter the Kingdom of God."

"Who then can be saved?" asked one.

"The things which are impossible with men, are possible with God," He
said.

"Lo, we have left all," said Peter, "and followed Thee," and then the Lord
gave to His disciples that promise that has been proven true by millions of
His children for ages past,—

"There is no man who hath left house or parents, or brethren, or wife,
or children for the Kingdom of God's sake, who shall not receive manifold
more in this present time, and in the world to come life everlasting."

CHAPTER XXXIII.

THE LAST JOURNEY TO JERUSALEM.

When Jesus and His disciples were finally on the way to Jerusalem Jesus went before them, and the shadow of the great trial He was about to suffer cast its shadow upon Him. The disciples saw it, and Mark says that "they were amazed; and as they followed, they were afraid." He told them all about the trial and the death that lay before Him, but so unwilling were they to believe it, and so sure were they that He would be made king of the Jews, that two of them brought their mother to Jesus to ask that her two sons might sit next to Him when He should come to the throne.

"Ye know not what ye ask," He said, "can ye drink of the cup that I drink of? and be baptized with the baptism that I am baptized with?" and they said,

"We can," not knowing that He spoke of suffering and death.

He told them that though they would indeed drink of His cup, He had no honors to give them.

Then, when the others were vexed with James and John for their foolish request, He talked to them all tenderly about the grace of humility.

"Whosoever of you who will be chiefest," He said, "shall be servant of all. For even the Son of Man came not to be ministered unto, but to minister, and to give His life a ransom for many."

It was the time of the Passover Feast at Jerusalem, and as they crossed at the Fords of Jordan and went over the Jericho plain they must have joined some of the groups of joyful people who were going up to the Feast, some on camels and asses, and some walking beside the beasts bearing tents or merchandise. The valley of the Jordan was bright with the freshness of spring, and as they came near Jericho with its rose-gardens, and orchards, and feathery palms, it looked like the gardens of Paradise. It was sometimes called Jericho "the perfumed" because of its great gardens of roses, and its balsam plantations from which they made perfumes that were sold in all the East. It was warm even in winter there, and no frosts destroyed its tropical fruits and flowers. The rich plain was made fertile by two springs that sent their waters through trenches all through these gardens and orchards. One is called the "Elisha Spring," because the prophet made its poisonous waters pure by casting salt into them.

And so the Passover pilgrims entered Jericho.

There was in Jericho a man named Zaccheus, who, like Matthew of Capernaum, was a rich tax-gatherer. He wanted to see Jesus as He passed, but the crowd was great, and he was a small man, so he ran before the people and climbed up into a sycamore tree to see Him.

As Jesus passed the tree He looked up and said,

"Zaccheus, make haste and come down, for to-day I must abide at thy house."

Zaccheus came down in great haste, and was full of joy to be able to entertain Jesus, though some complained that a sinner should have the honor of taking the Master into his house.

Zaccheus must have heard these cruel remarks, for he said humbly,

"Behold, Lord, the half of my goods I give to the poor; and if I have taken anything from any man by false accusation, I restore him fourfold."

Then Jesus said heartily, "This day is salvation come to this house, forsomuch as he also is a son of Abraham. For the Son of Man is come to seek and to save that which was lost."

It was just outside of Jericho that the bands going out toward Jerusalem passed a blind beggar who cried,

"Jesus, thou Son of David, have mercy on me!"

The Lord heard the cry and called him, and there by the roadside He opened the eyes of Bartimeus to see the beauty all around him, and the kind face of Jesus looking at him. And he followed Him.

The pilgrims came up the steep, rocky road from Jericho to Jerusalem, and they were fortunate who could ride, for the heat was great, and the road hard to climb. Jesus and His friends walked, for they were poor men, as riches are counted in this world.

It was a six hours' journey, and when they reached the green heights of the Mount of Olives they turned aside to the village of Bethany, and there Jesus rested in the house of Mary and Martha and the brother whom He had called back from the grave. The disciples were lodged in the town, no doubt, among their friends, and so grateful and happy were they of Bethany to have the Lord once more among them that they made a supper to show their joy at His coming. It was at the house of Simon, who had been a leper, and cured, perhaps, by Jesus, and Lazarus sat at the table with Jesus, and Mary and Martha served.

It was a holy, happy time, yet shadowed with sadness because of the words of Jesus concerning His death, which the disciples could not believe.

In the midst of the supper Mary brought an alabaster box of very precious and costly perfume, and poured it upon the head of Jesus and also upon His feet, wiping them with her long hair. Judas, one of the twelve, frowned upon her, and said it was a waste, for the perfume might have been sold for money to give to the poor.

But Jesus knew what Mary did.

"Let her alone," He said, "against the day of my burying hath she kept this ; for the poor always ye have with you ; but me ye have not always."

"She hath done what she could."

"Wheresoever this gospel shall be preached throughout the whole world, this also that she hath done shall be spoken of for a memorial of her."

CHAPTER XXXIV.

THE PRINCE OF PEACE.

It was in the lovely spring time of a land that scarcely knows winter that a strange and beautiful scene made Jerusalem still more beautiful. Over the Mount of Olives, where the olive and the fig-trees were in tender leaf, came a procession of people crying,

"Hosanna ; blessed is the King of Israel that cometh in the name of the Lord!"

The road was crowded with people who with lifted faces and songs of praise waved branches of palm as they walked before and beside Jesus, who was riding toward Jerusalem, seated upon a young ass, after the manner of the kings and prophets of ancient Israel.

After Jesus and His friends had left Bethany to go to Jerusalem He had sent two of His disciples to a village near by to bring to Him an ass, with its colt, that they would find tied there, and they were to say to the owner of the asses, "The Lord hath need of them," that the words of the prophet might be fulfilled,

"Tell ye the daughter of Zion, 'Behold thy king cometh unto thee, meek, and sitting upon an ass, and a colt, the foal of an ass.'"

While the Lord and His friends were coming up the Mount of Olives, many people from Jerusalem who knew that He was on His way came to meet Him, and when the two disciples brought to Jesus the ass upon which He was to ride they placed Him upon it, and spreading their garments in the way, and with waving palms and singing they came over the ridge of the Mount of Olives from which they could see Mount Zion shining before them. The Pharisees had come out to see what it meant and were angry. "See—the world is gone after Him!" they said, but Jesus, when they asked Him to stop the praises of the people, told them that the very stones would cry out if the people should hold their peace. As they came to a point in the road where from a smooth rocky height they could see the great city with its temple before them, the whole company stopped, and Jesus, beholding it, wept over it saying,

"If thou hadst known, even thou, in this thy day, the things which belong to thy peace, but now they are hid from thine eyes!"

And He spoke of the days when enemies should surround the Holy City, and lay it even with the ground, because they knew not the time of their visitation. Fifty years after the Romans took the Holy City and burned the beautiful Temple, and put uncounted people to death. And so Jesus went down through the valley of the Kedron and up through the city gates with the great procession that grew at every step until He came to His Father's House—the Temple. Then He looked about and saw the buyers and sellers again making the Temple a market, but He went silently away with His friends to Bethany again. He had entered the city as the Prince of Peace, not as a Roman Emperor would do, with sound of trumpet and the tread of armed legions, and they knew not the time of their visitation.

CHAPTER XXXV.

THE CHILDREN IN THE TEMPLE.

The next morning Jesus went early with His disciples to the Temple. It was on the way as they went over the Mount of Olives that they passed a barren fig-tree—one that bore nothing but leaves. It was like the Pharisees, who outwardly seemed to be religious, but were inwardly evil, and bore none of the fruits of a religious life.

"Let no fruit grow on thee henceforward forever," said Jesus, and it withered away. When the disciples wondered, Jesus said,

"If ye have faith, and doubt not, ye shall not only do this which is done to the fig-tree, but also if ye shall say unto this mountain, 'Be thou removed, and be thou cast into the sea,' it shall be done. And all things whatsoever ye shall ask in prayer, believing, ye shall receive." When Jesus came again to the Temple He drove out the buyers and sellers and the money-changers, as He had done before.

"It is written," He said, "'My house is the house of prayer, but ye have made it a den of thieves.'"

When they had been driven out, the people who had been waiting for Jesus, and the blind and the lame came to Him, and He healed all who came. The Pharisees looked on with hatred in their hearts, and talked with the priests of arresting Him then and there, but a clear, sweet sound of young voices singing came floating through the temple courts, and they saw bands of children who were crying, "Hosanna to the Son of David!" and it rang like heavenly music through all the place.

"Hearest thou what these say?" cried the angry Pharisees, and Jesus answered, "Yea; have ye never read, 'Out of the mouths of babes and sucklings thou hast perfected praise?'" Then He left them and went again to Bethany to rest in the house of His faithful friends, Martha, and Mary, and Lazarus.

CHAPTER XXXVI.

THE LAST DAY IN THE TEMPLE.

It was on a Tuesday that Jesus came again early to the Temple. It was the last day of His teaching there and He filled it with wonderful sayings that have been taught in thousands of Christian temples for nearly two thousand years. The chief priests and elders, who were full of anger because He had acted as if He had a right to say who should come into the Temple courts, came to Him as He was teaching and said,

"By what authority doest thou these things? and who gave thee this authority?" Jesus answered them by asking a question, "The baptism of John, whence was it? from heaven, or of men?" They could not answer, for

"HOSANNA!"

they said in their own minds, "If we shall say 'From heaven,' He will say, 'Why did you not then believe him;' but if we shall say 'Of men,' we fear the people, for all men hold John as a prophet." And so they said, "We cannot tell."

And Jesus answered, "Neither tell I you by what authority I do these things." They could not find what they wanted—something to accuse Him of before the Jewish Council and so they tried to lead Him to say something that would turn the Romans against Him. They came to Him with flattering words, saying that they knew that He taught the way of God truly, and would He tell them if it was lawful to give tribute to Cæsar or not? He saw their deceit and cunning, and said, "Why tempt ye me? Show me a penny. Whose image and superscription is this?" They told Him it was Cæsars. "Render therefore," He said, "unto Cæsar the things which be Cæsars, and to God the things which be God's."

They wondered much at the wisdom of His answer, and could find nothing whereof to accuse Him, but perhaps they never knew what He really meant to say to them—and to us also—that His Kingdom was not of this world.

CHAPTER XXXVII.

THE LAST WORDS IN THE TEMPLE.

On this day also, as Jesus sat near the treasury of the Temple and saw the rich, and the self-righteous casting their money into the boxes placed there, He saw a poor widow come with her mourning dress showing that she was the poorest of the poor—a pauper—and yet she had something to give : she dropped two "mites" into one of the boxes under the marble colonnade that surrounded the court of the women. Taken together these two coins were worth much less than a penny, but they were "all her living," and though the Lord did not speak to her, as far as we know, He saw her faith, and His blessing must have reached her in ways that we know nothing about. To those who stood about Him He said, "Of a truth I say unto you that this poor widow hath cast in more than they all ; for all these have of their abundance cast into the offerings of God ; but she of her penury hath cast in all the living that she had."

Jesus, who "spake as never man spake," preached the new Gospel of the Kingdom by means of stories, or parables, and on one long day of teach-

SHOWING THE PENNY.

ing in the Temple He told several stories that the people never forgot. Two of them were stories of the vineyard. One of them was of a man who sent his two sons into his vineyard to work. One answered "I will not," but afterward repented and went, while the other, who had said "I go sir," went not. Jesus taught in this that real sinners who at first refuse to enter God's kingdom but afterward repent and enter, are better than the heartless hypo-crites who talk much of their religion but are inwardly evil.

The other story was of a certain householder who owned a vineyard and let it out to some men while he took a journey into a far country. When the time of the fruit drew near he sent his servants to the men who had rented the vineyard, that they might receive the fruits of it, but the men beat one servant, and stoned another, and killed another. When the owner sent other servants they treated them in the same way. Then he sent his son saying, "They will reverence my son," but the men determined to kill the heir and take the vineyard for themselves, and they cast out the son of the lord of the vineyard and killed him. In this story He spoke of His own death, as well as that of the prophets and John the Baptist before Him.

The chief priests and Pharisees, when they heard this parable knew that the Lord spoke of them, and they tried again to take Him by force, but feared the people.

Another story told in the Temple that day was of the "Marriage of the King's Son" which you will find in the twenty-second chapter of Matthew. It shows first how the Jews were asked into the Kingdom of Christ, but refused to come, and their city was given over to their enemies to destroy. In the second part of the parable the call of all nations to come into Christ's kingdom is described, and the man who was found at the feast without a wedding garment, describes those who come into the church without real faith in the Lord Jesus, and are not prepared to enter heaven. "For many are called," said Jesus, "but few are chosen."

Knowing the wickedness of the priests and Pharisees, who stood before the people as more holy than others, the Lord ended His last day in the Temple with words to them that must have been sharper than a sword, and more burning than flames of fire. These words are in the twenty-third chapter of Matthew, and may no child who reads them ever live to deserve to hear them for himself. To the hypocrite alone the Lord was stern and severe, but to the sinner who truly repented He was full of forgiving love. After telling them of the sorrows and desolations that must fall upon the Holy City because of the sins of those who should be true and faithful teachers of their holy

THE TWO MITES.

religion, He sent forth these last words of love and sorrow through the Temple courts,

"O Jerusalem, Jerusalem, thou that killest the prophets and stonest them which are sent unto thee, how often would I have gathered thy children together, even as a hen gathereth her chickens under her wings, and ye would not! Behold your house is left unto you desolate, for I say unto you, ye shall not see me henceforth till ye shall say, 'Blessed is He that cometh in the name of the Lord.'" And He went out of the Temple to return no more.

CHAPTER XXXVIII.

AN EVENING ON THE MOUNT OF OLIVES.

Jesus and His friends went out from the Temple and Jerusalem to the Mount of Olives, and as they looked back upon the beautiful buildings of marble and gold that made the Temple seem like a great jewel shining in the sunset, the disciples turned to Jesus and spoke of it, but He said,

"There shall not be left here one stone that shall not be thrown down."

They sat down on the slope of Olivet where the olive and fig-trees were putting forth their new leaves, and in that quiet time Peter, and James, and John, and Andrew drew close about their beloved Master, and said, "Tell us, when shall these things be, and what shall be the sign of thy coming, and the end of the world?" He told them many things hard to be understood; of the sorrows of Israel when their city should be destroyed, and the people scattered; of the end of the age, when they should turn to the Lord they had rejected, and of His coming to the whole world.

"Watch, therefore," He said, "for ye know not what hour your Lord doth come," and He told them of the faithful and the unfaithful servants; that the one was found doing his duty when his lord returned, and was made ruler over all his goods, but the other, unfaithful in all things, was surprised by his lord's coming and cast out.

He told them another beautiful "watching" story of the Ten Virgins who went forth with their little lamps to meet the bridegroom on his way to the marriage feast. Five of them took oil to fill their lamps, and five took no oil with them. The bridegroom was long in coming, and they all fell asleep; but at midnight there was a cry, "Behold the bridegroom cometh! go ye out to meet him!" Then they all arose and trimmed their lamps, but five of the lamps had gone out, and the foolish maids who brought no oil to fill them begged it of the others, but they were told that they must go and buy it of those who had it to sell. While they went to buy the bridegroom came, and they that were ready went in with him to the marriage, and the door was shut. Afterward, when the five thoughtless ones came to the door crying, "Lord, Lord, open to us!" they only heard the answer, "I know you not."

After this He told them the story of the Talents, which you may read in the twenty-fifth chapter of Matthew. It is the Lord's teaching to all disciples about making the most of the life He gives us.

His last story was a picture of the gathering of the nations, and the separation of the good and the true from the false and the evil. The King's call to the good, "Come ye blessed of my Father, inherit the kingdom prepared for you from the foundation of the world," carried with it a strange reason. "For I was an hungered, and ye gave me meat; I was thirsty, and ye gave me drink; I was a stranger, and ye took me in; naked, and ye clothed me; I was sick, and ye visited me; I was in prison, and ye came unto me."

Then the good whom He had called were astonished, and cried, "Lord, when saw we thee an hungered and fed thee? or thirsty, a stranger, sick, or in prison?" and He answered, "Inasmuch as ye have done it unto one of the least of these my brethren, ye have done it unto me." To the false and the evil He could not say these things, but quite the opposite; and when they wondered when they had seen the Lord hungry, or thirsty, or a stranger, or naked, or sick, or in prison, and had not ministered unto Him, He said, "Inasmuch as ye did it not to one of the least of these, ye did it not to me." Those by a life of love and service had chosen eternal life, but these by a life of selfishness had chosen death.

CHAPTER XXXIX.

THE HOLY SUPPER.

There were two more days before the Passover Feast when Jesus would eat the Paschal Supper with His disciples. He spent the time with them trying to help them to bear the great trial that was before them, and which would shake their faith in Him to the utmost. They still believed that some great miracle would break around them like light in the darkness, and that Jesus would be acknowledged as the Messiah for whom the whole nation was waiting and yet the shadow grew deeper. The faith of one had failed. Judas had secretly hoped that Jesus would be made king, and that His disciples would be honored with riches and power, but little by little this hope had been dying, and little by little his heart had been turning away from his Master and his brethren, until, with the resolve to forsake the Lord, he opened the door of his heart to Satan, who began to enter in and possess him.

The high priest and the elders were plotting against Jesus in their council, and Judas, leaving Bethany and the company of the Lord and His disciples, went over the road he had so often walked with Jesus with a thought from Satan burning in his heart. He loved money more than everything else, and there was but one thing that would bring it now since all hope of Jesus becoming a king was past.

He went to the Temple and asked to be taken before the rulers, and he said to them, "What will ye give me, and I will deliver Him unto you?" There was a bargain made at once, and out of the Temple treasury they weighed him thirty pieces of silver, and he carried them away with the promise that he would watch Jesus, and tell them when and where they could take Him. He did not remember that five hundred years before the prophet Zechariah had written, "So they weighed for my price thirty pieces of silver."

On Thursday morning, the first day of the Feast, Jesus sent Peter and John to prepare a place where He should hold the Paschal Supper with His disciples in the evening. He told them to go into the city, and there they would meet a man bearing a pitcher of water, and if they would follow him he would show them a large upper room furnished. There they were to make ready the Passover.

They found it as He had said, and when the lamb had been slain at the Temple, the feast prepared, and the hour was come, the Lord sat down with the twelve. It was the last time that He would break the bread of the Passover with them before He suffered, and it was to be the first Holy Supper of the Christian Church. "With desire I have desired to eat this Passover with you before I suffer;" He said, "for I say unto you that I will not any more eat thereof until it be fulfilled in the Kingdom of God." Before Him were the cakes of unleavened bread, the wine, the water and the herbs, while the Paschal Lamb was on a side table. After the blessing and the thanks, the Lord filled a cup with wine and water, and blessing and tasting it passed it to His disciples. It was the custom for the master of the feast to wash his hands at this point, and Jesus rose, and laid aside His tunic, and tying a long towel around His waist, poured water into a large basin and going to His disciples knelt down to wash their feet. They had been contending as to who should sit nearest to the Lord, and so be accounted greatest, and He thus taught them a lesson of humility. He told them that they were not to be among those who hold authority. "But he that is greatest among you let him be as the younger," He said, "and he that is chief as he that doth serve." The disciples looked on astonished and distressed, for their Master was doing the work that slaves were in the habit of doing, and Peter cried, "Lord, dost *thou* wash *my* feet?" Jesus said gently, "What I do thou knowest not now, but thou shalt know hereafter." "Thou shalt never wash my feet;" said the loving, impulsive Peter, and Jesus answered, "If I wash thee not thou hast no part with me." "Lord, not my feet only," the humbled disciple said, "but also my hands and my head!" When He sat down with them again He talked tenderly to them of serving each other as He had served them, adding, "If ye know these things, happy are ye if ye do them." With a troubled spirit He said, "Behold, the hand of him that betrayeth me is with me on the table." Then the disciples began to inquire sorrowfully among themselves who it could be, and to ask the Lord in turn, "Is it I?" Even Judas, close beside Him, asked the same question, but the disciples did not hear the Lord's reply. Peter, beckoning to John, signed to him to ask the Master, for John sat next the Lord, and leaned upon His breast. When he asked, "Lord, who is it?" Jesus said, perhaps in a whisper to John.

"He it is to whom I shall give a sop when I have dipped it," and He gave it to Judas Iscariot. Then Satan entered fully into the angry, covetous heart of Judas, and when Jesus said to him in a low voice, "That thou doest do quickly," he rose and went out into the night. Alone with His faithful friends, the Lord took bread and blessed it and broke it, and gave to them, saying, "Take, eat, this is my body; this do in remembrance of me." And He took the cup, saying, "Drink ye all of it, for this is my blood of the New Testament, which is shed for many for the remission of sins."

And so the Lord founded the Holy Supper of His Church, the mystery and the holiness of which you will know more and more as you grow in the heavenly life, and receive through His Spirit the new wine of the Kingdom. John, the beloved disciple, kept for us the wonderful and precious words that the Lord spoke after the Holy Supper. They are full of a love for His children so deep and wide that we can never hope to measure it. They are written in the fourteenth, fifteenth, sixteenth, and seventeenth chapters of John's Gospel, and every child should hide them in his memory and heart before he is grown, and in after life they will be bread in time of spiritual famine.

Looking around upon their troubled faces at the table the Lord said to His disciples, " Let not your heart be troubled ; ye believe in God, believe also in me. In my Father's house are many mansions. I go to prepare a place for you. And if I go and prepare a place for you, I will come again and receive you unto myself, that when I am there ye may be also." He answered their questions, and He promised them the Comforter—the Holy Spirit of Truth, who would teach them all things, and make all the dark things clear. He also promised certainly to come back to them and not leave them orphans.

After they had sung a psalm they arose from the table, but they lingered for the Lord's last words and His prayer. He charged them to be steadfast and live from Him, as a branch lives from the vine, for He was the true spiritual Vine, and without Him they could do nothing. He told them of His great love for them, and that they must love one another through all the suffering and persecution that was before them, and trust to the Spirit of Truth, who would guide them in all things, and teach them the things He would say to them, but which they were not yet able to bear. And He promised that whatever they should ask the Father in His name should be given them. Then lifting up His eyes to heaven He prayed for His disciples, and for all disciples who should believe on Him through their word, that they might be one with each other and with Him as He was one with the Father, and, being made clean from the evil that is in the world that they should be with Him forever in heaven. After the prayer they went out of the city, and over the brook Kedron into a garden where Jesus had often sat with His disciples.

CHAPTER XL.

THE NIGHT OF THE BETRAYAL.

As they went out through the darkness down the valley and over the Kedron, Jesus still talked with His disciples. To Peter's question, "Lord, where goest thou?" He said, "Whither I go thou canst not follow me now, but thou shalt follow me afterwards." "Lord, why cannot I follow thee now?" said Peter. "I will lay down my life for thy sake."

"Verily, verily I say unto thee, the cock shall not crow till thou hast denied me thrice," said Jesus.

"Simon, Simon, behold Satan hath desired to have you that he may sift

THE HOLY SUPPER.

you as wheat ; but I have prayed for thee that thy faith fail not ; and when thou art converted, strengthen thy brethren."

"All ye shall be offended because of me this night ; for it is written, 'I will smite the Shepherd, and the sheep of the flock shall be scattered abroad.'"

Jesus and his friends had reached the olive trees of Gethsemane when He asked them to sit there while He went away a little distance to pray. He took Peter and James and John with Him ; and began to be very sorrowful, and He said,

"My soul is exceeding sorrowful, even unto death : tarry ye here and watch with me." He went a little farther, and fell on His face and prayed, saying, "O my Father, if it be possible, let this cup pass from me : nevertheless, not as I will, but as Thou wilt." He found His disciples sleeping for sorrow, and He said to Peter, "What! could ye not watch with me one hour? Watch and pray, lest ye enter into temptation." Again He prayed, "O my Father, if this cup may not pass away from me except I drink it, Thy will be done." And there appeared an angel unto Him from heaven, strengthening Him. Then there was the sound of the tread of many feet, and the light of torches moving among the olive trees, and Judas, leading a band of priests, elders and captains of the Temple came toward the little group, and kissed Jesus as a sign that He was the One whom they sought. Jesus turned to him saying, "Judas, betrayest thou the Son of Man with a kiss?" And to the others, "Whom seek ye?"

"Jesus of Nazareth," they answered. And when Jesus had said to them, "I am He," they fell backward at the sight of His face. "When I was daily with you in the Temple," He said, "ye stretched forth no hands against me ; but this is your hour and the power of darkness." Peter drew a sword and struck at the high priest's servant in defence of his Master, but Jesus said gently,

"Suffer ye thus far," and touched his ear and healed him. "Put up thy sword into the sheath," He added. "The cup which my Father hath given me, shall I not drink it?"

Then they took Jesus and bound Him to lead Him away, and the disciples forsook Him and fled, as had been written in the prophets. But John, the loving and beloved, came back and followed Jesus. So did Peter, remembering his vow, but he followed Him afar off.

GETHSEMANE.

CHAPTER XLI.

DESPISED AND REJECTED OF MEN.

Jesus was first taken to Annas, the old High-Priest, who sent Him bound to Caiaphas, who was his son-in-law, and High-Priest that year.

John went in with Jesus to the palace of the High-Priest, but Peter stood outside the door, shivering with the chill of the night, but more with fear.

A servant girl at the door said, when John came out to bring him in,

"Art not thou also one of this man's disciples?"

And Peter said, "I am not."

Restless and unhappy, he walked about, or warmed himself by the fire, until three had accused him of being a follower of Jesus, and three times he had denied his Lord. Then there came a sound that struck him through—he heard through the open windows the crowing of a cock. It had crowed once before, but he did not think then of what the Lord had said, but now his memory and conscience were wide awake, for, as he looked over the heads of the people towards Jesus standing bound and alone before the High-Priest, the Lord turned and looked upon Peter. That look broke Peter's heart, and he rushed out of the place, and wept bitterly.

There was a mock trial which would pain the heart of a child to dwell upon, and which we will not describe at length. It is enough to know that the Lamb of God, who had come to take away the sins of the world, was willingly in the power of His enemies, and going down to death. A wonderful description of the trial and death of the Messiah may be found in the fifty-third chapter of Isaiah, which was fulfilled in the trial and death of Jesus. The hatred of the priests, the scoffings, the blows, and the cruel words of the people we will not describe. "He was oppressed, and He was afflicted, yet He opened not His mouth. He is brought as a lamb to the slaughter, and as a sheep before her shearers is dumb, so He opened not His mouth." Finally Caiaphas cried,

"I adjure thee by the living God, that thou tell us whether thou be the Christ, the Son of God!" Jesus said,

"I am; and ye shall see the Son of Man sitting on the right hand of power, and coming in the clouds of heaven."

Then the High Priest rent his garments as if shocked at such profanity, and said,

(244)

JESUS BETRAYED BY JUDAS.

"Ye have heard the blasphemy; what think ye?" And they all condemned Him to be guilty of death.

There was another gathering of the priests in the morning as the day began to dawn. There were more cruel words and blows for the Divine Man who was bearing the sins of the world, and He was taken away to Pilate.

And where was the wretched man who had sold his Master into the hands of His enemies!

He could not have thought that he was bringing death on His Master; but when at last he saw the Lord coming, pale, suffering and bound, down the marble steps, and heard "Death! death!" on every side, he became terrified. He had no one to turn to, for he had not a friend among men. He ran to the Temple and, finding some priests, begged them take back the money they had given him, saying, "I have sinned, in that I have betrayed the innocent blood."

"What is that to us," said the heartless priests. See thou to that."

Then Judas cast the thirty pieces of silver over the marble floor, and fled from the place. Afterward he was found outside the city, where he had hanged himself. The priests could not put the price of blood in the Lord's treasury, and so they bought with it a field in which to bury strangers.

CHAPTER XLII.

THE KING OF HEAVEN AT THE BAR OF PILATE.

Pilate, the Roman Governor, who had come up from Cæsarea by the sea to keep order in Jerusalem during the Passover, was in his fine palace called "The Prætorium." Adjoining was "The Hall of Judgment," where cases were brought to the Governor to be judged, and just outside this Hall was a place called "The Pavement." It was a broad floor of many-colored marbles, open toward the city, and having an ivory judgment-seat.

While the morning was lighting the gold of the Temple roof to splendor, there was a deep shadow over the friends of Jesus. Their Lord was being led through the streets of Jerusalem by Roman guards, condemned to die. His mother and the women who believed in Him were in the city and saw Him, perhaps, as He was hurried by, pale and weak from the cruelty of wicked men. The priests would not go into the Judgment Hall for fear of defilement at the time of their Feast, so Pilate came out to "The Pavement"

JESUS CROWNED WITH THORNS.

and sat down upon the ivory judgment seat. He was a stern, proud man wearing a white toga with a rich purple border—the robe of a Roman ruler.

"What accusation do you bring against this man," asked Pilate, looking at the pure, pallid face of the Divine Man, and turning to the dark and evil faces of His accusers. To their complaining remark, "If he were not a malefactor we would not have delivered him up unto thee," Pilate replied,

"Take ye him and judge him according to your law."

When they replied that (under Roman rule) it was not lawful for them to put any man to death. Pilate did not wish to condemn that just One of whom he had known nothing but good, for he had heard of His miracles, and had doubtless heard his wife speak of the young Rabbi. He rose and went into the Hall, ordering the guards to bring Jesus to him. Then he questioned Him,

"Art thou the King of the Jews?" he asked.

"My Kingdom is not of this world," said Jesus. "If my Kingdom was of this world, then would my servants fight, that I should not be delivered to the Jews ; but now my Kingdom is not from hence."

"Art thou a king then?" said Pilate.

"Thou sayest that I am a king. To this end was I born, and for this cause came I into the world, that I should bear witness unto the truth. Every one that is of the truth heareth my voice."

"What is truth?" said Pilate, wondering, perhaps, what kingdom of truth this harmless man was dreaming of, and then he rose and went forth to the people on "The Pavement" who were saying that this man was stirring up the people from Galilee to Jerusalem.

Pilate, hearing that Jesus was a Galilean, sent him to the palace of Herod Antipas, who ruled over that province, and who was now in Jerusalem, but He was sent back to Pilate crowned with thorns and wearing a faded purple robe. The Roman soldiers had jested about His kingship, and Antipas had cruelly carried it out in returning Him in this dress to Pilate, through the streets of the city. He had been tried the fourth time and now Pilate made another effort to set Him free, He questioned Him again and heard the complaints of the Jews, but Jesus would not defend Himself.

"Hearest thou not how many things, they witness against thee?" said Pilate. "Answerest thou nothing?" If Jesus would only defend Himself!

Then Pilate thought he would scourge Jesus to satisfy His enemies, and let Him go.

"Ye have brought this man unto me," he said to the chief priests, "as one that perverteth the people, and behold, I, having examined him before you,

THE SIN OF PETER.

have found no fault in this man.   No, nor yet Herod.   I will therefore chastise him and release him."

The cry of "Crucify him ! crucify him !" rose again.

A message was sent to Pilate from his wife, which deepened the shadow on his face.   "Have thou nothing to do with that just man," she said, "for I have suffered many things this day in a dream because of him."

The people had been persuaded by the priests to ask for Barabbas, and when Pilate asked which of the two he should release to them, they cried,

"Barabbas !"

"What shall I do with Jesus, which is called Christ?" and all cried,

"Let him be crucified !"

"Why, what evil hath he done?" asked Pilate, but the cry was so great he could bear it no longer, and calling a slave to bring water, he washed his hands before them as a sign that he took no blame for the act, and said,

"I am innocent of the blood of this just person : see ye to it," but they cried,

"His blood be upon us, and upon our children."   And when Pilate had given the order to scourge and crucify Jesus, he went into his palace.

CHAPTER XLIII.

LOVE AND DEATH.

Jesus had been meeting and conquering evil all His life, and in the last hour of it the last enemy was overcome.   There were no children at the cross when Jesus laid down His life for us all, and we will not lead you there to point out all the means used by evil men to increase the suffering of our Lord.   It was greatest within the great Heart of Love which broke for the sins of the world, and when you have learned the nature of Spirit you will be able to understand that Jesus chose to pass through an earthly life of poverty and temptation, and die a painful and shameful death, that He might be the Brother of the poor, the tempted, the suffering and the dying. "He was taken from prison and from judgment:" "He poured out His soul unto death, and was numbered with the transgressors;" "He bore the sins of many, and made intercession for the transgressors."   So Isaiah wrote of the coming Messiah seven hundred years before.   But so blind were the

"ART THOU A KING?"

Jews that they could not see that the Redeemer had come to Zion, "He came unto His own and His own received Him not."

Bearing His cross He went forth meekly to death, and when He fell beneath the heavy cross, the Roman soldiers forced a passing stranger to carry it. All along the street women wept for pity as He passed, and there was sorrow in many hearts for the Man whom they had believed in as the One who was to deliver their nation.

But the eleven disciples—where were they? In deep grief somewhere ; but only one—John the Beloved—followed his Master down to death. With the suffering mother of Jesus and the faithful women disciples he kept near his Lord. They saw the rough soldiers as they took the Lord's garments and divided them among themselves, and when they put His body upon the cross they heard Him pray,

"Father, forgive them, for they know not what they do !"

Two robbers were crucified with Jesus, upon His right hand and on His left. One begged Him to save him, and reviled Him because He did not ; but the other said, "Lord, remember me when Thou comest into Thy Kingdom." And Jesus said, "Verily I say unto thee, To-day shalt thou be with me in Paradise."

His dying eyes also beheld His mother standing by the cross with the beloved John and the faithful women who had been His friends. The hour had come spoken of by Simeon in the Temple when he said, "Yea a sword shall pierce through thy own soul also." Jesus, looking at His mother supported by John said,

"Woman, behold thy son !" And to the disciple He said, "Son, behold thy mother !" And from that hour John took her to his own home to love and care for her through the rest of her life.

We will not look at the darkness that rolled over the sky, shutting out the light of the sun, or the sights and sounds of that day on Calvary. Jesus, thinking of the redemption He had wrought out for us, bowed His head and said,

"It is finished ! Father, into Thy hands I commend my spirit." Then the great veil before the Holy Place in the Temple was torn in two from the top to the bottom, as a sign that the Lord Jesus by His death had opened the way for us into life eternal.

JESUS BEARING THE CROSS.

CHAPTER XLIV.

LOVE AND LIFE.

There was a good man of Arimathea named Joseph who was a disciple of Jesus, but not a fearless one. He had not followed Jesus with the twelve, but he had loved Him, and when he knew that his Master, who had not where to lay His head in life, had not a place of burial in death, he lost all fear and went to Pilate and begged the body of Jesus. This Pilate willingly gave him, and he, bringing helpers, took the body from the cross and tenderly brought it to his own garden in which was a new tomb hewn out of the rock. In this peaceful garden-room for the dead they laid Him, wrapped Him in fine linen and spices, for another disciple who had not dared to follow Jesus openly had come with a mixture of myrrh and aloes of a hundred pounds weight to embalm the body of Jesus. This was Nicodemus who had a talk with Jesus by night among the olive trees about the breath of God in man. So these two rich men buried Jesus, and a prophecy was fulfilled.

We do not know that any of the eleven disciples helped to bury Jesus, but, while John took the mother of Jesus to a place of rest and safety, his own mother, Salome, and Mary, the mother of James, and Mary Magdalene stood looking on afar off. There were other women also, who helped to guard the body of the crucified Lord when it seemed to be forsaken of all men. They marked the place where He lay and went away, for the hours of "preparation" and the Sabbath were before them. On the eve of Friday they "prepared spices and ointments, and rested the Sabbath day (seventh day) according to the commandment. But Roman soldiers came and set a seal upon the tomb, and watched it night and day. On the first day of the week (now the Christian Sabbath) very early in the morning, while the streets were still, and there lay only a faint streak of rose in the purple east, Mary Magdalene hastened out of the city to the tomb in the garden, bearing her spices. When she reached the place she saw no guards there, and the heavy stone was rolled away from the door of the tomb. A great fear fell upon the woman who "loved much," and she ran to find Peter and John. "They have taken away the Lord out of the sepulchre," she said, "and we know not where they have laid Him."

Then Peter and John ran, and John the loving ran faster than Peter the believing, and was the first to reach the tomb. The other women also had

(254)

THE DESCENT FROM THE CROSS.

gone to the tomb early bearing their spices for the embalming, wondering on the way who should roll away for them the great stone that stood at the door of the tomb. But they found the stone rolled past the door, and entering the low vestibule they saw a vision of an angel, in a long white garment, and were afraid.

"Ye seek Jesus of Nazareth which was crucified," he said; "He is risen; He is not here: behold the place where they laid Him. But go your way, tell His disciples and Peter that He goeth before you into Galilee; there shall ye see Him, as He said unto you."

The Lord had left a special message for Peter who had denied Him so cruelly and had repented so thoroughly! As they looked to "behold the place where they laid Him," they saw another angel shining white through the gloom, "one at the head, and the other at the feet where the body of Jesus had lain." They also ran, glad, yet half afraid, to tell the disciples what they had seen and heard.

Peter and John found the linen that had wrapped the Lord's body laid carefully aside. They did not yet remember the prophecy concerning His resurrection from the dead, but they believed He had risen, and they went away, hoping perhaps, that He was seeking them.

Mary Magdalene could not leave the empty tomb until she had learned something more about the Lord. Weeping and desolate she stood at the low door of the cave-tomb, and stooping to look in again she saw the vision of angels that the other women had seen, "one at the head and the other at the feet, where the body of Jesus had lain."

"Why weepest thou?" they asked, and she answered,

"Because they have taken away my Lord, and I know not where they have laid Him." As she turned to go out into the garden she saw one standing there who said,

"Woman why weepest thou? Whom seekest thou?"

She thought as she looked through her tears that it must be the man who kept the garden, so she said,

"Sir, if thou have borne Him hence tell me where thou hast laid Him, and I will take Him away."

"Mary!"

It was the voice of Jesus—the same that once said to her, "Thy sins are forgiven," and she spread her arms to clasp His feet, crying.

"*Rabboni!*—my Master!"

"Touch me not," He said, "for I am not yet ascended to my Father:

THE ANGEL OF THE RESURRECTION.

but go to my brethren and say unto them, 'I ascend unto my Father and your Father: and to my God and your God.' "

It was while Mary Magdalene and Mary the mother of James, were still in the garden, perhaps, that Jesus met them and said,

"All hail!" and they fell at His feet and worshipped Him.

"Be not afraid," He said, "go tell my brethren that they go into Galilee and there shall they see me."

When the women told all these things to the apostles who had come together to mourn for their dead Master, they could not believe. But the first Easter had risen upon the world, and though the joy of it filled all heaven, only a few women knew the blessed secret on earth, and were saying over and over, "The Lord is risen! the Lord is risen indeed!"

CHAPTER XLV.

THE EVENING OF EASTER.

It was the afternoon of the same day in which the women had brought such strange stories from the tomb of the buried Christ, that two disciples went out to their home at Emmaus, a village about eight miles from Jerusalem. They had been in the upper room where they often gathered, and had heard the stories of Mary Magdalene, and of Peter and John, and they knew not what to believe.

As Cleopas and his companion (Luke, perhaps) went westward over the hills they talked of all these strange things with bowed heads and sad hearts, for Jesus, the One whom they had trusted was the Redeemer of Israel, was crucified, dead and buried, and as for the words of these women, they seemed like idle tales ; but what if they should be true?

Another step seemed to fall beside theirs, and looking up they saw a noble looking young Stranger who was following the same road. He greeted them and said,

"What manner of communications are these that ye have one to another as ye walk, and are sad?"

"Art thou only a stranger in Jerusalem," Cleopas said, "and hast not known the things that are come to pass there in these days?"

"What things?" asked the Stranger, and they said, "Concerning Jesus of Nazareth, which was a prophet mighty in deed and word before God and

THE WALK TO EMMAUS.

all the people, and how the chief priests and our rulers delivered Him to be condemned to death, and have crucified Him. But we trusted that it had been He which should have redeemed Israel: and besides all this to-day is the third day since these things were done."

Cleopas also told the story of the women who had come from the sepulchre that morning talking of a vision of angels, with that of Peter and John, who had gone also, and found it even as the women had said.

Then the Stranger began to speak to them of many things, and in words so full of wisdom and love and faith that their hearts were drawn with Him to believe that Jesus had risen from the dead. He told them that they were very foolish and slow of heart to believe all that the prophets had spoken. "Ought not Christ to have suffered these things," He said, "and to enter into His glory;" and He explained to them all the Scriptures that foretold the coming, the suffering, and the death of the Messiah, until the two hours' walk seemed as nothing.

As they came to the village where they lived, and the Stranger was passing on, they urged Him to come with them into the low white house near by which was the house of one of them. "Abide with us," they said, "for it is toward evening, and the day is far spent." And He went with them, and sat down with them to their evening meal.

Then another and strange beautiful vision was given at the sunset of the first Easter Day, like that which was given to the women at its dawn. The Stranger took bread and blessed it and broke it, and as He handed it to each disciple their eyes were opened, and they knew Him. It was the Lord! But in a moment He had vanished from their sight, and they could only wonder and believe. They began to recall His words. "Did not our hearts burn within us while He talked with us by the way, and while He opened to us the Scriptures?"

Perhaps they ate the bread that He had broken as they would take the sacrament, and then rose, though the day was fading over the hills of Ephraim and hurried back to Jerusalem to the friend's house where the disciples met. There in the upper room, the doors closed and guarded for fear of the Jews, they told the story of the Stranger to the eager disciples, and found that the Lord had also appeared to Peter.

In the midst of the joy and the wonder there fell a strange hush over the little company, for suddenly the Lord was seen standing in the midst and they heard the greeting so dear and familiar to them all,

" Peace be unto you!" and to them all He spread His hands having the print of the nails in them, and showed them His side that bore the mark of the Roman spear. That they might be still more sure He was the Lord and Master they had loved and followed (for they were afraid), He asked them to touch him ; and as they had been at supper together He asked to share their meal, and He ate of the broiled fish and of the honey-comb before them. After this He talked lovingly with them of Himself—of the fulfillment of the prophecies concerning Him and of the work of the kingdom that was before them. Again he blessed them, and breathed on them, saying, "Receive ye the Holy Ghost." And so ended the day of the Lord's resurrection from the dead—the first Easter of the Christian Church.

CHAPTER XLVI.

THE LORD'S LAST DAYS WITH HIS DISCIPLES.

On Easter evening, when the Lord's friends were gathered in the upper room where He appeared to them, one of the eleven was absent. There were others beside the apostles—Cleopas and his companion, and probably the women of Galilee, as well as Mary, and Martha, and Lazarus of Bethany, but Thomas was not there. The others had told him that the Lord had shown Himself to them and had broken bread with them, but he could not believe. He believed, perhaps, in a vision, but not in the return of the crucified Jesus. He declared,

"Except I shall see in His hands the print of the nails, and put my finger into the print of the nails, and thrust my hand into His side, I will not believe."

A week passed, and the disciples were again gathered in the upper room, and Thomas was with them. The doors were shut and guarded as before, but, as before the Lord suddenly stood in the midst, saying,

"Peace be unto you." Then He turned to Thomas with gentle rebuke,

"Reach hither thy finger, and behold my hands ; and reach hither thy hand and thrust it into my side, and be not faithless but believing." Thomas did not wait to touch the Lord, but cried,

"My Lord and my God !"

"Thomas," He said, "because thou hast seen me thou hast believed ; blessed are they that have not seen and have believed."

Soon after this the apostles went away into Galilee, as the Lord had commanded them to do. There by the Lake where He had called them from

their nets to follow Him they waited for Him.   Peter, and James, and John
were there, with Thomas, and Nathanael, and two others of His disciples.
The old love for the Lake came back to Peter, and he said,

"I go a fishing," and the others said,

"We also go with thee," and they went out for a night with the nets on
the Lake, but they caught nothing.   In the morning as they drew a little
nearer land they saw a dim figure on the shore and heard a voice saying to
them,

"Children, have ye any meat?"   They answered "No," and then the
clear voice came across the water saying,

"Cast the net on the right side of the ship, and ye shall find."   This they
did, and so heavy did the net become with fishes that they were not able to
draw it.   Perhaps John remembered another day on the Lake when the nets
broke with the weight of the fishes, and looking at the figure standing on the
shore in the sunrise, he said to Peter,

"It is the Lord!"

Peter did not wait to reply, but tying his fisher's coat around him he threw
himself into the Lake to swim towards His Master on the shore.   The others
followed in the ship dragging the net with them, and when they had landed
they found a fire of coals there, with fish laid upon it and bread, and the Lord
Himself standing there as one who served.

"Bring of the fish ye have now caught," He said.   And Peter, first to
obey, drew the net to land full of great fishes—one hundred and fifty-three—
and the net was not broken.   While they were silent for joy and wonder,
knowing that it was the Lord, and yet not daring to question Him, He said,
"Come and dine."   And there upon the sands the Lord for the third time
since He rose from the dead, broke bread with his disciples.   John, the beloved disciple was there, but it is not recorded that Jesus spoke to him person-
ally.   His heart was wholly with his Lord, and he did not need the loving
help that was given to doubting Thomas, and self-confident, wavering Peter.
To Simon Peter He said after they had finished their simple meal,

"Simon, son of Jonas, lovest thou me more than these?"

Peter must have remembered that he had vehemently declared, "Although
all shall be offended, yet will not I.   If I should die with Thee yet I will not
deny Thee in any wise," and had straightway forsaken and denied Him.   Now
he said simply and humbly,

"Yea, Lord: Thou knowest that I love Thee."   And the Lord answered,   "Feed my lambs."

THE ASCENSION.

Again the Lord asked him the same question, and Peter gave the same reply. And the Lord said, "Feed my sheep."

When the Lord had asked this question the third time, Peter, full of love and grief cried,

"Lord, Thou knowest all things: Thou knowest that I love thee." And the Lord answered again, "Feed my sheep."

By this Peter knew that the Lord trusted him to be an apostle, and teach the gospel of the kingdom to all men, but that he must have a steadfast love and faith. The Lord also said, "When thou wast young thou guidedst thyself, and walkest whither thou wouldest; but when thou shalt be old thou shalt stretch forth thy hands and another shall guide thee, and carry thee whither thou wouldest not." Afterward Peter was crucified as his Lord had been, and then John remembered these words of the Lord about him. As the Lord said to Peter, "Follow me," Peter saw John following also, and he said, wondering, perhaps, why the Lord had no word of counsel, of rebuke, or of prophecy for John,

"Lord, and what shall this man do?" And Jesus replied, "If I will that he tarry till I come, what is that to thee? Follow thou me." And they went away from the Lake, following the Lord, as they had done three years before when He called them to be "fishers of men."

CHAPTER XLVII.

"HE ASCENDED INTO HEAVEN."

Once more the Lord met His little company of followers and gave the apostles authority to found the Kingdom of God among men. "All power has been given to me," He said, "in heaven and on earth."

And this was the work that He gave them to do: "Go ye therefore and teach all nations, baptizing them in the name of the Father, and of the Son, and of the Holy Ghost: teaching them to observe all things whatsoever I have commanded you."

And this was His true word of promise to them: "Lo I am with you always, even unto the end of the world. And, behold, I send the promise of my Father upon you: but tarry ye in the city of Jerusalem until ye be endued with power from on high."

It was about six weeks after His death that the disciples were again in

Jerusalem where the Lord had told them to go and wait for the coming of His
Spirit. He led them out over the Mount of Olives as far as Bethany, where the
house of Martha had been a place of rest and refreshment for the homeless
Man of Sorrows while He was founding His Kingdom of Heaven on the earth.

As they ascended a hill just above Bethany, the Lord could see spread
out before Him the Hebron hills toward Bethlehem where He was born : the
great city with its golden Temple where He had taught and had been rejected ; Gethsemane, where He had suffered, and had been betrayed ; and
beyond the western walls the place where He had been crucified. Not far
from Golgotha was the garden and the tomb in which He had been buried,
and from which He had risen.

He was about to leave the little group that He had made the founders
of His Kingdom, and one of them ventured a question,

"Lord, wilt thou at this time restore again the Kingdom to Israel ?" And
the Lord replied,

"It is not for you to know the time and the seasons, which the Father
hath put in His own power. But ye shall be witnesses unto me both in
Jerusalem, and in all Judea, and in Samaria, and unto the uttermost parts of
the earth."

Then He blessed them, and while they were looking at Him He was
lifted above them, and a cloud seemed to come between them and their
Divine Master.

While they still gazed toward heaven hoping perhaps to see Him again,
two men in white garments stood by them and said,

"Ye men of Galilee, why stand ye gazing up into heaven? This same
Jesus, which is taken up from you into heaven, shall so come in like manner
as ye have seen Him go into heaven."

Then they worshipped their ascended Lord, and returned to Jerusalem
full of joy and praise, to meet the other disciples in the upper room, to tell
them of what they had seen, and to wait for the Promise of the Father.

CHAPTER XLVIII.

THE PROMISE OF THE FATHER.

While the disciples of Jesus waited in Jerusalem for the gift of the Holy
Spirit—the Comforter—who was to come and teach them all things, and

bring all the Lord's words to their remembrance, they were much in prayer, and looked to the Lord for direction about the things of the Kingdom.

Peter did much to help the others, for his faith had grown stronger, and he was no longer afraid. Many who had partly believed in Jesus before His crucifixion, and who had come to believe in the risen Lord, joined the little band, until they numbered one hundred and twenty at one of their meetings, and the mother of Jesus was among them. At this meeting Peter proposed that some disciple who could be a witness with them to the Lord's resurrection should be appointed to the place that Judas once held in the circle of the twelve. The ten disciples agreed with Peter, and two were chosen—Joseph and Matthias. Then they prayed that the Lord Himself would show them which of these two He wished to be an Apostle, and when they cast lots the lot fell upon Matthias.

When the upper room became too small they went to a larger one that was more public, and did not try to guard their doors, for the priests had become afraid of the people as well as of the signs at the time of the Lord's death, when the sky was darkened, the rocks rent by an earthquake, and the Temple veil by an unseen Hand.

The Feast of the Weeks came on, and at the end of May—the day of Pentecost (the fiftieth after the second day of the Passover), the Lord's little church had gathered in their large public room to pray and wait for the Promise. Suddenly there came a sound from the heavens like the rushing of a mighty wind, and with it came a flash of fire which was not lightning, but which divided into many, and sat above the brow of each like a soft, bright tongue of flame.

Then the silence was broken, and they all began to praise God in other languages, as the Spirit gave them utterance, for the Promise of the Father had been given, and the Lord Himself had come to dwell in His people—not only in these, but in all who should believe on Him through their word.

There were some good Jews present who had come from foreign countries to the Feast, and spoke other languages, and when each heard his own language spoken by these unlearned men they were astonished. The news spread and many came to hear. "Are not all these which speak Galileans?" they asked, "and how hear we every man in our own tongue wherein we were born? What meaneth this?" Others made light of it all, and said that they were full of new wine.

Then Peter, strong in the power of the Holy Spirit, stood up and spoke to the people. You will find Peter's sermon in the second chapter of Acts, and his text was a wonderful saying of the prophet Joel, beginning, as Peter gave it,—

"And it shall come to pass in the last days I will pour out of my Spirit upon all flesh: and your sons and your daughters shall prophesy, and your young men shall dream dreams; and on my servants, and on my handmaidens I will pour out in those days of my Spirit; and they shall prophesy. And it shall came to pass that whosoever shall call on the name of the Lord shall be saved."

Peter did not spare the enemies of our Lord in his sermon, nor did he fear them. He preached to them of Jesus of Nazareth, and whom they had taken and by wicked hands had crucified and slain: and whom God had raised up, having loosed the pains of death, because it was not possible that He should be holden of it. He closed by telling them that God had made that same Jesus whom they had crucified both Lord and Christ.

There were many among the people gathered there who were pricked in their hearts because of Peter's words, which had the power of the Holy Spirit in them. They looked at each other and said,

"Men and brethren, what shall we do?"

Peter encouraged them to repentance and baptism in the name of Jesus Christ, telling them that the promise was to them and to their children, and to all that were afar off.

It was a wonderful day for the Church of Jesus Christ, and for His Kingdom on the earth, for there were about three thousand who that day received baptism, and joined the little despised company of the followers of Jesus of Nazareth. And all that believed were drawn together by the love of the Lord Jesus, and no longer lived for themselves, but for each other. That there might be no rich and no poor among them, they sold their possessions and parted them to all, as every one had need. In the Temple, in each other's houses breaking bread together, wherever they were they were happy and strong in their new faith and in favor with all the people. Though great trials and persecutions came after awhile, they bore them as seeing their invisible Lord, and they joyfully met the loss of all things—even that of life itself with a smile, remembering the Father's House with its many mansions, and their spiritual Elder Brother who had gone to prepare a place for them.

AN AFTERWORD.

Dear Child:—God's Book is a Book of Ages, a Book of Races, and a Book of Nations ; but it is far more, it is a Book through which God Himself speaks to the soul of man. We begin to read it thinking that He is speaking to the mind ; afterward, when our conscience wakes, we believe He speaks to the heart, but at last we find that He speaks to the inmost spirit—the immortal soul. Then all that had seemed to be history, poetry, biography, philosophy, begins to be to us the voice of God in the inmost of the soul, speaking of the life of the spirit.

We find at last, too, that One has walked beside us all the way, teaching us by His Spirit as He taught the people on the hill-side, or by the lake-side in Galilee: the One who said, "Before Abraham was, I am"—the Child of Bethlehem, whose name was called "Wonderful, Counsellor, The Mighty God, the Everlasting Father, The Prince of Peace." That you, dear child, may find Him walking close beside your way, be in the habit of walking daily with Him in the paths of His Word, and He will reveal Himself to you there.

www.ingramcontent.com/pod-product-compliance
Lightning Source LLC
Chambersburg PA
CBHW031346070726
47496CB00017B/1796